Love me, remember me, forgive me . . .

"For argument's sake, let's say I agree to this. What makes you think he'll let me in? Let me help him?" Mia asked.

Lacey glanced out across the terrace before looking at her hands. "He will."

Why make me relive this again? Why make me consider ripping my heart out again? Ten years and it still felt like yesterday. Yes, she had grown up. Yes, she had moved on. She had made something of herself. But some things you just couldn't forgive. Forget.

Lacey dug into her pocketbook and withdrew something, setting it down on the table in front of Mia. "He had that on him when he got injured."

Mia turned over the small photo. She gasped and threw her hand over her mouth.

It was her on the Covingtons' private beach in Wilmington the last day they spent together. The edges were worn, the picture wrinkled and faded. It had been cut to wallet size, framing her face. Ten years and he carried this around? Why?

Lacey cleared her throat. "He never forgot . . ."

return
TO me

KELLY MORAN

BERKLEY SENSATION, NEW YORK

THE BERKLEY PUBLISHING GROUP
Published by the Penguin Group
Penguin Group (USA) LLC
375 Hudson Street, New York, New York 10014

USA • Canada • UK • Ireland • Australia • New Zealand • India • South Africa • China

penguin.com

A Penguin Random House Company

RETURN TO ME

A Berkley Sensation Book / published by arrangement with the author

For information, address: The Berkley Publishing Group,
a division of Penguin Group (USA) LLC,
375 Hudson Street, New York, New York 10014.

ISBN: 978-0-425-27687-7

PUBLISHING HISTORY
Berkley Sensation mass-market edition / March 2015

PRINTED IN THE UNITED STATES OF AMERICA

10 9 8 7 6 5 4 3 2 1

Cover photo by Image Source/Superstock.
Cover design by Lesley Worrell.

It is often said that freedom doesn't come free. It is also said that true heroes can come from both the most unlikely and obvious of places. I believe that. And so this book is dedicated to my heroes who fight overseas and at home.

My brother, Chuck (police officer); my brother-in-law, Nate (retired, U.S. Army); my friend David Wendler (retired, U.S. Army); my grandfather Powell H. McClure (deceased, Army); and my cousins: Charles Dow Jr. (Air Force Reserves); Hutchison Dow (Air Force Reserves); Mark Dow (Air Force Reserves).

Acknowledgments

I have to sincerely thank my friend David Wendler, for helping me to understand the military life and just what our soldiers go through while deployed and when they return. I could not have done this without you. Also to my friend Jacki Weinstein, a dedicated nurse who aided me in some of the medical aspects of this book. Any errors are my own, guys! To Dawn, my agent, who believed in me when I was forgetting how. And thanks to the team at Berkley, especially my awesome editor, Julie!

I'm blessed to have the best street team of wonderful people. I'd like to give a shout out to: Michelle Eriksen, Heather Moss, Ann Meyers, Lisa Mason, Nicola Woodhouse, Kathy Branfield, Kelly Sloane, Shawnee Robinson-Poling, Trinitee Mitchell-Dunn, and Michele Macleod. You guys are the best!

chapter
one

The sand beneath his hand didn't feel like the soft grains from the beach outside his Wilmington, North Carolina, home. This sand was packed, as firm and unforgiving as the region.

Okay, backtrack. Try to think.

He blinked and focused. There should be pain. That was an IED they drove over, right? He should be in pain.

Cole Covington was flat on his back, the goddamn unforgiving Iraq sun scalding his retinas. God, how he hated this place. He'd kill to see rain again. To smell the salt spray off the Atlantic in Wilmington again.

The last thing Cole remembered was heading back to camp. They were in the Humvee, bringing medical supplies to the unit just the other side of Samarra. Finn was driving. He had insisted after Cole nearly flipped the jeep on the last run.

The pansy ass wuss. He smiled. He might not like his life here, but he liked the guys he served with. He hoped they were okay. Panic started to form in his gut.

"Finn?" He couldn't hear his own voice. He cleared his throat and shouted out to his commander again. Nothing. Come to think of it, he couldn't hear anything. What the . . .

He tried to roll, but something was sprawled over his chest. Something heavy. His pack was pressing into his spine. Cole lifted his head, expecting a piece of the truck or part of the cargo.

Instead, Donny lay on him. Donny was almost bigger than the truck and just as stupid. Cole loved him to death. When they got out of there next month, he planned on keeping in contact with him. Donny was talking about signing up again. But hell, three years on this tour was enough for Cole. He was going home. Screw the U.S. government. He'd done his duty.

"Hey, man. Get off. Help me up."

Still no sound. The blast must've shot his hearing. Donny didn't budge.

Cole sighed and geared up to move the lug. He was probably knocked out. Wouldn't be the first time. He hoped Finn wasn't, 'cause no way in hell could Cole carry Donny alone.

He raised his arms and froze. Blood. A lot of it. Everywhere.

His chest tightened. He ran his hands over his arms, smearing the blood, trying to find the wound.

Where? Where was it?

No scratches. No gashes. And it didn't hurt. It wasn't his blood.

Oh no. Donny?

He wheezed in air, pressing his hands over Donny's shoulders to push him off. Donny rolled surprisingly easy, flopping to his right.

Cole edged up onto his elbows and looked in the direction of the Humvee. From forty yards away he could tell the supplies weren't salvageable. The truck lay on its side in flames, a crater next to it where the IED went off. So much for being safe by taking the same route back.

How the hell were they going to get back to base? There was nothing out here. In a couple hours night would fall. They'd be exposed. Three years here and he still wasn't used to the frigid nights, the blistering days. Third realm of hell, this country was. In more ways than one.

Hoping Finn had his portable radio on him, Cole set his hands down to stand and go in search of him. His hand slipped, causing him to flop face-first over Donny's prone body. All the damn blood. So sticky.

Blood.

Cole lifted his head slowly, his gaze raking over Donny's round, boyish face. The kid's mouth hung open as if he needed to scream but couldn't. Blue eyes stared blankly into the sky, fixated on the heavens above that he prayed to every night, like the good, God-fearing Southern boy he was.

Cole's hands shook as reality sunk in. His gaze darted down over Donny's body. Down, down. Past his chest, his stomach, and to his waist, where he stopped. Literally stopped. Donny's entire lower half was gone.

"Fuck!"

Cole scrambled to back up but got nowhere.

No. No. No.

"Come on, Donny boy. Wake up, man." He grabbed Donny's vest and shook the kid for everything he was worth. Donny's head rolled and drooped back, bobbing like a fishing float in the Cape Fear River back home.

A claw of terror ripped the beat from his heart. *Oh God!* His fingers relaxed and dropped to the dirt.

Cole ran a shaking hand over his face and tore his gaze away. The other half of Donny was near the crater. He saw it now. *Him* now. *Him.* Donny was a person. Even in two pieces.

Finn. Where was Finn? Cole called out again, but even if Finn called back, he couldn't hear him through the vacuum in his ears. His gaze searched the expanse of desert surrounding their location.

There! A hundred yards in the opposite direction was . . .

A leg. Part of an arm. More blood.

Adrenaline had him surging up. Searing pain reared him back down. Losing his leverage, he sprawled on his back again.

Fire. He was on fire. His whole left side burned in agony. His hands coursed over his chest. *No.* His face. *No.* Over his arms. *There.* His left shoulder. Marred layers of black flesh riddled the muscle of his shoulder and arm. So much pain.

Okay. Okay. Just the arm. You're fine, man. Get up. Breathe through.

Fuck. And his leg.

His hand instinctively clutched for the pain and couldn't reach it. He sucked in a breath and lifted his head. His uniform was shredded and burned, the tatters flapping in the wind. More blood.

His head flopped back down with the exertion of moving too much. He closed his eyes, counted to twenty, and tried again. Half of his left thigh was . . . gone. Muscles and tendons protruded like a morbid plate of spaghetti.

His stomach recoiled. His breakfast MRE came back up. He wretched and heaved until there wasn't anything left of the ready-to-eat crap.

His head slammed back down, his pack digging farther into his spine. He probably had a broken back. He was in pieces, too. How had he survived when Finn and Donny . . .

"Sweet Home Alabama" had been blaring in the Hum-

vee's CD player. Finn and Donny were arguing the seman-
tics of whether it was Lynyrd Skynyrd's best song. Cole
was in the back, laughing at their absurdity, trying not to
take sides. That was how he survived. He was in the back.
Protected.

Finn had a wife and kids at home. Donny a mother and
a sister. Why'd Cole make it? He had . . . nothing left to go
home to.

Pain flared again, stealing his breath. Fire and ice, puls-
ing and pounding. He wouldn't be alive for long either.
He'd lost a lot of blood. He was a mangled wreck. He wasn't
aware of anyone who knew they were out there. By the
time the base discovered they hadn't gotten back on time,
it would be too late.

Cole swallowed. The cold sensation of shock set in,
very different from the empty cold of the past ten years. It
settled in his bones before the tremors started. He'd seen
guys go into shock more times than he cared to count. No,
it wouldn't be long at all.

Alone. He was gonna die alone.

Once, he almost had it all. Even now, he had more than
most. Born with a silver spoon in his mouth, he was going
out with a rifle in his hand. He'd give it all up to have her
back again. To go back to that day he'd told her to walk.

Tremors turned into violent convulsions as he lay there.
So cold. His fingers crawled over his chest to get to his
breast pocket. That's where Mia was. In his pocket. In his
memory. The only two places he could have her.

He slid the photo out and raised it. The sun washed out
any distinguishable characteristics. All except her eyes. He
didn't need a picture to remember those. As turquoise as
the waters near Cozumel, and just as warm.

He'd wanted to take her there once, back before he

sucked all the hope out of her. Wanted to show her how the beauty of the Caribbean couldn't hold a lick to her.

For a moment, warmth enveloped him again, as he remembered.

What he'd give to take back that day again . . . He'd do it all different. He wouldn't be a coward the second time around. If only she knew how much guilt he lived with, how there wasn't a day that went by when he didn't think of her and wish he'd been a better man.

Spasms almost made him lose her. Well, the picture of her. It was the only personal item he had brought from home. He fisted the photo in his fingers, grasping it as long as he could.

His eyes were so heavy. The sun so bright. It wouldn't hurt anything to close his eyes and sleep. Maybe he'd die that way instead of in a heaving pile of pain, fighting to live. Survival was a basic human instinct, but even he knew there wasn't much for him to hold on to anymore.

He drifted in and out of consciousness, losing track of the blackouts after the fourth episode. Disappointment reared each time his eyes reopened. Still alive. Still here. He had no idea how much time had passed, but the sun was dipping lower now. The air was colder.

And then, without so much as a warning, sand kicked up, plastering his face. Damn sandstorms. He'd be buried. They'd never find any of their bodies. Finn's and Donny's families deserved the closure of burial. He struggled to cover his head with his arm as the grains cut at his skin like glass. Just as quickly, the wind died down, only to return moments later.

He was going numb. His limbs were blocks of ice. Not much . . . longer now. He was oddly at peace with dying. He'd atone for his sins to God. Maybe then he could forgive himself.

Just one more look at her first.

Shadows spun overhead, splitting the sky. Black, white. Black, white.

A helicopter propeller. Someone had found them.

He wished they'd leave him here to die. Hell, it didn't matter. He'd never make it as far as the medics.

Someone shoved his face in front of Cole's, a blurry mass. The face reared back, mouth moving with no words. The guy turned, waved an arm their way, and then the face was back in his. Cole didn't recognize the soldier, but he was one of theirs. His helmet had the U.S. flag on the side. Good ole Stars and Stripes.

He couldn't feel anything. Didn't even know if he was still shaking. Still breathing. The heli blades spun slower, until all that remained was the black. So this is what the end felt like. A void. No white light. No tunnel. No angels beckoning from beyond. Maybe he was going to hell. Except, he could've sworn that was where he'd been the past ten years.

Cole opened his eyes, and with the only strength he had left in reserve, he grabbed the soldier's sleeve and opened his mouth. "Please, tell her . . . I'm sorry."

Mia dropped her keys on the entryway table and kicked off her heels. Another interview a bust. This one had had potential, too. Head of nursing at Ridgeway Home. The salary would have been enough to make things a tad more comfortable.

Instead, she got the same story she had at the last ten interviews. She didn't have enough experience for a department position and they didn't have enough money in the budget to add another RN. Though there was a nationwide nursing shortage, not many were being hired. A testament to the economy.

She moved deeper into her apartment and plopped on the couch. It was the only item she'd taken from the trailer after Mama died. The only thing worth taking. Now it was falling apart, just like everything else in her life.

Mama wasn't worth spit when she was alive, but she was worth even less dead. The disability checks stopped coming a year ago. Mia was barely getting by before that. Now, being out of a job, she wasn't going to have the money to pay for Ginny's school.

She didn't know what she was going to do if St. Ambrose kicked her sister out. There weren't many decent options for severe Down syndrome teens. Her sister had been thriving there, finally getting the education, therapy, and social skills she'd never gotten at home. The public school system had already failed her, as had the state programs.

Mia stared at the stack of bills on the coffee table. After living in her car through most of college, she refused to be a victim of her circumstance, of her past. Because of the cost of Ginny's private school, Mia hadn't been able to put much in savings, but she did have a small cushion. She'd worked hard, made something of herself. She was a good surrogate mother to her sister and tried to give her everything. If they could survive on love, they'd be rich.

Didn't matter. She'd get through this. She was a great nurse with an excellent track record and several recommendations. The hospital's closing after the merger and Mia losing her job were just minor setbacks. Lord knew she'd been through worse.

She rose, aiming toward the adjoining kitchen. A cup of tea before she headed to the library to check job postings was in order. A computer just wasn't in her budget right now. She reached inside the canister and came up empty. Out of tea. She opened the cabinet to see if she had any instant coffee. All that lay inside was half a box of generic Wheat Thins and a can of tuna. She mentally added grocery shopping to today's to-do list. Since the layoff, she'd only been buying what was truly needed until she found another job.

She closed the cabinet and pressed her forehead to the aged, scarred pine.

She couldn't let Ginny down. Mia had to be the mother she herself never had. Someone had to love and care for her sister like no one had for Mia. The bubble of tears formed. She sucked in a breath and straightened. Tears were useless. Feeling sorry for herself was useless. Both had gotten her mother nowhere but an early grave. She looked at the phone on the counter. The answering machine light blinked. More bill collectors. More job rejections. Maybe good news?

Needing a pick-me-up, she dialed to check on Ginny. It was a bit earlier than she usually called, but hearing her voice would clear away the sadness and remind her what there was to lose if she gave in to pity.

Ginny's favorite teacher, Faith Armstrong, picked up on the second ring. "Oh, she's having a pretty good day today. Do you want to talk to her?"

"Yes. Thank you, Faith."

"I'm supposed to tell you when you call that her tuition is due Friday."

Mia pressed a hand to her forehead. The tuition would eat nearly the rest of her savings, but at least she would have another month to find a job. "I know. Thank you."

"Here's Ginny."

The slur of Ginny's voice came on to greet her and Mia nearly wept. She remembered when Mama came home from the hospital with her, just a bundle of pink blankets. She made squeaky noises and smiled when she pooped.

"Hey, pretty girl. Did you have art class today?"

"Uh huh. I made a bird."

Mia smiled. Before St. Ambrose, Ginny was almost completely nonverbal, never mind able to wield a crayon. Mia had worked with her as much as she could back then, but she worked two jobs and went to college to make a better life for them. And she had. "You did? What color?"

"Green. It flies."

"I'll bet it's beautiful. I'm so proud of you." Every chance she got, Mia repeated the words she would've given anything to hear. Just once. From anyone.

"When're you comin' to see me?"

St. Ambrose was clear on the other side of Charlotte and so was the home Ginny resided in. Mia was trying to save on the expense of gas so she only visited once a week. It killed her. "I'll come on Sunday, like always. I promise. I'll be there."

She never broke promises to Ginny either. Promises had been empty words for her growing up. They wouldn't be for Ginny. Ginny would know she was loved.

As always, Ginny hung up before Mia could say goodbye. She held the receiver and stared at it before setting it in the cradle with a smile.

The answering machine reminded her of reality. As long as it kept blinking, there was hope her résumé had gotten a hit.

She pushed Play and turned to fetch a glass of water.

"Ms. Galdon, this is Mark from Credit Services about—"
Delete.

"Hello. This message is for Mia Galdon. This is Faye from Human Resources at UNC. I wanted to thank you for your résumé, but we've hired internally for the position."
Delete.

She turned on the faucet and began filling the glass.

"Mia? This is Lacey. Lacey Covington."

The glass fell out of her hand, shattering in the sink.

"I know it's been a long time. It took me a while to find your number." Mia's gaze whipped to the machine and stared as Lacey's voice paused. "I . . . need to talk with you. Please. It's important. I know you probably don't want to hear from us, but . . . Oh, Mia. Please call me back. My number is . . ."

Mia's hands shook. Her mouth grew as dry as cotton.

She rewound the message and played it back twice more until her fingers were no longer numb. Until it sank in that the call was real. Until she was capable of writing down the number.

Covington. She hadn't heard a Covington voice in ten years. She'd never expected to again.

What could they possibly want with her now? She wasn't some seventeen-year-old kid with stars in her eyes anymore. She wasn't a doormat for them to wipe their feet on. They'd made it quite clear what they thought of her the last time she saw them.

She should ignore the call. She should grab her pocketbook and march right out to check on more jobs.

Lacey had been decent to her back then. At least more so than the rest of them. She sounded upset. Distraught. What had happened that she needed to contact Mia? What was so serious they resorted to calling her?

She was scraping the bottom of the barrel, but she still had her dignity. It had taken ten years to get that back. One phone call, one voice, and all that vulnerability returned. All the pain and embarrassment.

She looked at the door and then the phone, caught between the past and present. Between curiosity and common sense.

Her eyes slammed closed. Who was she kidding? They were the Covingtons. There was no choice.

Mia gave the hostess her name and waited. Garden View Country Club was full of Charlotte's elite, even in the middle of the Friday workday. She smoothed a hand down her yellow sundress, feeling underdressed and inadequate.

She hated this feeling. Like every eye in the place was on her. Silly, because no one in Charlotte knew her past. She'd moved here right out of high school to attend nursing school. No one in this city recognized her as the white trash girl from Wilmington.

No one but the Covingtons. She was an idiot for answering Lacey's call. For putting herself through this again.

"Your party is waiting for you," the hostess said. "If you'll follow me, please?"

Her party? Oh no. No, no. It was just supposed to be Lacey. Her feet followed the hostess through the dining room and out onto the balcony overlooking the golf course, while her stomach flopped like a worm on concrete.

Even amid the privileged members, Mia could pick out a Covington. Lacey sat at a cafe table for two with her back to the door. Alone. Thank God!

At the hostess's indication, Lacey rose and took Mia's hands, kissing each cheek. "Mia, so good to see you again."

Not trusting her voice, Mia nodded and sat across from her. Lacey's hair was the same champagne blonde and her eyes still just as dark brown as her brother's. Her face had thinned, making her look more mature. Her outfit clearly could've paid Ginny's school tuition for three months.

A waiter came by and unfolded a cloth napkin in Mia's lap. "What can I start you off with?"

Anything on the menu would hurt the remainder of her bank account. She glanced at Lacey. "Just coffee for now, please."

When he left, Lacey reached across the table and patted her hand. "It's been so long. Look at you! You cut your hair."

Mia ran her fingers through the short black strands by her nape. She had cut it all off years ago because the length drove her nuts working in the ER. She'd kept it short because it was less fuss. "I did. Keeps me cooler in this humidity."

Lacey tilted her head. "It suits you. Very chic."

Mia almost laughed. There was nothing chic about her.

Lacey sat back, her posture that of purebred, old Southern money. "We must catch up. Tell me what you've been up to."

Up to? Really? Lacey didn't call her to catch up. She wanted something. Covingtons didn't socialize with lower classes unless they needed something.

Yet Mia played along. "I went to nursing school after high school. Other than that, just working. The usual."

Lacey sipped her water. "I heard about your mom's passing. Two years ago? I'm so sorry."

Mia nodded. She just bet she was sorry. Strange thing though, Lacey sounded sincere. She looked sincere.

"Thank you. It was no secret. The years of drinking led to cirrhosis." Mia refused to hide behind her mother's shame. She was not her mother.

"And Ginny? How is she?"

Mia smiled. "Great. She's been at St. Ambrose for a couple years." Was this the part where she politely asked about Lacey's brother? She couldn't even say his name in her head. She wouldn't ask how he was doing. She told herself she didn't care if . . .

"I heard. Mother's on the board of directors at St. Ambrose."

Mia's eyes narrowed. "They're not kicking her out, are they? Please don't punish Ginny—"

"Gosh, no. Oh no, Mia." Lacey's long, elegant fingers closed around Mia's. "I just meant that's how I found you. I used Mother's influence to get your phone number from the school office. My parents don't know I'm here or that I called."

Mia removed her hands and folded them in her lap. She drew in a slow, deep breath and let it go.

The waiter came back and asked for their orders. Mia let Lacey handle it as Mia looked out over the manicured green. She didn't belong here. Not making idle chitchat with Lacey or at a table eating thirty-dollar salads with people who pissed money away.

The waiter left their table.

Mia wanted out. "I was surprised to get your call."

Lacey's smile grew wistful. The expression reminded Mia of summers in their clandestine little area of Wilmington Beach, nicknamed Covington Cove by the staff. Her mother used to be one of those staff. But Mia and Lacey were friends once upon a time. She'd watch Lacey play on the expansive estate, dreaming of getting out, while Mia dreamed of getting in.

How foolish they both were.

"I don't know how much you've kept up on with our family. Have you heard Father's running for governor next term?"

Oh, yeah. Mia heard. How appropriate. John Covington had presided as state senator of North Carolina for the past eight years. He could lie straight through a smile. A perfect politician.

"Mother has her hands full with several charities."

Mia nodded, not giving a damn about Kathryn Covington either.

"And Cole . . ."

At his name, Mia flinched. Lacey paused, staring her down with something close to sympathy. Mia took a sip of coffee, hating how her hands shook when she set the cup down.

"Did you hear he joined the army? Four years ago."

Mia's gaze whipped to hers. "Is that a joke?"

Lacey shook her head and stared at the table between them. "I wish it was. The ultimate punishment for our parents. Something they couldn't control. We kept it out of the papers, but it leaked out a couple years ago when a reporter looked into why he hadn't been seen at his usual hot spots. Dad spun a positive angle to the story. We're patriotic and wanted to do our duty."

Mia tried to picture the Cole she knew crawling through trenches and dodging enemy fire. The image wouldn't form. "I hadn't heard." In all honesty, she went out of her way to avoid press about the Covingtons. What did all this have to do with her?

"He was injured over there."

Mia's gaze searched Lacey's as her throat closed. She might have wished a lot of things on that family through the years, but not that. The seventeen-year-old girl inside her demanded answers. Remembered how much she once cared for Cole. She struggled for the calm she didn't feel. "Is he okay?"

Lacey shook her head, tears forming. Mia's heart sank like lead. The Covingtons didn't show public emotion. Not unless it served a greater purpose. If Lacey was crying, Cole was hurt bad.

Lacey sniffed and dabbed her eyes. "He was with two men from his unit when they drove over an improvised explosive device. I guess they're everywhere in the Middle East. The other two men were killed."

Oh, God. "Lacey, I'm sorry."

"They got Cole stable enough to fly to Germany. He spent a month there before he was well enough to come home. He has an honorable medical discharge."

Lord knows Cole had no business being over there in the first place. What was he thinking? He'd never had to wash a dish, take out the trash, or do anything else for himself a day in his life.

"At least he's home now."

"That's the reason I called." Lacey looked Mia in the eyes with what she could only decipher as a plea. "He's locked himself in the Wilmington estate. He won't see anybody, won't go to therapy."

Mia focused on the first part of Lacey's statement before she even tried to adjust to the second. "I thought your parents sold that estate."

"They did. They wanted nothing to do with . . ." As Lacey trailed off, Mia didn't have to ask why. "Anyway, it was a closed sale. Cole came into his trust fund that year. He purchased it outright. They didn't know he was the buyer until afterward."

Why would Cole want that house? Sure, there were plenty of great summers but, in the end, he wanted out. The bad outweighing the good. Nothing could replace the memory of that last tragic summer.

"Okay, and pardon me for being rude, but what does this have to do with me?"

Lacey reached down and then slid a manila envelope across the table. "Don't look at this now. Hear me out and read this at home later. Think about it and then decide."

"Decide what?"

Lacey's mouth firmed into a thin line. "You don't have a lot left in savings since your layoff. You haven't made payment at St. Ambrose yet this month—"

Mia stood, knocking her chair backward.

Heads turned their way.

"You have some nerve. You know that? Some nerve looking into my personal affairs."

Lacey never flinched. Not even a blink. "It was wrong of me, I know. But, as I said, hear me out."

Mia grabbed her pocketbook. "I don't want to hear anything you have to say." She turned to leave.

"Will you listen to me for Cole?"

She stopped, turned. Her gaze darted around the terrace, at all the faces looking at her.

"Sit, Mia. Please. I don't want to fight with you. I need your help."

A war waged inside. Part of her knew she never should've come. The other part knew she couldn't stay away. The Covingtons were her kryptonite. Always had been. She sighed and righted the chair, sitting back down. She'd listen and leave.

"I had to know I could still trust you, Mia."

"You didn't trust me back then and I sure as hell don't trust you now."

Lacey swallowed. "I had a background check done on you, too."

Mia's teeth ground. "You're not helping your cause."

"You need financial security. I need your help. I'll set up a trust for Ginny's school, payable for the next two years until she finishes and then an account to pay for her care until she dies. She'll be comfortable for life."

If she could move, her jaw would've been on the clean white linen tablecloth. "In exchange for what?" *My soul?* He already took that, ten years ago.

"In exchange for your help with Cole. You get him therapy. You get him back to normal. You rehab him until he resembles my brother again."

"You're not serious."

Her gaze softened. "I am serious. Over the past two months he's fired every PT and nurse I've hired. He refuses visitors, including my parents and me. The only person he's let stay is Rose Wendler, our former maid."

Dear, dear Rose. Mia hadn't seen her since Mama died. "For argument's sake, let's say I agree to this. What makes you think he'll let me in? Let me help him?"

Lacey glanced out across the terrace before looking at her hands. "He will."

"I'm not as confident as you." And there was a damn good reason for that.

Lacey tapped the folder. "Look at the file tonight. Call me tomorrow."

Mia shook her head. "You have more money than God. You could hire a nurse every hour if he fired them that fast. Why me?"

Why make me relive this again? Why make me consider ripping my heart out again? Ten years and it still felt like yesterday. Yes, she had grown up. Yes, she had moved on. She had made something of herself. But some things you just couldn't forgive. Forget.

Lacey dug into her pocketbook and withdrew something, setting it down on the table in front of Mia. "He had that on him when he got injured."

Mia turned over the small photo. She gasped and threw her hand over her mouth.

It was her on the Covingtons' private beach in Wilmington, the last day they spent together. The edges were worn, the picture wrinkled and faded. It had been cut to wallet size, framing her face. Ten years and he carried this around? Why?

Lacey cleared her throat. "He never forgot. He never stopped blaming himself."

chapter
two

Cole's arms slapped the water, one after another after another. Swimming his strokes, lap after lap, until the anger began to drain. His freakin' mother. Again. Never satisfied. If it wasn't his grades or his attitude, it was his posture, his clothes, his hair.

He swam until a slow, steady burn lit his muscles. Until he was sure the sun had kissed his skin too long. Until he couldn't hear Mother's incessant criticism anymore.

Gliding to the edge of the pool, there was a girl walking hand in hand with a baby toddling beside her. The girl had long, sleek black hair. Her eyes rounded as she noticed him. Eyes the deepest blue he'd ever seen.

"I'm sorry. I didn't mean to intrude," she stammered. "Ginny was getting fussy. I was just walking her so she wouldn't disturb Mrs. Covington's brunch."

He emerged from the pool and grabbed a towel, angry all over again that someone had seen him all worked up. "It's rude to stare at people, you know."

Her head shot down, avoiding his glare. "I'm sorry. You're just a really good swimmer. I never learned."

He glanced at the toddler and back to her. She was a couple years younger than him. Perhaps fourteen? What was she doing with a baby at her age? "Who are you, exactly?"

"Gloria Galdon's daughter. She's one of the day maids. Mrs. Covington said it was all right for her to bring us during the summer, as long as we stayed out of the way."

Gloria. He knew her. Mother had had her on staff a long time. The rest of the staff seemed to cover for her as of late. He remembered overhearing them talking about her having another daughter last year. A disabled one. He recognized the signs now. Down syndrome.

"Well, you're in my way." God, he was being a jerk, but his mother had just spent the morning belittling him again and he wasn't in the mood for company.

"I won't do it again. I promise." She grabbed the toddler's hand and walked toward the back of the estate.

He toweled off, watching her go, feeling terrible for treating her the way he did. She seemed like a nice girl. She'd be beautiful once she grew into her body. Long, lean frame. Smooth, tanned skin. And her eyes. Yeah—wow.

Between the house and the mimosa grove, the toddler threw herself on the ground, screaming and kicking her legs. The girl looked around frantically before kneeling in front of the baby. Even from thirty yards away, her voice penetrated. Lilting. Every ounce of Cole's residual tension fled in the ocean breeze. The toddler stopped screaming instantly and tilted her head to listen as the girl sang.

"Hey." He walked toward them. He had the strangest sensation in his gut, like the atmosphere was shifting.

Her eyes rounded again. Wide. "I'm so sorry. She's just a baby. I'm calming her down—"

"No, it's not that." He waved his hand. "I'm sorry for what I said back there. I was a jerk. Bad day, you know?"

Except, now he didn't know why he walked over. Several seconds ticked by as the sun beat down on them. Cicadas buzzed in the neighboring trees. Sweat beaded on her brow, trailing a path from her temple down her cheek.

"Bring a swimming suit tomorrow. It's hot out here. I'll teach you to swim."

"Really?" Her eyes lit to an electric, cosmic blue. "I don't want to be a bother."

He swallowed. "It's no bother." No bother at all. His mother was gonna love this. Fraternizing with the help. Or the help's daughter, be that as it may. Not that it was his reason for inviting her.

"But, Ginny . . . I have to watch her."

"Bring a suit for her, too." What was he doing? "What's your name?"

"Mia." She smiled.

That sensation from earlier morphed into a painful, wonderful ache. "Mia, I'll see you tomorrow."

Present

Mia swung her legs over the side of the bed to fetch her book and knocked the manila envelope to the floor. The solution to her temporary money problems. A guarantee for Ginny to be taken care of should anything happen to her.

Mia hadn't read the file after lunch with Lacey. She'd made up her mind not to get involved. Yet she brought it to bed. Could she do it? Could she risk reliving all that pain and humiliation again?

For Ginny. Just look at the file for Ginny's sake.

Reading the contents didn't mean she was agreeing to help. She picked up the envelope and pulled out the file. Knowing charts were typically in reverse chronological order, she flipped to the last page first. The dictation from a medic in Iraq was short.

Soldier arrived at 2100 by airlift. Patient was unconscious upon arrival. Suffered third degree burns on anterior of left shoulder and second degree burns on left side of neck. X-rays show compression fractures of C6 and C7 vertebrae. Patient was taken into surgery to assess necrotic tissue in left quadriceps. A muscle bypass was performed to save the leg and restore blood flow. Burns were treated in surgery by a skin graft from tissue of right buttocks. No complications from surgery. Patient will be placed in a medical coma for four weeks and given oxygen therapy.

Mia glanced over the nursing and physician notes after but found nothing useful. Cole had been hurt bad. A muscle bypass would mean severe to moderate pain for the rest of his life in that leg and limited mobility. Even with her nursing background, the pictures were hard to look at.

He was transferred to a German hospital while still in the induced coma four weeks later. There he got intravenous rehydration and was woken. He also got two more skin grafts before returning to the States. He refused cosmetic surgery for the burns and did just enough physical therapy to be released. The psychiatric notes showed severe PTSD. He was leaning toward the numb side of the scale versus anger, according to Dr. Melbourne, the psychiatrist at the VA in

Charlotte. Since Cole was uncooperative, the doctor was unable to determine any triggers or offer decent treatment. He'd tried cognitive behavior therapy without success. The nursing notes stated Cole had frequent nightmares, resulting in cold sweats and screaming through the night. Dr. Melbourne prescribed fluoxetine and clonazepam before releasing him. Cole hadn't returned for a follow-up.

Mia closed the file and leaned back against her pillows. The Cole she knew was pretentious but funny. She remembered how sweet he could be when someone bothered to look beneath the surface. He had a wicked streak of rebellion his parents barely sequestered. He didn't raise his voice. He rarely took anything seriously. Apparently the war and ten years had changed him.

It broke her heart all over again.

Things had ended terribly between them, but a lot had happened since then. Maybe she could help Cole. The nurse in her wanted to do just that. A man was hurt, in need, and she might be able to do something. She strove to set a good example for Ginny, to be a good person. What did it say about her if she refused?

Plus, she was between jobs at the moment. She wouldn't be giving anything up or putting anything on hold if she was to take Lacey up on this offer.

Besides, she could make things right with Cole and bring some peace back into her life. Back then she would've given anything for the chance. Now it lay before her. They were adults. No longer playing in fairy-tale dreams. Why had the Covingtons and that summer set the course for her life? They were just kids back then and had made some terrible mistakes. Yet, in some ways, she continued to let them rule her life. Maybe going back would help her realize those feelings weren't as strong as she thought, that the misguided notions she formulated about her past didn't have to be all there was to her life.

She hadn't thought about the Covingtons in a long time, wouldn't allow herself to. She'd told herself she'd forgiven them, forgiven herself, but obviously she hadn't or these thoughts wouldn't be on her mind now.

She bit her lip. Was she a bad person if part of her wanted to show them she'd made something of herself? She had finished college, gotten a degree, and become a great nurse who took good care of people. She sighed. She shouldn't care what they thought.

Sitting upright, she set the file aside and headed toward the kitchen. Sucking in a deep breath, she dialed Lacey's number before even realizing she had made the decision. Ginny's future would be secure, which, in the long run, was all that mattered.

The thirty-foot wrought iron gate buzzed open the moment Mia's car pulled up. Lacey was to tell Rose that Mia was coming, but the plan was not to tell Cole until she arrived. Lacey wouldn't be here to greet her as Lacey thought her presence would only infuriate Cole more.

The gate closed in her rearview mirror and suddenly Mia was trapped. She forced her gaze ahead, pulling the car forward down the long, palm-lined drive. She breathed in the salt spray from the ocean. The surf pounded the sand as her tires crunched over the crushed-oyster-shell drive.

The lane ended in a paved circular driveway and the sprawling mansion came into view. The Covingtons' estate in Pineville near Charlotte was bigger, but even after all these years, she still thought this one was the most beautiful thing she'd ever seen.

A stick-built home, the house was contemporary, and despite its size held a cottage feel. At the same time it was ostentatious. Two stories, five bedrooms, four baths, a library, weight room, four-car garage, swimming pool, and guesthouse, right on the beach, overlooking the Atlantic. The exterior was white stone with cobalt accent shutters. The previous owners had made sure the roof was metal and the windows double-paned to withstand a hurricane.

Once she'd dreamed of living in such a place. Now it made her sick to think how immature she was then and how cruel the world could be. Money didn't buy anything but loneliness.

She pulled around the twenty-foot decorative fountain toward the guesthouse to park. Part of her agreement with Lacey was that she didn't stay in the main house. Lacey had complied with that easily, along with giving her Sundays off so she could drive the four hours back to Charlotte to visit Ginny. She hoped her car survived the extra miles.

Leaving her bags in the trunk, she drew in a breath and exited the car. The humidity from Charlotte was gone, replaced with a sea breeze and slightly cooler temperatures. The small white flowers from the loblolly-bay and the orange red blooms of the gaillardia checkered the edging of the front walk. Yaupon holly bushes lined the front of the house up to the pillared front door.

The place looked exactly the same. She'd bet the wild sea oats were still at the base of the porch facing the ocean, to prevent erosion, swaying unceremoniously with the sea grass.

As she stood by the foot of the front steps, the door opened. Rose Wendler filled the doorway, wiping her hands on an apron tied around her round frame. Her dark black skin was sheened with sweat, same as Mia remembered. Mia nearly wept. Rose had always been more of a mother to her than her own. She'd taught her, bathed her, and fed her. Showed her the beauty in life when ugly things emerged.

"Come here, child. Let me look atcha." She smiled and opened her arms.

Mia climbed the steps, walked into her embrace, and, for a minute, forgot her unease and fear. She was home. Mia backed away and shook her head. "Rose, I missed you."

Rose's assessing gaze traveled down the length of her. "You're still too skinny. I'll put meat on yo bones."

Mia laughed. "I'll hold you to that."

Rose wasn't the Covingtons' cook back then, but she'd often brought Mia and Ginny a meal at their trailer, since they all lived in the same trailer park on the other side of town. The woman made cornbread to die for. Rose's skin was still beautiful, her nails trim and short, but around her whiskey eyes the wrinkles of time had set in, showing her almost seventy years. There was more white than black in her fitted bun.

"How's your family?" Mia asked.

"Big. Loud."

Mia laughed.

Rose pulled a key from her pocket and passed it to Mia. "That opens the guesthouse and the main house." She pointed. "Come on, let's get you settled in."

Mia's stomach dropped as she followed Rose to the guesthouse. Just being back here had her nerves in a riot. Mia pulled her suitcase from the trunk and met her at the door. Rose unlocked the house and stepped inside.

It smelled like Pine-Sol and gardenia potpourri. The living room and kitchen, separated by an island, were tastefully decorated in sea-foam green. Conch shells and sand dollars were set on the white mantel over the small fireplace. Matching white wicker furniture was arranged in the center of the room, facing each other. Four paintings of the ocean at sunset hung, one on each wall, the colors nicely contrasting.

Lacey had painted those long ago, back when her mother sometimes allowed her to do frivolous things like indulge in hobbies. She had a lot of talent, even as a young teen. The brushstrokes and oil paint jumped off the canvas.

Lacey had run across the driveway once, holding a canvas. Mia had watched from her perch under a mimosa tree as she bounded over, long blonde hair flowing behind her. "Look, Mia. I think I got it right. How does it look?"

Mia stood and straightened, and her jaw dropped. Besides the actual view, it had been one of the most beautiful things she'd ever seen. Such detail. Such emotion. "It's amazing, Lace! Amazing!"

Her smile spread to a full, wide grin. Something Mia rarely got to see. Her mother had been grooming Lacey more and more, and more and more the light was draining from her eyes.

"Mia?" Rose's voice snapped her back. "Child, come on."

"Sorry." She headed down the short hall to meet Rose in the only bedroom. Rose set Mia's suitcase by the queen-sized, four-poster bed.

The air whooshed from Mia's lungs in one hard, swift breath. A steady humming drummed in her ears, like a thousand cicadas on a July afternoon.

The bed. She'd almost forgotten.

Hands moving. Mouths kissing. Sheets tangled.

"Mia Galdon!"

She sucked in air, shaking her head, and staggered. Rose stood in front of her.

Quickly, Mia wiped the tears from her eyes. "I think I made a mistake. I can't do this."

Rose pursed her lips. "Yes, you can, and you will. That boy needs you."

"Oh, Rose. I didn't expect it to still hurt this bad." She clutched her chest, the motion not stopping the sharp ache.

"Well, get over it. You were stronger than them then and you are now. That's why I told Miss Lacey to call you. She didn't want to. Didn't think you'd do it. I told her you would."

Mia blinked and held Rose's gaze to ground her, not at all surprised it was Rose's idea to bring her back. Rose had always known best, had always guided her toward the correct path and choices, but Mia was having a difficult time believing this was the right move.

"Time will heal." Rose's simple statement was backed by as much emotion in her voice as Mia held in her heart.

Mia nodded. She focused on the room. A small desk and laptop were in the corner. The white pine dresser and armoire were the same design. The rocking chair by the window was original. She looked away before those memories swamped her again.

"Miss Lacey left you a note." Rose handed her an envelope. "I can update you on other matters later."

She slid the envelope between her fingers. "How is he?" She should remain objective. She was here to help him, then leave. *This is a job.*

Rose studied her with a trained eye. "Follow me. We'll have a cuppa coffee at the house and then I'll take you to see him."

Every nerve in her body went hyperalert. They exited the guesthouse and walked across the drive into the main house. The aroma of chocolate chip cookies baking wafted across the hall. To her left were the library and weight room. To her right was the sitting room.

Everything inside the main house seemed different. The wallpaper had been replaced by rich, deep-hued paint. Above a chair rail in the entryway and staircase the walls were burgundy. The sitting room walls were navy. She stepped inside.

White leather furniture and stained-glass-top tables. When she was young, the furniture had a floral print. She used to squish her toes in the plush carpet when no one was watching. Mahogany hardwood had been laid throughout now.

"He did a lot of work renovating before going overseas," Rose said, as if reading her mind.

Mia nodded. "It looks nice."

A loud crash resounded from the ceiling, followed by an earth-shattering growl lasting longer than her breath could hold out. The walls vibrated as more booms resonated from the second floor. Mia turned toward the staircase, but Rose grabbed her arm and shook her head.

"But, he may be hurt—"

Rose shook her head again. "Come into the kitchen. We'll talk."

Hesitant, Mia did as asked and followed Rose down a long hall and into the kitchen. The kitchen was completely different, too. Bright yellow walls, finished white oak cabinets, blue tile countertops. The entire house had been decorated with traces of Cole's personality. The island in the center of the kitchen had cookies cooling on a rack.

"Chocolate chip still your favorite, child?"

Mia smiled, near tears. "Yes."

"Have a few. You go ahead and read Miss Lacey's note while I make a pot of coffee."

Mia placed a cookie on a napkin and walked to the table. She opened Lacey's note and sat down.

Mia,

Please, you are my last hope. I know things there seem rough. He's not the man we used to know, but if anyone can bring him back, you can. Mother and

*Father don't know I've hired you. If possible, that
must remain between us.*

*Rose knows the doctors' information at the
veterans hospital if you need anything. They're
expecting a call from you. I am Cole's power of
attorney for healthcare, but I haven't put forth the
action to activate it. I won't take away his rights
unless I have to. He can make his decisions as of now.
It's his house you are in, but I hired you.*

*Ginny's trust has been set up. There is a laptop in
the guesthouse, which is yours to keep, regardless of
how things turn out.*

*I've left a credit card with Rose. Buy anything you
need for yourself or Cole's care. Please call me with
updates. I'm so worried, Mia. Thank you. You'll never
know how much this means to me.*

Lacey

Mia refolded the note, processing the information. Though
a weight lifted from her shoulders over Ginny's tuition, guilt
consumed her. What if Cole wouldn't see her? What if she
couldn't help? Mia had never taken a free ride in her life.
She'd slaved for everything she and Ginny had.

Rose set a cup of coffee in front of her and sat across the
table. "I'm here from nine until nine, Monday through Friday. I cook the meals and keep general order. Jake, the
landscaper, comes on Wednesdays. There is no one else.
I've been with him since he returned three months back
and he trusts me not to let anyone else in, including his
parents."

Ten years had changed things. Cole used to like people
around. His friends, anyway. On the off chance he needed

privacy, those moods didn't last long. Cole was at his best as the life of the party. The class clown.

"Tell me what that banging was about."

Rose set her cup down. "He sleeps in late. Nightmares wake him. He throws and breaks things until he realizes he's in his bedroom."

"Is he dangerous?" She'd heard about violent outbursts with returning vets. She didn't know a lot about post-traumatic stress disorder.

"Only to himself."

That was a relief. The only thing she'd ever feared from Cole Covington before now was how he made her feel. "How's his appetite? Does he exercise?"

"He doesn't leave his room. I bring his meals up."

That could only be exacerbating his condition. Isolating himself couldn't be good. She'd have to talk to his doctors and do some research now that she had the Internet at her disposal. Most of her nursing experience was in geriatrics and emergency medicine.

She rubbed the back of her neck. She needed to go up and see him. He'd be angry. The last time they saw each other he had ordered her out of his life. Had laughed at her naive tears. Then why did he carry a picture of her through the Iraqi desert?

She met Rose's gaze. "Take me to see him."

Winded, Cole hobbled over to his wheelchair by the patio doors and sank into it, waiting for the blind panic to ease. Though they were becoming less frequent, in this last nightmare he'd done more damage. The ceiling fan lay in a heap on the floor, wires protruding like a cobweb. The dresser was on its side.

Turning his head away, he glanced at the ocean. How many times had he wished to be right here? To feel the sand between his toes? To hear the lull of waves crashing in at high tide? He hadn't gone down to the beach even once. Hell, he could barely walk.

Ever since he'd opened his eyes in the hospital, screaming in agony from his injuries, he'd been emotionally numb. There was a tightness in his left arm now from the burns. They'd left a large, protruding, discolored scar over half his arm and up his neck. A constant reminder every time he looked in the mirror. His left thigh shot darts of pain through his leg with even minor movement. There was a giant chunk of flesh missing where that had healed—it looked more like a moon crater than a limb.

He sat there, staring at his beloved ocean, and tried to summon some kind of emotion. Anything. Aside from random, infrequent spurts of anger, there was nothing. Something had hollowed out his insides. A shell waiting to be collected and displayed. If not for the throb in his leg, he'd swear he was dead.

He should've died.

Footsteps landed on the stairs. Probably Rose, bringing his breakfast. He ate only because food filled him. For a few seconds anyway. In moments, the emptiness would return. At least he had that.

She knocked on his door. She always did, not that it mattered what she would have walked into if she didn't knock. She'd seen him in a violent rage, tearing apart the small piece of his world that was this room. She'd seen him at his worst. He didn't have a best. He didn't allow anyone else to visit. Couldn't. He was a monster. Rose was the only one who didn't demand anything from him. She left him alone.

"Mister Cole?"

He didn't bother turning to face her. "Come in, Rose. I'm sorry about the mess."

Three months, and always the same conversation. *Come in, Rose. Sorry about the mess.*

She'd clean it up without a word and leave him in silence until lunch. He thanked her every day for taking care of him, but she deserved a better job than this.

"Someone's here to see you . . ." Most likely she trailed off to examine his latest damage.

Her strange words floated over him, rolling in his mind until he repeated them back to himself in order to comprehend. "Send them away. I don't want to see anyone. You know that." He tried for the kindest tone he could muster.

"Yes, sir, but I think you'll want this visitor."

He sighed. "No, Rose. There's no one I want to see."

The bedroom door closed. He assumed he was alone until a shuffle scraped the floor. His responses went on alert. Soft breathing emerged from several feet behind him. Rose didn't ever close the door when she cleaned the room. The foreign scent he barely detected wasn't hers, nor was it his morning coffee.

No, wait. Not foreign. *Jasmine.* The smell and memory overtook him until a voice called out from behind.

"Hello, Cole."

It couldn't be.

Slowly, he turned his head, and right then and there he knew his nightmare wasn't over. He was still asleep. His mind still trapping him in a horrid, wretched state of what-ifs and could-have-beens.

Except, she looked different. Her body still had the curves he remembered, but her face had thinned out. Her black-as-midnight hair, which once trailed all the way down her back, was pixie short. She stood there in a sleeveless yellow dress, hands folded in front of her. In his previous dreams, she'd always worn the black dress he'd last seen her in. The one she wore to the funeral.

It wasn't her. His fucked-up brain was torturing him again. But, he didn't turn away. Didn't look her in the eyes. If he looked in her eyes, she'd disappear. Like every dream before.

"It's been a long time," she said.

He'd recognize that voice in a sea of others. In his dreams, she never spoke. His brain slowly began to thaw. He followed his gaze up her neck to her perfect pointed chin, over her wide, pink mouth, up past her button nose and to . . . *those eyes.*

"Mi—*Mia?*"

She didn't dissolve away. "Yes, it's me."

Air wheezed in and out of his lungs. *I missed you. I'm sorry. I should never have sent you away.* "What are you doing here?"

She didn't step any closer, but he reached out to touch her, remembering the petal-like caress of her skin. His other hand fisted on the wheelchair arm. He rocked forward to stand, but pain shot down his leg and he flopped back.

He wasn't dreaming.

"Lacey called me. I'm here to help."

At his sister's name, he devastatingly snapped back to the present. His hand dropped.

Lacey. He ground his teeth. It wasn't bad enough she shoved nurse after nurse in here. Threatened him with Mother and Father. Pleaded with tears and promises, as if any of those things would make him feel something. Would make him normal again. Would erase the past.

Bringing Mia Galdon back was an all-time low. Probably

Lacey's last-ditch effort. He'd fucked up his life and Mia's enough for two lifetimes. Why couldn't Lacey just leave him to live out the rest of his miserable existence in peace? Alone with his demons as punishment.

Because she was his sister. Family. The only family who truly gave a damn, instead of just pretending to. He'd do the same for her if things were switched. God, Lacey meant well. She really did.

He could only imagine what he looked like to Mia after all this time. He'd let his hair go, and it had grown way past his collar. He hadn't shaved in months either. It had been at least a week since he'd showered or dressed. His bathrobe smelled almost as bad as he did. The thin terry fabric didn't hide the ugly scar crawling up his neck. His appearance should have made him ashamed. Somewhere inside he knew that. Instead, he couldn't drum up anything.

"Please, Mia. Just get out." His gaze dropped to the floor to avoid looking at the pain in her eyes. Pain he'd put there and, it seemed, was still able to instill.

"Cole—"

"Get out." He hated himself.

She stepped back.

"I don't want to see you." Oh, such a lie if ever he'd told one. And he'd told her a lot of lies.

He flinched at the click of her swallow when she turned.

"I'm not leaving this time, Cole. I'm staying until you're well. Then I'll go back to my life, and you can go on with yours."

Once, they'd planned a life together. A childhood dream never to come true. Her back was to him, so she couldn't see how his eyes were shut tight with pain. Couldn't see the regret slamming into him, just like it had ten years before. Couldn't see he loved her still, even if only the memory.

The door closed and he forced his eyes open. Forced himself to breathe.

Forced himself to feel.

chapter
three

The Covingtons were back in Wilmington for the summer, and in true Covington fashion, Mrs. Covington had her annual tea and brunch at the estate earlier that day. Mia, as she had the summer before, hid herself away by the mimosa grove until the guests left.

Now, as the heat of the day simmered away, she walked along the edge of the surf while the bonfire raged behind her. Cole had invited her this year. He had previously, too, but she'd made excuses. Cole and Lacey's friends drank expensive beer and laughed at inside jokes she didn't understand. As before, she felt left out around them.

This summer was the first year she didn't have Ginny with her. Wilmington's public school system had her enrolled in the special needs early preschool program all day. Mia didn't have to go to work with Mama anymore either, yet she came. Sometimes she helped out Rose or the other staff. Most of the time she hung out with Lacey, trying to spot Cole.

Cole had invited her to his summer kick-off bonfire and promised to drive her home afterward. He'd seemed so excited she'd agreed to come. But he'd been drinking and she didn't know what to do. Mama would be passed out at home by now.

"Hey," a voice called out from behind.

She turned and squinted through the dusk. Dean jogged over. Lacey and Cole's older brother shared all their genetic traits, and was boyishly handsome. He'd been away at college most of the time she'd been there, so she'd only seen him a handful of times. Dean had been so nice to her, like his siblings.

"Hey, back." She smiled.

"What are you doing over here by yourself?"

She shrugged. "I don't really know your friends." She did know them actually, but she wasn't from their side of town, didn't have their money. Most of the time they snickered behind her back. Cole's were the worst. He wasn't anything like them and, again, she wondered why he hung out with that crowd.

Cole had taught her how to swim that first summer. He'd even been sweet to Ginny, letting her splash him. They spent time together on and off, talking about stupid things. They watched movies she'd never seen. Last summer he introduced her to a few of his friends, even went driving around once or twice. During the day he stared at her while she was reading in the grove. What would they do this year?

Dean matched her pace and walked beside her. "You want me to drive you home?"

She hadn't seen him drinking. "I don't want to be a bother."

"I have plans later. It's not a problem."

Cole was the only one who had seen where she lived. How she lived. In a run-down trailer smaller than the Covingtons' master bath. She was so embarrassed. Cole had even suspected her unease once and waited until everyone had been taken home before dropping her off last summer.

"It's pretty far," she said evasively.

"Waiting for little brother, eh?" Dean winked.

Heat crawled up her cheeks and she hoped it was masked by the dark.

"I tell you what, if he hasn't offered by the time I leave, I'll come and get you. Deal?"

She smiled. "Deal. Thanks, Dean."

They headed back toward the bonfire. Cole was waiting for them, arms crossed over his chest.

"Uh oh," Dean said. "Looks like little brother's jealous."

Jealous? Of what? Cole hadn't said so much as a word to her since his friends arrived, which was an oddity for him. They were always able to talk to each other. Dean was nice enough to offer her a ride, but that was all.

"What's going on?" Cole demanded when they reached him.

Mia didn't know what to say. Cole had never been mad at her before. She looked to Dean for answers.

Dean's grin widened, which only seemed to infuriate Cole. "Just offering your friend a ride home."

"I'll drive her."

"Suit yourself."

"But," Mia cut in, "you've been drinking, Cole."

"What are you, a poster child? I had one beer two hours ago. I'm fine."

The words made her want to shrink inside her sweater.

He'd never been harsh, not unless he was upset at his mother, and he'd never taken it out on her before.

"Okay," she said. "Thanks anyway, Dean."

Dean jogged off toward their friends, leaving her standing under Cole's glare. "He always has to take what's mine."

"I don't understand."

His sigh was unforgiving and impatient. "Never mind. Let's go."

As they walked over the dunes toward the house, one of Cole's friends shouted, "Taking the trash out?"

Her steps faltered before she caught herself. The jab hurt her more than it should have. She crossed her arms over her chest and pretended not to hear as tears clogged her throat. This was a mistake—coming tonight, thinking she could be one of them.

Cole whirled and stalked back to the beach. Heated words were exchanged and, by the time Cole had finished, his friend was pulling his keys out of his pocket with a scowl.

"He's not leaving, is he, Cole?"

"He was being a jerk anyway." Cole strode to his car and held the door open. "You coming?"

She ran over and climbed in.

He peeled out before she had her seat belt on.

"Thanks for driving me home." She grabbed the door handle as he took the first turn too fast. "Next year I can get my license. Maybe you won't have to drive me."

"I don't mind."

He acted like he minded. He drove like it, too. The tires squealed as he took another turn and headed over the bridge. She pinched her eyes closed, as if that would slow him down. By the time they were clear of the other side of town and had pulled up to the trailer, her stomach had lodged in her throat.

She tried to summon the courage to talk to him. "Why did you invite me tonight? You obviously didn't want me there."

His gazed fixed out the windshield at the trailer as he swallowed. "I did want you there."

When he didn't elaborate and tears threatened again, she unbuckled her seat belt and slid out of the car. She jumped when his door slammed.

"I said I did want you there!"

She was wary of this new side she was seeing of him, directing the anger her way. When he was upset, he looked to her for comfort and came to find her if she was at the house. They talked or swam or went for a walk on the beach until his anger drained. They were at her place now and couldn't do those things. Cole usually got quiet and broody when he was angry. This yelling was so unlike him. It would help to know what flipped his switch.

"What did I do, Cole? Tell me and I'll fix it."

"Look at you. Why are you so damn nice? Look at this place. Look at how my friends treat you."

So it was about that. She was trailer trash, only worthy of talking to if his friends weren't around. She ached. So, so bad.

"I'm sorry you're embarrassed by me." She was more ashamed of her tears than the trailer. Some day she was gonna get out of here, but she'd always remember how he made her cry in front of him. "I won't go back to the estate anymore. You won't have to see me again."

She turned to go and had almost made it to the front door.

"I don't care where you live, Mia. I care how you let them treat you."

"They're your friends, Cole, not mine. If it bothers you so much, change the company you keep."

He seemed appalled. For the third time, she turned to head inside, but he closed the distance and took her arm, desperation on his face. "You're so much better than them. I could never be embarrassed by you. I didn't mean to yell at you." He cupped her jaw and her insides turned to pudding. His warm, firm hands held her cool cheeks. "You're the only one who gets me. The only one who understands."

She had no idea he felt this way. No clue he felt anything for her beyond friendship. They only saw each other in the summer. Casual friends of convenience. This declaration made her heart speed so fast she thought she'd explode.

His hands dropped as he backed away, a look of pure horror on his face. His gaze darted to the ground before looking at the trailer and then his car. "I have to go."

He peeled out as fast as he had pulled in. All she could make out after the dust cleared were two taillights fading in the night.

Present

In the early afternoon, as Rose prepared dinner at the kitchen island, Mia read over Cole's medical file again, charting a list of questions for his VA doctor.

"Has he come downstairs at all?"

Rose expertly chopped peppers for the sweet and sour chicken. "No."

"What does he do on the weekends when you're off? How does he eat?"

Rose frowned. "Sometimes he doesn't. I make a bunch of sandwiches and a bowl of fruit to bring upstairs. Sometimes they're still there on Monday."

"How often does the bedroom look like that?" She shuddered, remembering the ceiling fan and the dresser lying on the floor.

"Not so often now. Once or twice a week."

That was a relief. "Is he taking his meds?"

Rose glanced up. "I don't know. The bottles are in his bathroom. Come to think of it, I haven't refilled them."

"Okay. I'm going to put a call in to Dr. Melbourne. I'll be in the library if you need me."

Rose nodded and went back to chopping.

Mia left the kitchen. She walked down the hall and past the weight room before coming to a halt. She opened the door to take stock of what machines he had. Keeping up on exercises would help the leg from stiffening. After making notes, she closed the door and stepped into the library.

She used to love coming in here. Floor to ceiling shelves cased the small twelve-by-twelve room. A crystal chandelier hung from the vaulted ceiling. Two leather-back chairs centered the space, and a redwood table stood between them. As a teenager she hadn't dared to linger in the room, but she used to borrow books to read in the grove.

She dialed the number to the VA and sat in one of the chairs. A secretary patched her through immediately and Dr. Melbourne's voice boomed in her ear.

"I was expecting your call. Cole's sister tells me you're an old family friend. I sure hope you can help. He needs to come back for in-treatment."

"I'm afraid he's not going to comply with that." She told the doctor what she knew of how Cole had been doing the past few months. "Essentially, I need to know what I can do from here."

"It sounds like his triggers are still nightmare related. You need to identify what sets off the anger. Look for facial changes such as staring off into nothing. Loud noises or certain smells and pictures can set off an episode. Be very observant. Once you identify the triggers, you need to replace them with something else. Tapping him on the hand or using a sound to draw him out will most likely help. Maybe try a bell or chimes, something soothing. This type of cognitive behavior therapy often replaces the negative images. Because this happens primarily at night, you'll probably have to sleep in a nearby room or monitor his sleep, if he allows it."

That would mean moving into the main house, not something she wanted to do, but she would if it would help. "Okay, what else?"

"He needs coping skills. This means he needs to talk about what happened overseas. He may not come right out and tell you, but you can listen for subtle comments. Replace the negativity with assurance. Use reality and logical scenarios."

"How long are we talking?" Cole had kicked her out of his room in less than a minute. She had a feeling it would take weeks just to get him used to the idea that she was there.

"Most patients with PTSD recover within six months with therapy, but some can become chronic. We've lost a lot of time with Cole because he wasn't compliant. He needs help now. Keep at it. Don't give up. Make sure he takes the scripts."

She sighed. That should be as easy as pulling teeth without novocaine. "Okay. What about the physical end? He has a treadmill, a stepper, and a rowing machine."

"I'm not familiar with what PT orders he had, but all of those sound fine as long as he doesn't overdo it. Try once a day for three days a week then steadily increase to five days. I recommend massage therapy as well. That can help his mood and physical pain."

Oh no. Touching Cole like that was out of the question. He'd never allow that anyhow. She'd talk to Lacey and maybe hire someone when Cole was ready for physical touch. "I'm thinking diet modification. Fruits high in vitamin C and proteins for muscle and cell regeneration."

"Yes, definitely."

She hung up after assuring the doctor she'd email him progress notes once a week and try her best to get him back to Charlotte for therapy.

But first, she had to get him out of his room.

Cole turned his head at the knock on his door. "Come in, Rose."

The door swung open, but it wasn't Rose. Mia stood there with a tray. "I've got your dinner."

The embarrassment that had taken all afternoon to bank down surfaced again. "I told you to get out."

She set a tray down on his nightstand. She wasn't wearing the dress from earlier. Instead, she had on a pair of baggy shorts and a white T-shirt. The makeup had been scrubbed off her face.

She straightened and turned to face him. "And I told you I wasn't leaving. Can you move to that chair, please?"

He looked at the wingback chair in the corner, then at her. "Get out of my house." She had to go. He couldn't face her now, not after all this time.

"I don't work for you." She pointed to the chair again.

He'd envisioned a number of things should he ever see her again. Fantasy after fantasy after delusion. None of them compared to the reality of seeing her when he was nearly wheelchair-bound, looking as clean as the floor of a bus, and scarred just shy of a hell beast.

"Get the hell out, Mia!" Guess he did still have feelings.

"We can do this the easy way or the hard way."

She'd grown a pair since he last saw her. He wondered what her hard way was, but kept quiet. "Why do I need to move from the wheelchair? It's comfortable."

Her eyebrows raised in answer. She crossed her arms. She wasn't leaving.

He set his hands down to stand. Her eyes widened as she took a step back. And there it was again. That pang in his chest. The same pang he had this morning when he realized she wasn't a dream. The first tinge of emotion in months.

"Jesus, Mia. I'm not going to hurt you." Never.

She swallowed and glanced away. With great effort, he stood and hobbled over to the wingback chair, gritting his teeth against the pain. She set the tray in his lap and collapsed the wheelchair. Before he knew what she was doing, she had it out of the room.

"What are you doing?"

"Do you have a cell phone?"

"Answer my question."

"Answer mine," she huffed back.

Now he was curious. "Top drawer of the bedside table."

She walked over and pulled out the cell. Then she went to the other nightstand and unplugged the landline phone. She took both out of the room.

"What the . . . bring those back!"

"So you can call reinforcements in to haul me away? No thanks."

She reentered the room, this time with a ladder. She unfolded the thing by the foot of his bed then stepped out again. When she returned, she had a candle in her hand. She set it on his tray and lit the wick.

"Dinner by candlelight."

Dinner by . . . "What are you doing, Mia? Stop screwing around."

She walked to the hallway, completely ignoring him.

"Okay, Rose," she yelled.

The lights cut out, surrounding them in low light from the waning sun. She climbed up the ladder with a screwdriver. After examining the wires from his ceiling fan, she climbed down and grabbed the fan then climbed back up the ladder.

He sat in stunned silence as she twisted, turned, and reattached the wires. After reconnecting, she grabbed the screwdriver and remounted the fan.

From the top of the ladder, she called out to Rose to hit the breaker. The lights flickered on and the blades started spinning. He stared at them as all sound filtered out of the room, replacing it with a vacuum.

The heli blades split the sky. Black, white, black, white. Searing pain in his shoulder, his back and his leg. The dry sand pelted his face, smelling like a wasteland for forgotten souls. Fear reared up, stopping his heart . . .

Someone tapped his hand. That hadn't happened before. The smell of jasmine overtook the musk of sand. Humming. In the distance. Then he wasn't in Iraq, he was in the grove, watching Mia sing to Ginny . . .

"Cole."

He blinked and stared up into the bluest eyes he'd ever seen. Familiar, loving eyes. Eyes that never judged him. She was back. Mia had come back. He reached up to cup her face. "God, I missed you."

"Cole!"

He jerked. Blinked again.

Mia backed away and stared at him. He darted a glance around, but it was only his bedroom. The dresser was still knocked over, but the ceiling fan was repaired. Yes, Mia had fixed it.

She walked over to the wall and flipped the switch, turning the fan off. "Look at me, not the ceiling."

He swallowed and did as asked. The fog cleared. His heart rate slowed. He hadn't thrown anything this time. Hadn't broken a lamp.

Hadn't hurt her, thank God.

"I think the fan is one of your triggers," she said.

"Triggers?"

She nodded. "You have post-traumatic stress disorder from your tour in Iraq. Certain things trigger an emotional response. That's why you get angry."

"All I saw was the helicopter blades."

She crouched in front of him, so close her jasmine perfume teased his nose. "We'll keep the fan off for now, until you readjust better."

"I heard you, singing to Ginny."

"Dr. Melbourne gave me some ideas to replace the negative triggers with positive images and sounds."

He blew out a breath. Whatever she did had worked.

She rose and walked into his bathroom. She came back out seconds later with his prescriptions. She handed him a small yellow pill. "Clonazepam. Very mild. It will help."

He hadn't taken any of the pills the shrink gave him. Didn't want to. What was the point? He wasn't going to get better. Had nothing to live for. He just wanted to be left alone. But for some reason, no matter what he said, Mia wouldn't leave him alone.

Still, she had taken away the fear from before. She'd

done something to pull him out of that hell. Maybe she knew what she was doing. He took the pill and swallowed it.

After setting the bottles down on his bed, she walked over to the upturned dresser. She crouched next to it before he realized what she was up to.

"Mia, don't!"

She smiled, holding up her hand. "I've got it, Cole." She righted the dresser and, with a final grunt, slid it back to the wall. Brushing her hands together, she nodded at his lap. "You need to eat. And you better enjoy it 'cause that's the last meal you're eating in this room."

It took a second for her words to sink in. "What are you talking about?"

"Rose will not be bringing your meals up here anymore. If you want to eat, you come downstairs."

His face heated. His pulse beat like a drum against his temple. "We'll see about that."

Her eyes narrowed as she grinned. "Yep."

As Mia entered the kitchen, Rose looked up from washing the dishes. "I didn't hear no yellin'."

"Not yet anyway." She plopped in a kitchen chair and snagged a cookie. She could still feel Cole's hand on her cheek from when he'd touched her before coming out of his flashback. For a stranded second, she'd flashed back, too.

Rose grabbed her lower back and stretched before returning to her task. Sixty hours a week was a lot to ask of her. And she'd been carrying on almost completely alone for three months. She needed a break.

"Why don't you take the rest of the week off, Rose? I can take care of things here."

Rose cut the water and dried her hands. "No. Mister Cole won't have it."

"I can handle Cole. You need a break." Rose had two grown daughters with families of their own. "Where are you living now?"

"With my eldest daughter, Cynthia. She don't much have room for me, but I get to see the kids."

Mia nodded, an idea blooming. "I'll have to talk to Cole about this, but why don't you move into the guesthouse? It has plenty of room for you and you won't have to drive at night. The doctor said I should be in the main house to monitor him anyway."

"The privacy would be nice, and less driving, too." She shook her head. "I don't think Mister Cole would like it."

"If Cole says it's okay, will you? It'll make me feel better."

Rose gave her one of her many assessing glares. "If Mister Cole says all right, then I'll think about it."

Mia glanced at the clock. It was almost seven. "Head home, Rose. Take the rest of the week off. He won't come down for a few days out of sheer stubbornness."

Rose sighed. "You call me if there's any trouble now."

Mia nodded, understanding she was just given an order and not asked a question. She grinned. "I missed you, Rose."

"Aw, child. I missed you, too."

chapter
four

Cole stood by his bedroom window, looking down at Mia while she sat reading in the grove. He'd been doing a lot of that lately. Watching Mia. These feelings for her had been stirring in his gut since the first time he saw her. He'd already received the warning glare and talk from his mother. Covingtons were set to higher standards than where Mia came from. Meaning, the trash should be kept out, where it belonged.

According to Mother.

He hadn't touched Mia. Not since the night of the bonfire last year when he'd almost kissed her. But damn, he wanted to. She was only sixteen. He was eighteen. Bound for Harvard and great things. In so many ways, she was just a kid. A kid he had no business dreaming about.

The winters in Charlotte were long, this last winter the

longest. He'd thought about her often and wondered what she was doing. Who she was with.

Their long summer talks remained in his head. Her voice, so soft and innocent. It didn't matter what crap his mother threw at him, Mia could calm him down. Make him forget. He'd spent less and less time with his friends and more time with her. She didn't care what car he drove or what school he went to. There was no competition with her. He could be himself.

Mia had more class and dignity than the whole of Father's country club. Yet, to his parents, she'd always be the help's daughter. A person to acknowledge only in private, to be polite. He'd done that for three years.

Dean was being groomed for the family business now that he'd passed the bar. Cole had already gotten the career lecture from Father. He had no interest in finance law. He didn't know what he wanted to do. And what in the hell was wrong with that? What eighteen-year-old knew what he wanted to do with his life?

That was completely unacceptable for a Covington. Cole was sick to death of being a Covington. What major would Mia think he should study? She knew him so well. She was the only one who knew him. Their time together, their world, felt like a cherished secret between just them.

He pressed a hand to the glass, wishing it was her skin. But that couldn't happen. If his mother got bent out of shape over a few glances, imagine her rage if she found out he did more than look.

Still, a guy could dream.

At the knock on his door, he turned. "What's up, Sis?"

Lacey walked across the room and followed his gaze out the window to the grove. A knowing smile crossed her face. "Why don't you tell her how you feel?"

Cole barked a laugh. "As if. Imagine what people would say."

Lacey shook her head in disappointment.

He didn't have the heart to burst her bubble.

"You're a snob."

He wasn't. He just pretended to be for the sake of family reputation. One day—one day he'd say to hell with that and go after what he wanted.

"Hey, kid," Dean said from the doorway.

Both he and Lacey turned, but Cole knew his brother was talking to him. "Hey. Thought you weren't coming in till next week."

"I'll catch you two later." Lacey gave Dean a quick hug.

Dean closed the door. Cole raised his brows in question. He crossed his arms and leaned against the windowsill.

"Mother wants me to have a chat with you."

Cole tipped his head back, thunking it against the window. "What now?"

Dean laughed. "She comin' down hard on you, is she?"

Cole straightened. "Just lay it on me."

Dean sat on the edge of the bed. "Where to start? Your grades? She thinks you're distracted." Dean cleared his throat. "By the maid's daughter."

"Jesus, Dean. Not you, too."

Dean lifted his hand, his face saying this wasn't coming from him. "Look, Mia's a great girl."

"But?"

Dean shrugged. "No but. She's a great girl. My advice to you is to make sure you know what you want before she realizes you've been watching."

Unsure how to interpret this, Cole stared at his brother. "You don't care if I chase the help's daughter? Mother does."

Dean sighed. "Here's the thing with Mother. She's an

unhappy woman, which means she's only happy making everyone else around her miserable, too." Dean stood. "You know why she's so hard on you, more than Lace and me?"

Cole shrugged in nonchalance, but inside he was dying to hear Dean's thought.

"Because you stand up to her. You don't fit her perfect mold. Lacey and I do what we can to keep her off our backs." Dean's eyes lost their spark, leaving an almost dejected absence in its place. "Don't lose that edge, Cole. It's what makes you so passionate, so unique."

Cole didn't know whether to hug him or laugh at him. The perfect son, in a roundabout way, had just told the black sheep he envied him.

Cole turned and looked out the window again, but Mia wasn't sitting in the grove anymore. She and Lacey were walking toward the beach, laughing at some joke. Damn, she was beautiful when she laughed. Made his chest ache in a sweet, painful way.

He sighed. Better to watch from a distance.

When Cole looked back to ask Dean if he wanted a swim, too, Dean was gone.

Present

"Rose!" Another crash hit the floor. "*Rose!*"

Two days and Cole still hadn't come down. Two days of yelling for Rose. Two days with no human contact, no food.

Mia waited him out downstairs, hoping to hear his door crash open. Hoping this plan of hers wouldn't make her fall flat on her face. She'd moved her things into the bedroom next door to his. She didn't think he noticed. One of the nights was a loud one, but she didn't step one foot inside his room.

She was waiting for him to come out, to acknowledge he needed help. Then she'd do what she could if he let her.

After a few more crashes, Cole quieted down again. She closed her eyes and sighed. He needed to eat. Hopefully that basic human need would be enough to drive him out.

She finished the last of her sweet tea and rose to rinse out the glass. She stared out the window at the darkening sky and tried to remember when she last saw the sunset over the ocean. The answer came immediately. Ten years ago, since she hadn't had the heart to return to the coast after what happened.

She glanced up at the ceiling. He was quiet now. She could slip out for ten minutes. Sliding into her flip-flops, she closed the kitchen door behind her.

The smell hit her first. The distinct scent of saltwater and seaweed. The cry of gulls above could barely be heard over the crash of the tide. She closed her eyes as a breeze hit her face, humid and soothing. She'd forgotten how peaceful this place could be. How healing.

Opening her eyes, she stepped off the porch and onto the sand. As she edged the water, the red and purple sky melted into the green blue of the water until a thin, black line separated the heavens from earth. Their last day together had been like this.

Warm. Beautiful.

Her cell buzzed. She pulled it out and answered, hoping everything was okay with Ginny.

"It's Lacey. I just . . . wanted to see how things were going."

Mia kicked off her flip-flops and sat on the beach. Cole's house was in a private area of Wilmington Beach. Not a soul was around to hear her.

"It's going. He's on a hunger strike currently." Mia elaborated for Lacey's benefit.

"That's brilliant. He hasn't kicked you out yet?"

"Oh, he has. Several times, in fact."

Lacey laughed, a sound from deep in her belly, one that Mia hadn't heard in too many years. They'd been friends once. Mia didn't realize how much she missed that, having been too ravaged by the hurt to see past it. Cole wasn't the only thing taken away from her back then.

Mia didn't have any friends. She'd never really had friends. There were a few women from college she talked to once in a while, but over the past couple years that had dwindled down to Christmas cards. She had no one. The truth hurt. There was only Ginny.

"How are you holding up?" Lacey asked at length.

"Oh, you know. Slumming it like this is hard."

Lacey didn't laugh this time, but Mia heard the smile through her words. "It is beautiful there, isn't it? I miss it so much sometimes." She paused. "Oh, Mia. You deserved so much more than you got in life."

Mia wasn't expecting that, nor the swift wave of tears clogging her throat. Lacey didn't say what she did out of pity, and Mia knew that. Lacey, Dean, and Cole weren't like the other Covingtons. She pressed her lips together until she could speak. "That's nice of you to say, Lace."

At hearing her long-ago nickname, Lacey must've been feeling sentimental also. Lacey sniffed. "I have to go. I'll check back in with you soon."

He was freaking starving and she was strolling on the damn beach. She made quite the vision though, standing there against the sunset. He'd pictured that in his head about a thousand times, too.

He still couldn't believe she was here. Like a crazy hallucination. Part of him was so damn relieved he wanted to weep. Maybe he'd get to say all the things he didn't before. Amend the past and let her know how very sorry he was that he couldn't be stronger for her. The other part of him just wanted her gone. Back in his memory, where he couldn't hurt her again. Either way, he wasn't so numb anymore. Bits of emotion seeped their way through the cracks.

Seeing her out there made his chest splinter wide open.

He kept waiting for her to disappear. Dissolve into nothing, making him realize this was all a cosmic joke at his expense. He blinked his eyes, looked again. She was still there.

And the nimble little minx wasn't going to feed him. He'd have to go downstairs. He hadn't tried stairs in months. He needed to go down now while she was out, so she couldn't see how weak he'd become.

He rose and stood in place for several seconds to get his bearings. Once he felt ready, he bore weight on the left leg and quickly transferred to the right. This concentrated form of walking was how he got to and from the bathroom. Stairs were an entirely different matter. He made it out of the bedroom and stared down the curving staircase, which was too wide to grasp each railing with both hands.

He scooted to his right to hold the railing with his strong side. He hopped down the first step, landing only on his right leg. When that seemed to work, he repeated the motion until he reached the bottom step, sweating and completely out of breath. After waiting a good minute, he hobbled into the kitchen doorway just as Mia came back in from the beach.

Her eyes widened. "You're out of your room."

"And you're still here. Where's Rose?"

She walked to the sink to wash her hands. "I gave her the rest of the week off."

"You gave her . . . You had no authority to do that!"

Drying her hands on a towel, she shrugged. "She's getting up there in years, Cole. You can't keep her on those hours. I'm here."

Yeah, she was. Why? He should be pissed. She'd barged in here after ten years, pushing her way back into his life and throwing his world into chaos. Looking at her, at everything he wanted and couldn't have, he just couldn't hold on to the anger.

Through the years, he'd come to idolize the memory of her. Put her up on a pedestal. What they had was so long ago and they were so young. It still got to him, either because of how it ended or because of the thought of what could have been. He hadn't had anyone in his life since she walked out that he could trust as openly as he did her. No one he connected with on such a deep level.

"What's for dinner?"

"BLTs."

He made a noncommittal sound.

She fisted her hands on her hips. "I thought you'd hold out at least another day. I wasn't planning on something special."

He didn't need special. He just needed sustenance. "It smells good."

"I haven't started cooking yet."

Right. He hobbled to the table and plopped down in a chair as she pulled a package of bacon out of the fridge. After she laid the strips in a pan, she turned to face him. "I was wondering if it would be okay with you if Rose moved into the guesthouse? She's staying with her daughter and could use the privacy. Plus, it would save her from driving."

"Aren't you staying there? Where would you sleep?"

A crooked smile creased her mouth. "Not kicking me out today?" He didn't respond, so she shrugged. "I've been in the bedroom next to yours the past two nights."

The bedroom right next to his. A whisper away.

"Is it okay?"

He couldn't concentrate with her around. "Fine, fine."

"She needs normal hours, too. Nine to five."

"Fine." He should've done that long ago, but he'd grown too dependent on Rose.

Mia poured a glass of orange juice and set it in front of him. He drank it as she sliced tomatoes. The smell of applewood bacon filled the kitchen and he damned near leapt for the pan. She finished compiling two sandwiches and set them in front of him. He had just enough manners left to wait for her to join him. They ate in uncomfortable silence until she pushed away the second half of her BLT.

"You still eat like a bird," he mumbled.

"And you still eat like a famine is coming."

She glanced at his empty plate then up at him, and a smile traced the corners of her mouth. He almost choked. The smile eventually made it to her eyes. He couldn't look away from all that blue. Somewhere in the space between them the past collided with the present.

"Your eyes are still blue." He hadn't realized he'd said it aloud until her smile fell and her eyes rounded in painful memory.

Long ago, when either was having a bad day, he would tell her, *Your eyes are still blue*. And she'd retort by saying . . .

"And you're still rich."

His gaze dropped to her mouth. Back to her eyes. "Yeah."

Abruptly, she stood and cleared their plates, pulling him from the past. A dull ache throbbed behind his eyes. She loaded the plates into the dishwasher and then sliced some strawberries into a small dish. After adding whipping cream, she set them in front of him.

"Dessert."

This wasn't his idea of dessert, but he took a bite and chewed.

"Now that you're done brooding upstairs, I'm making some changes around here."

He dropped his fork and stared at her. "Like what?"

"Tomorrow, you shower and shave. You look like a vagrant. Afterward, I'll cut your hair. And we're burning that robe."

He looked at himself, unable to argue. He'd let himself go to hell. He hadn't even cared. Strange thing, he kinda cared now. If the last memory she had of him wasn't bad enough, this one would trump it. He needed to start complying with her demand to help him, show her he could be a good guy again. Then at least when she left this time around, it would be under better circumstances and with a better image of him.

"I'm implementing a diet high in calcium, vitamin C, and protein. You're also doing one hour a day in the gym with me three times a week. The days we're not in the gym, we'll take a walk. I'm off on Sundays, so you are, too."

He'd barely made it down the stairs tonight. "And if I refuse?"

Her grin was wicked.

He sighed. The sooner he complied with this, the sooner she'd be gone. Though that thought broke a chunk of his heart away, he knew she had to go. They were all wrong for each other as kids and nothing on that front had changed. The longer she stayed, the blurrier the line became. In *his* mind anyway. She still hated him.

He sucked in a sharp breath when his leg suddenly

throbbed, not in the usual spot, but lower in the calf. It intensified until he cried out.

She knelt by his feet. "What's wrong?"

"Hurts," he ground out.

"Where?"

He pointed.

"Does it usually hurt there?"

He shook his head.

"Does it feel hot or more like a cramp?"

"Cramp."

She stood. "It's a Charlie horse. Bring your toes up and flex your foot."

He did as she said and the pain lessened. He blew out a breath.

Mia walked to the fridge and pulled out a Gatorade. "You're dehydrated. Drink this tonight. If the pain returns, just flex your foot. With your injuries, you have to watch for blood clots. If it ever feels hot, sharp, and stabbing, you call the doctor right away."

He nodded, bringing his foot down. The leg still cramped, but not as harshly as before. She knelt by his feet again, this time with a bottle of hand lotion from the sink. "What are you doing?"

"Rubbing the calf to loosen the muscle." She squirted a quarter-sized amount of lotion into her palm.

"No."

"But, Cole . . ."

She could *not* touch him. He'd lose it. "I said no!"

The roaring tone of his voice careened her backward. He felt like an absolute shit but couldn't bring himself to apologize.

Several seconds ticked by before she straightened. She rubbed the lotion into her hands. The silence continued.

"I'm going upstairs to straighten your room. The next time you have a flashback or an episode, I'll be there. We'll see if we can get you through it."

She was still too damn nice for her own good.

As she walked past, he grabbed her arm. "Why are you doing this?"

She didn't look at him. "Closure."

chapter
five

Late Summer: Twelve Years Before

Lacey brushed another stroke down the length of Mia's hair and sighed. "They want me to go to this all-girls prep school in the fall."

Mia opened her eyes and stared at the ocean. The day was blistering hot, cooled only by their dip in the water an hour ago. "I'm sorry, Lace."

"Father says I don't have to, but Mother's persistent. She says I need to learn to be a lady and stop my fruitless leisure."

Lacey had better manners than Cole did. Lacey was Mia's age, too, so it seemed odd to pull her from her current school when she only had a couple years left. "What about your friends?"

"I don't think I'd miss any of them. Maybe I should go." Her voice was so wistful, so sad. Mia used to wish for the things the Covingtons had, but they seemed just as lonely as she was. "Can you paint at the new school?"

Lacey had shown Mia some of her paintings and for a sixteen-year-old who was self-taught, she was good.

"Probably not. Mother says I need to be more active in social clubs."

Mama had been spending less and less time sober. Mia had been making dinner after Mama drove them home and then giving Ginny her bath. Mia suspected Mama was drinking at work. She hardly noticed Ginny was finally starting to do normal things other kids did, like babble and feed herself. Mia had been working a lot with her at night. At least her mama never forced her to do something she didn't want to. Compliments were hard to come by, but at least she got them on rare occasion. Poor Lacey. She just wanted acceptance.

Mia turned in the sand to face Lacey. "I think you should do whatever you want to. You are so talented, it would be a shame to waste that. Painting makes you happy."

Lacey shrugged and glanced back at the house. "You make Cole happy."

She'd spent a lot of time with Cole this summer. Unlike with Lacey, who wrote Mia letters over the winter, her only contact with Cole was in summer. They'd made up for the long time apart, though. They did all the things they usually did together, like swimming and walking, but they also talked more. He told her about college. He loved it at Harvard, like his father and brother before him. Finally out of his mother's grasp, he could be himself. He even told her about a few girls he dated. He claimed they were different than the debutantes his mother tried to pair him with. Though the thought made her stomach hurt, she was happy for him.

"It's not me, Lace. He's got his own life now. That makes him happy."

Lacey shook her head and stared at Mia. "He doesn't smile like that at home on holidays. Not like when he looks at you."

That stole her breath away and somehow made her giddy inside. That was silly. Cole wouldn't like a high school girl romantically, especially one so out of his class. No, they were meant to be summer friends, who came and went with the tide.

Yet, she smiled at the possibility.

Present

Mia looked up from her laptop as Cole stepped into the kitchen. She assessed him with such clinical preciseness he wanted to turn right back around and say to hell with her help.

"Well, you smell better," she said.

He'd thrown on a pair of old army sweats and a T-shirt after his shower. He held out the robe for her. "To burn, as you said."

She rose and pulled out a kitchen chair, patting the seat. "Let's cut your hair. We'll use the robe as a cape. Then burn it." When he didn't move, her eyebrows rose. "I can't make you look worse, Cole."

True. He walked over and sat, trying to hide a wince when his leg gave a painful jolt. She placed the robe over his shoulders and pulled out a pair of scissors from a nearby drawer. She stared at him so long that she forced his eyes to meet hers. God, it hurt to look at her.

"You look better without all that scruff on your face."

He wiped a hand over the freshly shaved skin on his

jaw. "It's hard to shave with the scar." He immediately regretted the slip. It was still so easy to talk to her, even after all the years apart.

Her gaze darted to the ugly marring of skin on his neck, which rose above the collar of his T-shirt. "I'll pick up an electric razor when I go out. That should be easier to use, with less irritation."

He doubted it.

Stepping behind him, she ran a comb through his still-damp hair. Her fingertips brushed his scalp. His body remembered that touch. He gritted his teeth and closed his eyes until the sound of the shears slicing through his hair echoed inside his brain.

The static from the portable radio crackled as Finn adjusted the frequency, a cigar wedged between his teeth, his left arm completely missing. Blood trailed down his side and pooled in the sand. Gunfire rang out in the far distance. Donny handed him a beer. The top portion of his body leaned against a rock, but the lower half was lying on the other side of the campfire. Cole's heart painfully lodged in his throat.

Over the laughter of the other men, a humming started to grow. And grow. His gaze whipped around to find the sound. There. Behind him. He turned, finding Mia where Finn had just stood.

The desert dissolved until all that remained was her.

"Cole."

He blinked and looked at the sheers and comb in her hand. She smiled, still humming, and moved to the side of the chair. She tugged his hair, the scissors snipping when they opened and closed, but her sweet, sweet voice blocked out the rest.

"The memories are all jumbled in my head."

"What memories?"

He didn't answer, unable to put into words what was going on.

Her hands stilled. "Just describe them to me." She started cutting again.

"At night, the men used to light a campfire to ward off the cold. We drank beer if we had it and tried to laugh away the shit we'd seen, but the guys who died are there in the memory, with their injuries, carrying on as if they're not dead. Then you're there, humming."

"You see the men as they are now in a memory of how they were. It's a coping skill. You see me there because you hear me humming. Your brain recognizes the difference and pulls you back. It's replacing the images. In time, the flashbacks should be less frequent."

Before he could process that, her hip brushed his arm and every touch, every caress from that summer slammed into his head. His pulse sped, his eyes burned with unshed tears, his skin heated, and his dick jumped. Christ, he didn't even know that organ still worked.

His hand snaked out and grabbed her arm, pulled her into his lap. He cupped her cheeks and stared into her widening eyes. There was fear there.

His arms dropped to his sides. He became increasingly aware she was sitting right on his thigh. It hurt to freaking hell, but she wasn't moving, so he didn't either. He hadn't meant to touch her, hadn't meant to pull her against him. But he did. Like an instinct bred deep within his soul, his need to be near her overwrote everything else. The fear in her eyes edged away, replaced by surprise and . . .

And.

God. He'd always described her eyes as tragic. Tragically

blue. Tragically sad. Tragically sweet and loving. It was all still there. Right there. He could've loved a thousand other women, seen a million more horrors, but those eyes would bring him back. He'd remember them.

Remember her.

"Mia," he whispered. Pleaded.

She drew in a breath and his gazed dropped to her mouth.

"Mia." He wanted, needed to do so much more than say her name.

Recognition dawned in her eyes. "Oh God." She fumbled off his lap, dropping the comb and scissors to the tile.

Reality slammed hard into his chest. She hastily picked up what she'd dropped and ran it to the sink.

"I'm done with your haircut." She talked faster than his heart was racing. "You'll want a professional one eventually. For now, it'll do." She walked back over, removed the robe draping his shoulders and shoved it in the trash can. "Um. Let's go take a walk."

Oh man. He'd almost kissed her. And she'd almost let him.

It took ten years to get over this man. And now she wondered if she was really over him at all. She'd only been in the house three days and she felt like a teenager again, wishing he'd touch her and at the same time scared he would.

Not having the closure she needed was making her mind think their previous relationship was more than it was. A secret romance apart from the outside world, and one so young it didn't have any basis in reality. She knew that in her head. Forced herself to remember that.

Swallowing hard, she stepped out onto the back porch and waited for Cole to join her. After he closed the door behind them, he stared out at the ocean with an unreadable expression, acting like he had nothing better to do than just stand there. She could wait.

He was still a head taller than her, his chest in her direct line of sight. He'd always had a great body. Not muscular in the magazine sense, more like a lean baseball player. He moved with the same athletic grace from before his injuries, but now, with his pronounced limp, he seemed to walk with purpose. Determination. Nothing he did was without careful thought and planning. He'd filled out, too. His body was no longer that of a boy, but a man.

After the shower, shave, and haircut, he seemed more like the man she used to know. Seeing him as he was before, a disheveled, broken man, was unbearable. He'd given up before she arrived. She hoped she could bring him back.

"I haven't been out here yet. Not since I returned home."

Home. How strange, she always thought of this place as home, too.

The coarseness of his voice trailed over her skin. She followed his gaze to the water, watching the surf catch the early morning light. "Why?"

He shrugged.

She thought about letting it go, but the doctor said to try to get him to talk. "Tell me."

A smile quirked one corner of his mouth. "Still persistent as ever. Nothing ever got past you." His smile fell. "Too many memories out here."

Yeah. Pesky memories. "They weren't all bad."

He looked directly into her eyes and held her gaze so long she forced a swallow. Dark, dark brown eyes. Once full of mischief. His gaze returned to the water. "No, they weren't all bad."

There was something she'd been wanting to ask him

since Lacey had first told her he owned the estate, and he'd just left the opening. "Why'd you buy the house, Cole?"

Nothing about his stance changed, but a muscle ticked in his jaw. His eyes glazed over, as if he'd gone somewhere else completely. She was pretty sure where. Worried she might be wrong, though, she called his name.

"I'm here." He wasn't regressing. He cleared his throat. "I guess I bought the place 'cause it killed me to think about someone else having it. The only time I can ever remember being happy was here."

Oh God. Oh wow. She tried not to read too much into his comment, but the way he said it, in that direct tone she remembered so well, it was hard not to infer meaning. "You can be happy again, Cole."

He barked out a laugh, so harsh she flinched. "I see you're still an optimist. I used to admire that."

Okay, enough innuendo for one day. She'd been rattled to her limit. "Let's walk. Can you handle the sand?" She hadn't thought of that before coming outside.

"I'll manage."

"Have you tried a cane? The support might help."

"I don't need a cane," he ground out, leaving no room for argument.

Okay, fine.

He hopped down the five steps and stopped at the bottom to rest before continuing. She trailed after him in silence until they got over the dunes and she could walk beside him.

"How's your sister doing?" he asked.

She smiled, partly because he was initiating conversation and partly because he was being polite enough to ask. "She's great. I was able to get her enrolled in a private school, so she's progressing."

"Where's she been living since your mom died?"

Mia's steps faltered. How did he know Mama died? According to her calculations, he would've been in Iraq at that time. Mia, Ginny, and Rose had been the only ones to attend the funeral. It was a pathetic end to a pathetic life.

He looked at her when she stopped walking. "I've been . . ." He ran a hand through his dark blond hair, a fleeting look of surprise showing he registered the haircut. He sighed. "Sometimes I just wanted to see how you were. I've looked you up a time or two."

So he'd kept tabs on her. She didn't know how to feel about that, so she answered his earlier question. "Ginny lives in a group home. With my work schedule, she wasn't getting the attention she needed. They take her to and from school. I wanted her to have her own life, too. I visit on weekends."

"That must be hard on you, being away from her." No judgment. No condescending tone. Just understanding.

It was strange, even after all these years had passed, how much she wanted to lean into him like she used to do. To sit down with a Coke and slip into their comforting conversations. He'd known every dark secret, every wish she'd ever had for herself. And she'd known his. But that was a long time and a thousand heartbreaks ago. Too much had happened since then. Turning to resume their walk, she decided not to get personal this time around. She'd get him back on his feet and move on. After she left, he'd need someone in his life.

"You should think about letting Lacey visit. At least return her calls."

He drew in a deep breath and released it. "I don't know what to say to her anymore."

His honesty was unexpected. "Start with 'hello' and go from there. She loves you. You're the only brother she has left."

He stopped so abruptly he flinched and grabbed his leg. Dean and Cole hadn't always gotten along. They rarely saw eye to eye on anything, but Cole loved him. Admired him. In a strange way, Cole wished he was more like his older brother. Dean had fit into the Covington dynamic, understood his role and what was expected of him. Dean didn't complain but rather paved his own way, seemingly making everyone happy in the process. Cole used to tell Mia that he felt like the outcast, never measuring up. So, when Dean was ripped away from them, she knew how hard it was on Cole. On the whole family.

She'd accepted her part of the blame for what happened to Dean. In fact, it took years to realize his death was no more her fault than it was Cole's.

She looked at him, eyes closed, jaw wrung tight. Cole still wasn't done blaming himself. Nothing she said would change the past or make him see the truth.

"I'm sorry. I shouldn't have brought it up. How's your leg? Do you need to head back?"

He opened his eyes and stared at the water. "The leg feels better," he said, barely a whisper.

She nodded. "It'll take some time, but motion will help."

He looked at her through hooded eyes. Eyes so dark brown they were almost black. She wanted to squirm under the direct gaze, but she remained calm, waiting him out. He used to look at her like that and she always wondered what was going on inside his head. Part of her wanted to ask him now, but that bridge had been burned.

"Ready to head back?"

His mouth opened and closed again. "There is no going back. No matter how much I wish we could."

We. Her heart all but stopped. There were more demons chasing him than what he had seen overseas and what had happened to Dean. Their shared past haunted him, too. She'd believed him all those years ago when he'd ordered her out of his life, claiming what they had was nothing. But now, that all seemed like a lie.

Everything between them felt like a lie.

Mia awoke in the middle of the night to screaming. Feral, guttural sounds that had her insides vibrating.

Cole.

Shoving the covers aside, she rushed from her bedroom, detangling her legs from the sheets, and hopping down the hall. She threw open Cole's bedroom door. He was still in bed, asleep. Whatever nightmare had him trapped was a nasty one. Cold sweat laced his face; his fists clenched the bedding. His back was arched as if in demonic possession.

Rushing over, she clicked on his bedside lamp. She'd caught him before he destroyed the room. She looked back at Cole. His face was twisted in pain, but his eyes were still closed. Remembering what the doctor said, she tapped his hand and called his name. His muscles relaxed, but he didn't fully wake. The humming seemed to work before, so she did it again now. Behind his closed lids, his eyes darted back and forth. A whimper emerged.

The sheet fell to his waist. The sight of his bare chest brought out all kinds of buried emotions. Every time she looked at him it seemed like another secret diary page had been opened in her mind. She remembered the feel of his chest crushing her breasts in an embrace, the hold both sweet and demanding. Memories she'd spent years trying to repress. It didn't matter how much time had passed, it was impossible to forget your first love. That's what Cole had been to her. He'd been the only man she'd ever loved. Looking at him, it tore her apart to see him like this.

He screamed. She'd stopped humming. She sat next to him on the bed and began humming the chords again, but he kept howling, unable to hear.

Flustered, scared, she pressed her palms to his cheeks and leaned over. "Cole. Cole, wake up. You're safe."

His eyes flew open, panicked. His pupils dilated against the dark brown of his irises. Drawing in a breath, his gaze swept the room before landing on her. Okay, there. He was back. Before she could remove her hands, however, he shot to a sitting position and cradled her face.

Little things she thought she'd forgotten started to trickle through. The way he smelled like sandalwood. The softness of his large hands. The small cluster of freckles that dotted his jaw. And the way he held her, looking not at her but through her. Intense. Unwavering.

"God damn, I missed you."

She opened her mouth to confirm she'd felt that very thing . . . *No*, to deny it, but he crushed his mouth over hers.

chapter
SIX

Early Summer: Ten Years Before

One of the maids interrupted their silent lunch to announce Jason's arrival. Cole set his napkin down and stood.

"Sit, Colton," his mother demanded. "Your friend can wait until our meal is through."

"I'm finished and this can't wait."

The crease deepened Mother's brow before it smoothed out and her usual, placid expression returned. Heaven forbid she got a wrinkle and showed her true age, or undid her surgical attempts to combat time. Lacey watched the two of them, probably waiting to see who'd give in first.

Mother sighed her resignation and disapproval. "Very well."

Weaving around the dining room table, Cole walked down the hall to address Jason. His friend—laughable—had been a thorn in his side. They'd grown up in Charlotte together, both raised among the elite, and their families had summered together in Wilmington.

That was where their similarities ended. Jason was an arrogant prick who thought the world belonged to him. With them attending colleges on opposite sides of the country, he hadn't seen Jason since last summer. Still, Cole had heard the rumors Jason spread. Rumors that involved Cole's taste in women, his errant GPA, and his surprisingly deplorable change in majors. As if Jason knew a thing about Cole's life.

Cole didn't give a crap what people thought of him, but he did care about the constant condemnation from his parents that was propelled by the rumor mill. He cared a lot about what the papers were printing based off those rumors. And he cared about Mia.

Father's recent bid in politics had thrown the whole family into the eye of the media. Now that he was in the running for state senator, the family was even more conservative and harshly protective of the Covington name. The tabloids were evasive about Cole's supposed secret affair, but if Jason kept flapping his mouth, Mia's name would be splashed all over the front page and possibly ruin Father's campaign. They weren't even having an affair. Not that he hadn't thought about that very thing a million times over. He didn't care about the politics, but he wasn't going to stand in Father's way. If it was up to Cole, he'd take Mia to a deserted island and never be seen again.

Jason wasn't in the hall or the foyer, but the maid pointed to the front door. "He's waiting by the fountain, sir." Cole nodded and stepped outside.

At first, all he saw was the hood of Jason's roadster behind the fountain, but closer inspection showed Jason himself. And Mia. Up against the cherry red sports car. For

an instant, jealousy lurched like a shroud. As he stepped
forward, Mia ground out a harsh, "No," followed by a
whimper so helpless it shot through his heart.

"Come on, trash. You spread 'em for everyone else."
Jason had her pinned against the driver's door, her black
hair thrashing as she tried to fight him off.

Rage. Unlike anything he'd ever felt before. It clawed
through his chest and out his throat. One minute he was on
the porch, the next he had Jason on the ground, his fist
pummeling the jerk's perfect face. Too soon, hands tugged
at his arms and pulled him away.

Mia.

Breaths heaving out, he glared at the sack of shit he
once called a friend and shrugged Mia off.

Jason swiped a trickle of blood from his nostril.

"We're done. You and me. *Done*. If I ever see you or so
much as hear your name in our circles, I'll finish what I
just started. And if you try to slip this or her name to the
media, I'll show them the security footage."

Jason's gaze whipped to the surrounding trees and the
house, his face paling when he spotted the subtle cameras.
"What the fuck's gotten into you, man?" He rocked to a
stand and stared Cole down. "She's fucking trash."

"You called her that once before and I threw you out. I
should've kept you out. You've got ten seconds. Ten, nine . . ."

Jason swiped his keys from his pocket, muttering, "Whatever, man." He climbed behind the wheel and peeled out of
the drive.

Cole waited until the car was out of sight then closed his
eyes to suck in air. His pulse was still hammering, his fists
still clenched when Mia squeaked. He whirled to see those
wide, haunting blue eyes swelling with tears. Wrapping her
arms around herself, she trembled, lips quivering.

"Jesus, Mia." Everything but her was forgotten. Marching the two paces to her, he ran his hands up and down her arms. So soft. She was so, so soft. "Are you all right? Did he hurt you?"

She shook her head violently, obviously not hurt but scared witless. Any minute now someone was going to emerge from the house after hearing the ruckus. That or one of the help was gonna talk. He needed to get her out of here.

Glancing over her shoulder, he looked around. "Come on." He directed her toward the beach.

She nearly crumpled in his arms.

"Okay, Mia. Hold on to me." Sweeping an arm under her knees, he cradled her back and carried her past the side of the house and down to the beach. He climbed the dunes and headed south of the house, where the view would be obstructed by the palm trees and sea grass. Nestled in a bed of sea oats, he plopped on the sand and held her in his lap. She curled against his chest, burying her face in his neck.

God, how long had he wanted to hold her? How many times had he kissed other girls, sank himself in their wet heat and pretended it was her? He'd fought the urge, the fantasy. Oh, how he'd fought it. But now, here she was, smelling like jasmine flowers fresh off the vine and fitting so perfectly against him. His arms instinctively tightened around her.

There was an urgent need to protect her, so powerful, so deep, he nearly wept. "Are you sure you're okay? He didn't hurt you?"

She shook her head. "Just . . . embarrassed."

He wanted to pound Jason all over again. "You shouldn't feel embarrassed."

Her face pressed deeper into the crook of his neck.

"Mia, look at me."

Her head lifted and, if ordering her to look at him wasn't the stupidest, sweetest mistake he ever made . . . "God, do you know how beautiful you are?"

Her lips parted. Time stopped on a dime. He stared at her mouth. Red, full lips, begging to be kissed by the right person. Cole sure as hell wasn't him, but damned if he was strong enough to fight this anymore.

Fitting his mouth over hers, he waited for her to adjust to the change between them. In the atmosphere around them. After only a brief hesitation, her lips opened and he dipped his tongue inside. And he was lost. Her fingertips brushed his scalp, threaded his hair through her fingers, and tugged him closer. She moaned, deep. His chest rumbled with the vibration through their kiss. Her nipples pebbled through her bathing suit, the peaks teasing his chest, then crushing between their bodies.

His hand fisted around her silky strands, and he nearly laid her out on the beach. Instead, he tugged her head away.

She stared at him with clouded eyes, as out of breath as Cole. "What are we doing?" she whispered.

"I don't know, but I've wanted to do this for a long, long time. Can we analyze it later?" He didn't give her a chance to respond.

Present

The familiar press of Mia's lips against his was a shock. He knew the exact instant she stopped hesitating and melted. His hand skated down her back, vaguely aware her long, gorgeous hair was gone. That's right. She'd cut it all off. It was short now, framing her high cheekbones and beautiful face.

His fingers reached the hem of her shirt and dipped

under to the petal softness of her skin. Skin that smelled like jasmine and felt like heaven. He drove his hands under her shirt, up her back, and pulled her flush against his chest. She squeaked out a moan, a sound that raged his hard-on to the point of pain.

The nightmare in Iraq had faded, replaced by their first kiss on the beach eons ago. He wasn't dreaming anymore. His leg hurt, his dick throbbed, and it was all because Mia was in his lap, kissing him again with the same innocent heat he'd nearly died without. He never stopped wanting her, but why was she kissing him back? She hated him. Had every right to hate him. She should go right on hating him . . .

He drew back and waited a few seconds for her eyes to open. There, the electric shock to his solar plexus. All that blue. "You still taste the same."

"I . . . you were having a nightmare."

"This doesn't feel like a nightmare."

Her hands fell from his neck to his shoulders and her gaze dropped to his scars. She touched the mangled, hard flesh beneath her palm. He knew what the scars looked like, had stared at them a thousand times in the mirror. Closing his eyes, he clenched his jaw. Her fingertips traced the white, thick skin over the worst of the burns on his shoulder then spread out to the red, disfigured patches surrounding. Over his collarbone, up his neck . . .

He grabbed her hand and yanked it away but held her wrist tight. "I'm not so far gone, Mia, that I forgot how to fuck you. We're not kids anymore. I told you before not to touch me. Unless you want me to lay you out on this bed right now, stop. I came back a monster. I won't be gentle."

Shit. He hated being so tactless, so . . . crass. Beauty such as hers never belonged with someone like him, even before he looked like this. The moment his words sank in, the edges of her eyes shifted down. Her eyebrows drew together. When her lips pressed tight into a thin line, he tore his gaze away.

Oh, but the pain came anyway. The memory. For the first time in months, years probably, a slow burn churned his stomach, igniting a path up his chest and wedging in his throat. She'd had the same look that night in the rain ten years ago. His guilt hadn't subsided for one day since. He'd torn her to pieces, humiliated her, and walked away.

She needed to walk away now, before this escalated. Before he broke her heart. Before she broke his. No, they weren't kids anymore, playing around in an adult world. What they had then couldn't hold a lick to what could be now, if given half the chance.

Except the result would be the same.

"You're not a monster," she whispered.

His gaze flew back to hers.

She swallowed. "No matter what you think, Cole, you're not a monster."

Holy hell in a handbasket. It used to infuriate him how damn sensitive she was. Compassionate, gifted, caring. She raised her disabled sister when her mama was too lazy or drunk to deal with life. She dished out every excuse for the way people treated her, claiming they didn't know any better. But this was too much. Not even she could possibly find any beauty in what he'd become.

Slowly, she rose, the bed shifting in her absence. Her glance darted everywhere but at him, pink tingeing her cheeks. "I won't touch you again. Goodnight, Cole."

In the humming quiet, he decided enough was enough. From now on, he was going to be more honest with Mia and less defensive. If that was all he could offer, he'd do that much.

Mia walked into the kitchen and scrubbed her hands over her face. She'd never been able to function on little sleep and last night she'd had none. After what happened in Cole's bedroom, she tossed in her bed for hours before eventually giving up. She poured water to start a pot of coffee while looking out the window. The sun wasn't even up yet.

Deciding to go for a walk to clear her head, she donned a sweater and stepped outside while the coffee brewed. She closed her eyes, listening to the roar of the surf hitting the shore. The air was damp and cool. Fall would set in soon, bringing hurricane season upon them. Though tropical storms could hit anytime in June through November, they were most likely to strike in August through October, with September being the peak. The Covingtons used to leave at the end of August to head back to Charlotte. She'd never been to the estate during fall. The trailer park where she grew up was much farther inland, on the west side of the county. They'd seen their share of storms and hurricanes, even had to evacuate to the elementary school overnight a time or two. She'd have to watch the weather reports and keep an eye on the radar in case the house needed to be closed up.

Noticing an empty basket on the porch, she picked it up and headed toward the water. Maybe she could make a wind chime out of seashells for Ginny. It would give her something to do in her downtime, besides thinking of Cole.

Walking along the surf, she kept her eyes trained down for shells, the warm foam hitting her feet. The task gave her a purpose and kept her focused for a short while until she had filled the basket and headed back. Halfway to the house she paused, her gaze directed at a patch of sea oats just left of the house.

He'd first kissed her there. One of his friends had tried the unthinkable and Cole had stepped in. Her feelings already in an emotional summersault, he'd kissed her as if she was something more than a friend. She still felt his arms around her, holding her close, chasing away the uncertainty.

Mia knew coming back here wasn't going to be easy, knew she'd have to relive the painful memories, one by one by one. But that kiss last night didn't bring pain. Instead, it left her reeling in all the sweet, pleasurable time they once shared. Time that was too short, yet left an eternity of scars. Maybe her inability to let go stemmed from the fact that they could never be more. It was a doomed relationship from the beginning. A relationship that could never amount to anything more than stolen kisses and hidden caresses. Perhaps because he was her first, or that he had way more to lose than she did by crossing that line so many summers ago.

As much as she told herself coming back here was to help Cole, to secure a future for Ginny, part of her knew it was about closure. About shutting down the past so she could move on without the Covington shadow looming over her. More than half her life had been spent on bitter regret and anger. She needed to let that go.

Sighing, she glanced up at the house, shocked to see that Cole stood on his bedroom balcony. He made no attempt to hide, just leaned his forearms on the railing and wove his fingers together. After staring at each other for several moments, he broke the contact first and glared in the direction of the sea oats. Her pulse sped. He was thinking of the same memories. He had to be.

Last night he'd acted like he still wanted her. In fact, he'd so rudely pointed out how much he'd like to . . .

Which contradicted what he'd said when he'd ended things ten years ago. Before she could think too deeply about that, Cole straightened and walked back inside.

Closing her eyes, she took a moment to let the sound of the waves and the feel of the sand beneath her feet ground her. Sucking in a deep breath, she opened her eyes and made her way to the house.

Cole was at the counter, pouring himself a cup of coffee when she walked in. She set the basket of shells on the table and went to the sink to wash her hands. He didn't back up or give her any breathing room, just watched her over the rim of his cup as he drank. Hating the on-edge feeling he gave her, she backed away to dry her hands.

"Morning. I'll get you some breakfast and then we need to hit the gym. Working out in the morning is better for—"

"I'm sorry about last night." Just like that. No interlude, no warning. The gruffness in his voice set her nerves on fire and he just stood there stoically, as if not fazed in the least.

He was sorry. Sorry he had kissed her? "It was just a kiss, Cole. You were confused—"

"I wasn't confused." Very direct. Very sure. "I'm not sorry I kissed you either. I'm sorry for my words after."

Her mouth opened and closed three times before a wayward, "oh" popped out.

A slow, steady grin spread as his direct glare held her frozen.

Wow. She remembered that smile. It transformed his whole face.

"Yeah. So what's for breakfast?"

Breakfast? He plowed over her with an admission like that then asked about breakfast? "Um, eggs. Sit down. It'll be a minute." *Yes, back away from me. Give me some breathing room.*

Walking over to the table, he eased into a chair.

She didn't realize she was still watching until his eyebrows shot up in question. "Your limp is better."

He nodded once. "Doesn't hurt as bad."

Whirling, she opened the fridge and removed the necessary items. "How do you like your eggs?"

"Scrambled."

Funny, that was how her brain felt. She cracked the eggs into a bowl and whisked them before adding salt, pepper, and a touch of milk. Once they were in the skillet, she sliced some melon and set it on a plate.

He watched her every movement.

"Would you stop, please?"

"Stop what?"

She turned to face him. "Stop staring at me." Now she sounded like a child.

His gaze dropped to his coffee. "I used to watch you all the time. Mostly while you were in the grove or walking on the beach."

She never knew that. She wished he'd kept that to himself. Turning back to the stove, she stirred the eggs, hating how her hands shook. "That was a long time ago."

"Doesn't feel so long ago now."

Her hand stilled.

"Having you back here . . . it reminds me how easy you were to talk to. Still are."

She gripped the spatula with such force she was surprised it didn't snap. Transferring the eggs to a plate, she set them in front of him and sat down across the table. He wasn't staring at her now. God, he looked so lost. So lonely.

Cole had a lot of friends. Or at least he used to. Mia suspected they were mostly for show. Not really the kind of people he trusted with secrets and deep discussions. Not like the conversations they used to have. Did he have no one in his life anymore? Army buddies? Anyone?

"Is that what you want to do, Cole? Talk?"

He stared at his plate, that vacant expression hollowing his eyes.

Worried something had triggered a flashback, she set her hand over his. "Cole?"

"I'm here." He slid his hand out from under hers and picked up his fork. He said nothing more as he ate his breakfast, so she let the subject drop.

She wondered, and not for the first time, what was going on inside his head. Thousands of questions ran rampant in hers, but he wasn't ready to answer them yet. She wasn't sure she was ready to hear them either.

Her gaze dropped to the scar on his neck and her throat closed with emotion. It must've been terrible being over there. Watching soldiers die, the conditions they lived in . . .

With a sudden, jerked movement, he slapped his hand over the scar. "Now who's staring?" The tone in his voice nearly cut her.

Refraining from the urge to pull his hand away, she looked right into his eyes. "You shouldn't be ashamed of your scars, Cole. You fought and almost died for our country. You're a hero."

He stood so swiftly the plate careened across the table. "Tell that to the wives and mothers of the men who died. I'm no hero, Mia." He turned to leave.

"Why did you enlist?"

He froze in the doorway, every muscle wrung tight. She thought he'd turn around, thought he'd give an explanation when he stood there so long. Instead, he mumbled, "I'll meet you in the gym."

chapter
seven

Mia finished helping Rose make the bed in the master bed-room and straightened. "You need anything else, Rose?"

"No, child. You've done enough of your mama's work today."

Mia smiled and turned to leave. She was supposed to meet Cole by the pool in a few minutes. He said he had a surprise for her and she couldn't wait to find out what it was. Mrs. Covington stepped into the room before she could make her exit.

She wore powder blue slacks and a fitted silk blouse buttoned all the way to her neck. A strand of pearls tucked under the collar and lay over the first button. Matching earrings were posted in each ear. As always, her makeup was carefully applied and her smooth, coifed blonde hair styled neatly into a bob. "May I have a word with you, Mia? Alone."

Mia looked at Rose, for what, she didn't know, but Rose ducked her head and left the room.

Mrs. Covington closed the door with a quiet click. "You've been helping the staff a lot lately, I noticed."

Mia's heart pounded. What was she expecting her to say? "Um . . . yes. Mama's been a bit under the weather, so I thought I'd help out."

Mrs. Covington sniffed as if a stench had entered the room. "Under the weather. Is that what we're calling it?" She waved off Mia's excuse. "Is this your ambition, Mia? To clean houses for a living?"

"No!" Mia answered, a bit too loudly. There was nothing wrong with that profession, but she wanted more. She wanted . . . out. "I want to be a nurse, ma'am."

Her eyebrows rose so slightly Mia thought she'd imagined it. "High expectations, don't you think? That involves college and college costs money."

"My guidance counselor helped me apply for grants and a student loan. I've been accepted at UNC for fall."

"I see." Her gaze assessed her from head to toe. "You've been spending a lot of time with my son as of late." Mia opened her mouth to respond, but Mrs. Covington raised her manicured hand. "You're a bright girl and I'm no spring chicken. You'd do well to remember Cole's place in society in comparison to yours. Things will go smoothly for you if you do."

Mia's blood turned to ice. She might not have the education of the Covingtons, but she darn well knew when she'd just been threatened. Mrs. Covington had enough power to get her kicked out of UNC before she even set foot in the door. And Mama—she could fire her. Would do it, too. Where would that leave Ginny?

Her stomach rolled, but she looked her square in the eyes. "I understand."

With a curt nod, Mrs. Covington left the room. Mia stood there for ten grueling seconds before stepping out and descending the stairs. She needed to get the hell out of here. The staff didn't come and go through the front door, but if she went out the side door, Cole would see her. That was, if he'd waited for her.

Of course he'd waited. Their kisses after that first one had been building. He'd told her many times how much he wanted her and she'd admitted her feelings as well. It was exciting and raw and . . . new. They'd been careful with where they met. Someone must've seen.

Mia opened the front door, the humidity slamming into her, but it did little to chase away the cold inside. Without wasting time, she bolted down the porch steps and around the fountain. She made it halfway down the drive before a car pulled up beside her. The passenger window glided down and she looked into Dean's kind whiskey eyes.

"Where are you off to, Miss Mia?"

"Um . . ." God. She hadn't thought that far ahead. She just needed to get away. The trailer on her side of town was easily twenty miles. "I was just walking home. I'm a bit tired."

When his eyebrows rose, she knew he saw through her lie, but instead of calling her out, he leaned over and opened the door. "Hop in. I'll drive you."

"Oh, um . . ." Flustered, she ran a hand over her ponytail. Did Mrs. Covington's warning extend to Dean, too? Or Lacey? She looked over the roof of the car. Cole glared at her from the corner of the house.

After a few seconds, he began walking over.

"Okay." Diving into the passenger seat, she shut the door. "Thanks, Dean."

Shifting gears, he pulled ahead before Cole could catch them. As they drove through the gate, Cole's reflection in the side mirror showed his arms crossed, mouth firm. In his eyes was . . . hurt. She bit her tongue hard enough to draw blood and keep the tears at bay then tore her gaze away.

Present

In the gym, Cole stepped out of his sweats, leaving on only his nylon running shorts. Not that he did any running. If Mia wanted him to start on these machines again though, he'd suffocate in sweats. The shorts, loose and tapered just above his knees, barely covered the crater-like gouge in his thigh. She'd see it. And just like before, when she saw the other scar, her eyes would cloud with pity.

Screw pity. He didn't need anyone's pity. He'd made his choices. Everything he touched turned to shit. Including his life. Why was he bothering with all this anyway?

Mia's jasmine perfume hit him before she entered the room. Man, it still made his gut clench.

"Which machine?"

"The treadmill." She walked over. "Step on."

He did.

"Now, place your feet on the side of the tread when you start. This will keep you balanced. Even after you work back up to a jog, you need to start at a slow pace to allow your leg time to adjust." She set the dial to a snail's pace and backed away. "Let's do ten minutes."

"Fine." Placing his feet on the runner, he kept up with the easy stride.

After a few minutes of watching him, she sat in a chair a few feet away, apparently satisfied he wouldn't go flying backward into the drywall. "If the leg ever cramps up or you can't go on, move the right leg to the side of the tread and raise the left before turning off the machine. You'll be less likely to fall—"

"I've got it, Mia!"

Her tiny red mouth popped open before she pressed her lips firmly closed. A trace of hurt crossed her face before her features smoothed out. Shit. He needed to stop snapping at her. This wasn't her fault. She was only trying to help. He felt so, so . . . *emasculated*. Before his injuries he had a solid body. Defined muscles and strength. Though a trace of the corded muscle tone was still there, he wasn't the lean, strong man he used to be before enlisting. Then there were the scars . . .

"I'm sorry. I'm not trying to kill your pride, Cole."

She could still read him. Even after ten years she could still look at him and know everything that was going on in his mind. God, no one knew him like Mia. No one. Every secret, every wish for his life had rested in her hands and heart. Then she was ripped away and there was no hope left.

Closing his eyes, he counted to ten slowly. "Don't apologize. I'm sorry." He opened his eyes.

She nodded but wouldn't look him in the eyes. Leaning back, she glanced at her watch. "Five minutes to go. You doing okay?"

"Yes." Strangely enough. There was still a dull ache, but it wasn't nearly as bad since she had arrived at the house. Since she made his ass get out of the wheelchair and move. He looked over at her. She was staring at her hands in her lap. Guilt—the emotion he'd grown so used to through the years that it was woven into his very soul—rose inside. They needed to talk about something else, something in her comfort zone. "So, you became a nurse like you always wanted."

Nodding without looking up, she crossed her arms over her chest. The movement caused her perfect breasts to rise near the neckline of her fitted blouse. "Yeah. I started out in the ER, but the hours were rough. I worked at a geriatric clinic after that. Until I got laid off."

He forced his mind off her breasts and focused on what she said. "How long ago was that?"

"A couple months back."

"So now you're doing private duty for crazy vets?"

Her smile nearly made him fall on his face. "Something like that."

He wondered what Lacey was paying her. It had to be substantial to get her beautiful ass back here to help him. Whatever it was, it wasn't nearly enough.

"I might apply at the veteran's hospital when I leave here. To be honest, before you, it never crossed my mind. I think I could make a big difference helping soldiers."

When I leave here. That thought ate him raw.

He tried to focus on their conversation. He remembered her excitement when she was accepted to UNC. So long ago now. She'd gone into nursing because she wanted to help people. Always the savior, his Mia. *His. Not anymore, asshole.* "Is the work everything you'd thought it would be? Are you saving the world one patient at a time?"

A look, something like doubt, crossed her face. "Sometimes."

She was lying. One more thing had let her down. He didn't know much about her life now, but Mia's early years had been a series of constant disappointments. Once, he'd thought he could change that. Instead, he'd only made things worse.

He didn't know why his life had been spared in that

godforsaken desert. He didn't know why Mia chose to come back, but he was handed a second chance and he was going to rectify the past. The only thing that got him through the hell overseas was her. She'd never know. He'd make sure of that. Somehow Cole would make up for what he'd done, for the lies he told to spare her a lifetime of guilt and pain. To avoid her ending up like him.

Hesitantly, she glanced at him. "Did you get your degree?"

If not for her insistence back then to follow his dream, he wouldn't have. For all the good it did him now. "Yeah. I earned a master's in English literature. I worked at a New York literary agency for a year, specializing in mysteries and memoirs. Then I came into my trust and bought this house."

Something flickered over her face.

"What?"

A shrug. "Nothing. Just thinking."

"I know that look, Mia. What are you thinking?"

"Time's up." She stood. "Let's move to the rowing machine. Only five minutes on that one."

Stepping down, he walked over and sat on the rowing machine. He placed both hands on the bars and his feet on the pedals. When he pulled back, pain shot down his left leg. Before he could contain it, a roar erupted.

In a heartbeat, she was kneeling next to him. "I'm going to touch you, and you're *not* going to freak out, Cole."

The sharp order stunned him enough to freeze. Her palm came down on his thigh and pressed, temporarily quashing the pain. To her credit, she didn't try to examine the scar or say anything soothing. She'd been very careful not to stare at his injuries or coddle him with false words. It made him respect her even more. Bringing her other hand over, she gently kneaded the thigh until he was gritting his teeth, not from pain, but from her touch. Damn, how he missed her touch. He drew in a ragged breath and she released the pressure.

"Better?" She still looked down.

When he didn't answer, her gaze shot to his. In those deep, deep blue eyes of hers he didn't see pity, only concern.

She must've taken his expression all wrong because her hands flew up. "Cole?"

She thought he was having a flashback. Truth be told, he hadn't had many since she came back. Probably because his overloaded brain could only pull her out amid the craziness. "Guilt." If he was going to mend things between them, he had to start somewhere. "That's why I enlisted in the army. I couldn't take the guilt anymore."

Sighing, he looked away. "I'd only just come off an internship at the agency and had my own desk for six months. I went back to an empty apartment with too much time to think. I saw this commercial for the army and on a whim I signed up. Just like that."

Her lips parted and her hand fell to his knee. She withdrew like he'd electrocuted her. Taking her hand, he placed it over the scar on his leg. Through the shorts, his skin heated from her touch. "I thought these scars were a punishment. Part of me wanted to die. In the back of my mind I knew getting killed was a possibility. What started out as guilt morphed into a way out, Mia."

Her hand trembled under his. "Cole." The way she said his name, like a statement, still had the ability to stop his heart cold.

He could still know what she'd say, even after ten years. "You're going to say Dean's death wasn't my fault, that it was yours. No matter what she told you, Mia, she was wrong."

Her gaze leveled on his, so intense he couldn't draw in air. "No. It wasn't my fault. And it wasn't yours."

He opened his mouth.

She abruptly stood. "Shut up, Cole. On this one subject, please, don't argue with me. Now, row." She pointed to the machine.

Guess she was done discussing it. Hearing wasn't believing, but he did as she asked and didn't correct her. It *was* his fault. His brother was dead because of him. Because of a chain of events he'd set into motion, his brother died, and he lost Mia forever.

"I'm going to head to the market after lunch. Why don't you come with me? Get out of the house for a while?"

It took a lot of concentration not to falter his movement. "Um, no. Thanks though."

"Why?"

Damn her persistence. "I'm not up for it, okay?" He focused on the hardwood floor, the gray walls, anything but her as he rowed. Forward. Back.

"You haven't been out since coming home, have you?"

He should have let one of Lacey's other nurses help him—someone who didn't know when he lied, who didn't know his every quirk and nuance. But then he never would have seen her again.

"An answer, Cole."

For that, he did stop. "I walked on the beach with you yesterday." Maybe she'd drop the subject. No such luck.

"Why won't you leave the house?"

Rising, he grabbed a towel and wiped the sweat from his face. "Let it go."

"I will not."

Aw man. The Southern drawl still thickened when she

got angry. They used to have wonderful, satisfying arguments back in the day. He grew hard just thinking about it. Dropping his hand to the waistband of his shorts, he covered himself with the towel, hoping she wouldn't see.

"Take off your shirt." Out of nowhere. Just like that.

"Uh, look." He cleared his throat. "Mia—"

"I'm not going to molest you, Cole. Take off your damn shirt."

"What if I want you to molest me?" Why the hell did he go and say that? Out loud.

Her perfect-for-kissing mouth formed an O, her Mediterranean blue eyes wide, wide open. Then she . . . Well, hell. She laughed. Long, loud, and with the same gut-wrenching smokiness that had him wrapped around her finger all these years. His dick jumped.

"Oh, Cole. Nice try." After several attempts, she sobered. "Honestly, it's just you and me here. Take off your shirt. Please."

It was the *please* that did him in. His heart pounded against his ribs with such force it hurt. "Mia, I don't know what point you're trying to make, but—"

"Don't make me do it for you."

Huh. She had grown a pair since he last saw her. No more meek Mia. He wanted nothing more—God, nothing—than for her to close the distance between them, slide her long, delicate fingers under his shirt and tug it over his head. "You're killing me."

You said thoughts out loud again. He needed to quit that.

She took a step forward, but he held her in place with his palm up. With utter mortification, 'cause his hands shook like hell, he reached behind his neck and pulled off his T-shirt. His eyes slammed shut as he dropped his chin to his chest. His hands fell on his waist. The other night, when she looked at him after the nightmare, she saw the ugliness only in the dim lamplight. In the harsh daylight, she would be able to see everything. The pitted flesh, the purple and red splotches, the jagged, raised surgical scar where they'd tried to fix him. The plastic surgeon had told him they could minimize the damaged flesh, but Cole wouldn't let them. This was his punishment. An everyday reminder of his sins.

He finally looked on the outside how he felt on the inside.

"Look at me," she said.

His teeth ground as he shook his head.

"Cole, look at me."

His name on her lips. A shiver tore from deep within. Opening his eyes, he looked at her. There was no trace of what he'd been expecting. Truly, he hadn't known what to expect, but it sure wasn't . . . heat. Understanding.

"You're just as handsome now as you always were," she whispered. "No scars can change that." A swallow clicked from her throat. "Your clothing hides most of the scars. No one is going to see. And if people stare, then let them. You have nothing to be ashamed of."

So there was the point she was trying to make. From the start she knew why he didn't leave the house, but she tried to get him to say so on his own, without her interference. He wasn't ugly to her. God, that felt as good as it hurt. Looking at her, though, damn if she didn't mean every word she'd just said. The warmth of her words sank deep, making him *want* to believe.

She blew out a breath. "You're not ready yet." She nodded in acceptance. "We'll try again another day." Her gaze darted around the room. "I think we're done here. Come on, I'll make you some lunch before I go shopping."

Mia set a bag of groceries on the counter, surprised Cole still sat at the kitchen table. He'd eaten half his sandwich and two bites of apple.

"Not hungry?"

"Guess not."

Unable to decipher his expression, she began putting the groceries away. When finished, she set out the makings for subs and got to work slicing the fresh Italian bread.

"What are you doing?"

Without looking up, she spread mayo over the bread. "Making you a sub for over the weekend. I have to head home tonight, remember?"

"When are you coming back?"

The hint of desperation in his voice had her looking over at him. "Monday morning. Rose will be back then, too."

"Oh."

She set the knife down, staring at him. "You'll be fine. I'm making lunch for tomorrow and there will be enough leftovers from dinner tonight." His expression didn't change, almost like he was . . . afraid. Maybe he'd finally gotten used to her being here, which was a giant leap in the right direction. "I bought you a donut for breakfast tomorrow." She wiggled her brows.

He laughed and the sound drifted across the room, settling inside her chest. He hadn't laughed once since she got here. What a great laugh he had.

"What about this new diet of yours? Doesn't that break the rules?"

"You never cared about rules before, Cole Covington.

Don't pretend to now." She smiled and turned back to her task, laying ham on the bread. She topped that off with some provolone before slicing the Roma tomatoes. "I'll let you cheat your diet on Sundays."

"You'll *let* me? You're putting more veggies on that sub than meat."

She grinned, satisfied his smug tone had returned. The hollow weariness was so unlike him. "Guilty. You'll get over it." After adding lettuce and cucumber, she wrapped the sub in cellophane and set it in the fridge.

The camaraderie they'd once had was slowly seeping back into this new relationship. Being together was almost easy. She hoped leaving for a day wouldn't backtrack all the progress they'd made.

"Why are you staring at me?"

She hadn't realized she was. Dropping her hand from the fridge door, she sighed. "So, I have an idea."

"I get the feeling I won't like this idea."

Shaking her head, she smiled. "Follow me into the library, would you?"

Without question, he stood, making her grin widen. It felt good not having him challenge her for once. They made their way down the hall and into the library. Powering up the computer on the corner desk, she waited for the PC to reboot. Going into the settings, she opened a blank Word document and waved him over.

He sat in the computer chair and looked at her with raised brows. The close proximity had her pulse thumping. Close enough to smell his sandalwood scent, to see the muscles working his jaw. Another inch to the left and their arms would brush. The kiss the other night rushed to memory and, for an insane, haggard second, she wanted to lean over. Brush her lips against his. Feel his hands threading her hair.

No. Don't do this again.

Straightening, she cleared her throat. "Um . . . I think you should write down your thoughts."

"Come again?"

"Part of full recovery means talking about what happened. There are some things you may not want to talk about, to me, to anyone. That's okay. If you write them out, they'll help you process and move on."

"You want me to write a diary?" His tone was incredulous.

She sighed. "Or . . . a memoir." His expression hardened, so she quickly clarified. "No one has to see it but you. You have a lit degree and worked as an agent. You know how to format and write a book."

"Being an agent and an author are two separate things."

"I know. A lot of agents become authors and vice versa. Write a memoir, Cole. For you. If you choose to let others read it afterward, then that's up to you. Either way, it might help."

As he looked between her and the screen, a lock of his blond hair fell to his forehead. So, so badly she wanted to brush it aside, just to touch him again. She needed this break from him. Badly.

"It'll also give you something to do while I'm gone. There's only one television in this house and you haven't turned it on. I haven't seen you read either."

He opened his mouth and closed it again. "It's been hard to focus on a book and sometimes a movie will . . ."

"Movies trigger memories." She nodded. "I'll make you a deal. You do this memoir thing and I guarantee the focus will return. After exercising, we'll watch a movie in the afternoons. See if we can't get you past the flashbacks."

As he looked at her, she sensed not only the hesitation, but the hope. Not once this week had she witnessed any trace of hope in his dark eyes. With a sudden jolt, sympathy consumed her, and with that emotion came a determination to make him whole again. This mission was no longer about Ginny's future, though she'd do anything for her sister. Being here was about Cole and about herself. As the determination grew, happiness didn't seem so much like a dream anymore.

"Mia, I don't know if I can do this. Even trying to seems . . ."

His words brought something to mind and a memory struck. They used to talk in quotes to each other. Something silly to make a point or one-up each other in a battle of wits. "Do or do not. There is no try."

He blinked and reared back. A corner of his mouth lifted. "Let me guess. Obi-Wan Kenobi?"

"Close. Yoda."

As he laughed, she walked to the door. "You work on that. I'll go start dinner."

"When a man falls into disaster, he did it himself."

Her steps faltered, realizing the hidden implication in his quote. She sucked in a slow breath before turning. His gaze darted to his lap, unable or unwilling to look at her. Emotion clogged her throat. "Hemingway?"

"Mark Twain."

Okay, fine. He wanted to go there, well, she could counter. She searched her brain. "To be wrong is nothing unless you continue to remember it." Before he could ask who, or before this conversation and subtext went any deeper, she turned and said over her shoulder, "Confucius."

Cole stared out the library window as the waning sun dipped west. For the hundredth time, he ran a hand over his jaw and glanced at the cursor on the computer screen.

The page was still blank. The idea to write down what happened would be the equivalent of raking his soul over hot coals. He didn't think he could do it.

Mia wanted him to. Thought it would help. Most of all, she had faith he *could* do it.

The problem didn't lie solely in the memories. Rehashing everything that happened would be the hardest thing he'd ever done. He couldn't simply write about Iraq, his injuries, and how he escaped death. In all honesty—and that's what Mia wanted from him—his time in the military was only a glimmer of what haunted him. The story started long before enlisting. With Mia. With Dean. And, dear God, with his parents.

Mia said no one else had to read his words. Just him. For Cole to drum up the courage to write down his memoir, even if he was the only one to see it, he had to fall back on what he knew. He knew manuscripts. The task would be tolerable if he wrote in book form. Yes, they'd be his words, his story, but to hold on to sanity, he could keep himself detached if he wrote it as a book, pretending the characters were just people in his head.

He shook his head and stood. It was too late in the day to start something like this now. The nightmares would be terrible if he opened himself to this. Plus, he'd be alone in the house tonight. She'd be gone for one day and two nights. It was strange how quickly he'd grown to depend on her again. On having her scent in the house. Her lilting, soothing voice wafting over his skin like a breeze.

Leaning over, he saved the document on his desktop as "Project Mia" and left the room. The closer he got to the kitchen, the stronger the Italian scents grew. Tomato, oregano, garlic. His mouth watered.

He stopped in the doorway. "It smells good in here."

Her smile came easy as she looked over her shoulder. "And it's done, so have a seat."

Making his way to the table, he sat and watched her.

"How did it go in there?" She had her back to him as she dished out whatever she'd cooked.

He thought about the blank page. "Okay. I have some ideas."

Turning, her brows rose. "Ideas or words?"

He laughed. "I'll work on it, Mia."

"I'll hold you to that."

Of that, he had no doubt. She set a plate in front of him. Picking up his fork, he glanced down. On his plate was the greenery of fresh salad and, beside it, spaghetti. The edges of his vision grayed. The smell of smoke and diesel and burnt flesh rose up. Before the images could fully form, he roared, sending the plate across the room and shattering against the wall. Red sauce dripped down to the floor.

A pause. "Cole?"

Dammit. Burying his face in his hands, he mumbled an apology. A long silence followed before her feet padded across the tile. The clinking of ceramic filled the quiet kitchen as she collected the shards of the broken plate. The mess hit the bottom of the trash can, then the kitchen faucet was running. Mortified, he couldn't look at her, just kept his head buried in his hands. Before long, he not so much heard as felt her sit down in the chair next to him.

"What happened, Cole?"

He shook his head.

She gripped his wrists and forced them down. "What happened?"

Unable to look her in the eyes, he stared at the curve of her throat, remembering how soft the skin was there. He swallowed. "I'm sorry." At this point, he didn't even know what he was apologizing for anymore.

"You said that already. What happened?"

He glanced up, trying to determine if it was anger or disdain in her tone. Surprised to find neither on her face, he looked at her long fingers around his wrists. Dammit again. The horror he'd seen over there should never touch her, but he'd already brought it to her attention. What would one more hurt? Fact was, he found it oddly comforting talking to her about the flashbacks. Somehow, she took them away. The ceiling fan in his room no longer reminded him of the heli blades. It was just a ceiling fan. His nightmares weren't about Iraq anymore. Instead, other areas of his past, their past, crept into his dreams.

Suddenly, telling her about the dinner he ruined wasn't so daunting. In fact, it was preferable to what else haunted him. Forcing his gaze to hers, she just looked back at him, patiently waiting for an explanation.

He sighed. "After the IED went off and I was lying in the sand, I tried to assess my injuries. When I finally got the strength to look at my leg, the first thought that came to mind was how the damage resembled a plate of spaghetti."

There. Now she knew. Like him, she probably never wanted to eat it again.

"Okay. Wow."

"Yeah."

Her fingers slid from his wrists to his palms, cupping their hands together. "Close your eyes." He did after only a second's hesitation. One of her fingers circled his palm, sensual and comforting. "What do you smell? Describe it for me."

Trying to direct his focus off her caress and shift to other senses, he inhaled. "Garlic and tomato sauce." Not diesel or charred flesh.

"All right. Keep your eyes closed." Her chair scooted across the floor and she walked away for several seconds before returning. "Open your mouth."

Naughty, naughty images floated to mind. Despite an effort not to, he grinned. At her sharp intake of breath, as if she were just as affected, he wondered what she'd do if he closed the space between them and kissed her. "Is this the part where you cover me in whipped cream? 'Cause I'd like my eyes open for that."

"Lord. The old Cole *is* still in there."

One of his eyes peeked open. "You don't sound disappointed."

"Relieved," she mumbled, then shook her head like she was appalled to admit so aloud.

He closed his eyes and opened his mouth expectantly, pleased that he wasn't the only one who couldn't hold his tongue. Maybe she wasn't as calm as she appeared. Maybe being around him again was drawing her back, too.

Something touched his lips, and for a blinding moment, he thought it was her mouth. Everything south of his waist responded. Tomato sauce and herbs settled over his tongue, shifting desire to hunger and back again. Swallowing hard, he fought the physical response to her, a battle he'd lost long ago, although not for lack of trying. Over the smells of Italian food, her jasmine scent pulled hard at his groin.

"Are you okay?" she asked.

Fight. Harder.

But as his eyes opened, he cupped the back of her neck and pulled her to him. Just before he kissed her, common sense kicked in and he pressed his forehead to hers instead. Her eyes widened. Blinked. Their breath mingled, hers so very warm against his parted lips.

She didn't pull away. Didn't even try.

Barely containing a growl, he blew out a breath and reared back. To avoid looking at her and doing what his body desperately craved, he glanced at the plate on the table. Spaghetti. It was just spaghetti. She pressed a hand to her chest. He dragged the plate closer and took a bite.

Her hands were shaking as she set them down to stand. In silence, she filled two Tupperware bowls with the leftovers and put them in the fridge while he ate.

"Aren't you eating, too?"

Her eyes were still dazed, a look he remembered well. Guilt rammed his gut. This desire for her had not abated, but he would overcome it. He had to. He could not touch her again. Thinking led to touching. Touching led to . . .

"Um, no. I'm not very hungry and I have to hit the road."

He dropped his fork, panic causing his heart to pound and his throat to close. "You'll be back?" He hated this. Hated the desperate feeling inside at losing her all over again. Hating depending on a woman he could never have, who was never truly his to begin with.

She must have sensed his anxiety because she claimed the seat next to him again. "Cole, you have my word, I'll stay until you feel well again. I won't leave. You're safe. You will overcome this. I promise. But I need this time for Ginny. You understand?"

Looking into the endless depth of her eyes, he saw truth. If he trusted no one else, he could trust her. One more thing to feel guilty over. He didn't deserve her or her help. He never had. "Yes. Of course you need to see your sister. I shouldn't keep you here all week like this. Why don't you take the whole weekend off from now on?"

Oh God. Say no. Please, please say no. Say you need to stay. Stay.

A smile traced the corners of her mouth. "We'll work up to that. For now, let's stick with Sundays."

His stomach recoiled as he watched her pick up her pocketbook and her overnight bag. Following her to the front door, he forced a smile. "I'll see you on Monday."

"My number's on the fridge."

He closed the door behind her. *You will not use it. You will not call her. She has her own life.* A life without him.

But God, the past ten years fell away as he watched her car disappear down the drive.

chapter
eight

"You've been avoiding me for more than a week."

Mia jumped and slammed backward into the dryer, toppling the stack of towels she had just folded. To avoid looking at Cole, she bent to retrieve the towels. "I've been busy. Um . . . helping the staff, you know?"

"No, I don't know."

She briefly closed her eyes before daring to look at him. Anger furrowed his brow, his mouth a tight, thin line. She wanted to smooth her fingers over the hurt there so badly. "I'm sorry."

What else was there to say? Of all the emotions she was feeling, sorry wasn't one of them. She wasn't sorry for letting him kiss her. She wasn't sorry for the deep friendship they'd forged these past few years. She wasn't sorry he made her heart come alive, or for the weak measure of happiness she finally had from just being near him.

The only thing she was truly sorry for was that she couldn't give him any more than the gift of walking away.

"Sorry for what, Mia? Leaving me in the driveway staring after you? Leaving me to wonder what in the hell happened?" His hands balled into fists. She watched him battle back the frustration. "Meet me at the guesthouse in a few minutes."

"I can't. Rose is driving me home as soon as I finish this laundry."

"Then tell her you have a ride. Meet me at the guesthouse, Mia."

No one was staying in the guesthouse currently. No one ever really went over there. Mrs. Covington wouldn't know. Mia could meet him in private and say her good-byes. A forever kind of good-bye. Oh, that hurt so bad. The Covingtons were heading back to Charlotte in one week. She was no longer needed here at the house after today. She'd made the decision not to come back next year, whether Mama needed her or not. She'd start college in the fall and leave Cole to find some other girl to love. A girl who fit into his world.

Slowly, she nodded her head, consenting to the meeting. He stormed off. Blowing out the breath she didn't realize she was holding, Mia finished refolding the towels and went in search of Rose. After she told her she had a ride, she glanced around the grounds nervously and headed to the east side of the guesthouse.

Feeling a wave of relief for not being seen, she crossed her arms over her chest and stared at the ocean. Tide would be in soon. The staff stayed much later these last few weeks of the season to prepare for closing the house for winter. Her muscles ached. She rubbed her neck, trying to fight off anger at Mama for the drinking. Mia had spent the whole summer cleaning up her mama's mess.

Cole's hands settled over her shoulders and kneaded. She didn't realize he'd come up behind her. Closing her eyes, she let her head fall back to his chest.

"You're tense."

"Yeah."

A long silence and then, "What did I do wrong, Mia?"

Tears formed behind her lids as his thumb traced circles at her nape. No matter the circumstance, he always looked at her, touched her, like she meant everything to him. "Nothing, Cole. You did everything right. I'll remember you always."

His hands stilled. "That sounds like good-bye."

"It is good-bye," she whispered, barely able to hold back a sob.

"No." He spun her around and cupped her face. "No." This time he ground out the word.

"Cole, come on. We knew this was coming." How she hated the quiver in her voice. "We live in different worlds."

"We don't have to."

If only. She shook her head and pressed her cheek to his chest where his heart pounded. After a few moments, his arms came around her. "I . . . love you," she stammered.

His arms tightened, cocooning her in his warmth. "God, I love you, too. Come inside with me."

This summer had changed everything. She'd fallen in love and had her heart broken. It was breaking still. They'd kissed in secret, but they hadn't crossed that line. Had never said the words to each other. She knew what he was asking, knew it would destroy what was left of her heart afterward.

"I've never—"

"I know."

The tremor in his voice, the tenderness, made the

decision for her. She nodded, her cheek still pressed against his heart. He bent over, swept his arm under her legs and carried her inside. He locked the patio door, swept his gaze to the front door to check that lock, and walked into the only bedroom. Carefully, he set her on her feet and walked to the window, drawing the blinds to half-mast.

She swallowed hard, fought the nervousness coiling her belly as he strode back to her side of the room. His fingers threaded her hair when he leaned in to kiss her. All her uneasiness evaporated. This was right. This was Cole. He'd never hurt her. Her first time should be with him.

Breaking their kiss, he removed his shirt and she spread her hands tentatively over the smooth muscles of his chest. "Yes, Mia. It's okay to touch me."

The conviction in his tone gave her courage. Unbuttoning her jeans, she let them and her panties drop to the floor and kicked them away. When she reached for her shirt, he stopped her with his hands. "Let me."

Wide, large hands wrapped around her waist, slid up, up, up, taking her tee over her head. Then his arms came around her back, unfastened her bra, and she was bared fully. She tried to cover herself, embarrassed at the new experience, but he took her hands in his and wove their fingers together.

And then she was crushed to his chest, his tongue seeking every crevice of her mouth. Heat pooled between her thighs and her legs gave out. He caught her, carrying her to the bed and pulling back the comforter before setting her down. Her trembling gave way to quaking as he removed a condom from his back pocket, stripped out of his jeans and underwear and slid the condom over his intimidatingly large erection, all while watching her intently.

Fear filled her chest, knowing this would hurt, not

having the experience or knowhow to make this good for him. "Cole . . ."

"Shh," he quieted, crawling over on his hands and knees and rising over her.

The heat radiating off him calmed her nerves, warmed her cooling skin. He pressed his forehead to hers and smoothed the hair away from her face. Reaching back, he pulled the comforter over the both of them, forming a tent, so all that remained was the two of them. Everything else fell away. He kissed her with such tenderness she wanted to weep. His fingers brushed across her body, taut with tension and want.

For the longest time that's all they did, touch and kiss until her body was screaming for more. For them to continue to the next phase. He must've sensed her readiness because he gently nudged her legs apart and centered himself near her opening. Reaching for her hands, he wove their fingers together once more.

His mouth hovered over hers. "Take a slow, deep breath in, Mia." When she did, he glided his hips forward and entered her, painfully stretching her inside until their hips joined and he stopped. "Breathe, baby. I've got you. Just breathe."

She drew in air as her body adjusted to his size, to the full, thick, hard length of him. He stayed there, hovering over her, gazes locked together until her muscles relaxed and there was no more pain, just a tender ache.

As if knowing her body, her mind, he drew back, pulling out until only his tip remained inside. "I love you," he whispered and slid back inside her heat with as much sentiment as his words.

Releasing her hands, he nudged one hand between their bodies and touched her nub, causing an electric charge of need to spiral her into oblivion. His other arm snaked behind her back, drawing them even closer yet. Before she knew what was happening, her muscles contracted around him, clutching him like a fist to hold him there. Her back arched off the bed. His face pressed into the curve of her neck.

"Ah, Mia . . . I can't . . ." His arms compressed, stealing her air, but she didn't care. She rode it out with him until the shudders ceased and he collapsed. His breathing came out in shallow pants. "Mia. Mia, Mia," he said against her shoulder. "There are no words . . ."

"So, I was . . . okay?"

"No," he muttered.

Dread and shame pitted her stomach.

He lifted his head to look down at her. "*Okay* is not even in the same category. I've wanted you for so long . . ." He cut off and shook his head. "That was amazing. It was . . ." His eyes widened. "Did I hurt you?"

Her heart swelled, filling her chest. "No."

But he rolled off her anyway, taking the comforter with him. He discarded the condom in the trash and snuggled up beside her again before her skin could have time to cool. He wrapped his arm around her and drew her against his side. She rested her cheek on his chest and they lay there until the light was gone and only shadows remained.

"I can't lose you," he said, his tone determined. She lifted her head and rested her chin on his peck. "I graduate in two years. I can support us. We'll just have to keep our relationship a secret until then."

Hope blended with trepidation. "Your family will never accept me. I can't take you from them. I won't—"

"They will not take *you* from *me*." He sat up, placing her in his lap to fully face him. "They can't do anything if they don't know. We can do this, Mia. Say you will." He cupped her face. "Stay with me."

Could they do this? Him in Massachusetts for two more

years, her in Charlotte for four? Would it even be possible to stay apart that long, catching only glimmers of each other on school breaks? The alternative was no Cole. The pain of possibly, inevitably losing him if they didn't try pummeled her nerves raw. Tears filled her eyes.

"They'd disown you, Cole. Can you live with that? Can you live without your family?"

His jaw clenched. "I'll have you. It'll be tough those first few years, but we can do it. Together."

We. He wanted to be a *we.* For the long haul. "Okay," she whispered, tentative, unsure. Then the warmth spread, making her feel giddy and never more sure of anything. "Yes," she said with more confidence. "Forever, Cole."

Present

"But it's not Sunday."

Mia smiled at Ginny from the easy chair in her sister's bedroom at the group home. It was decorated in muted shades of yellow, Ginny's favorite color. A row of stuffed animals lined the headboard behind her sister. She'd just listened to twenty minutes of what Ginny was doing in art class at St. Ambrose. Ginny loved art, which made Mia think of Lacey. She wondered if Lacey kept up on painting like she used to.

Mia had driven straight from Wilmington to Charlotte to see her sister, not even bothering to stop at her apartment first. She needed to see Ginny, to remind herself of what she could lose if she gave her heart over to Cole Covington again. After only one week, she felt like she was losing the battle.

"I know," she said easily. "But I was thinking we could have a sleepover at my place tonight. What do you think?"

"Yeah!" No hesitation.

Mia rose and shifted over to sit next to Ginny on the bed. Ginny's features had all the markers for typical Down syndrome, but her hair was dark like Mia's and her smile twice as lovely. Her eyes were hazel like Mama's. "You're so pretty, Ginny girl. You know that?"

Ginny played bashful. "You told me that already."

"Well, a girl can never tire of hearing she's pretty." Lord knows she didn't hear it near enough. "Can you pack a bag by yourself or do you need help?"

"I can!"

She kissed her sister's forehead. "So smart, too." She stood. "I'm going to let the staff know you'll be gone tonight. I'll come back in a minute."

Mia walked down the short hall and into the country-style kitchen where Karen, the group home manager, was setting up the med trays for the evening. "If it's okay with you, I'm going to take Ginny home for the night. Girl time."

Karen flipped her blonde ponytail over her shoulder and waved her hand. "Oh sure," she said with a smile. She signed off in a red binder and glanced up, looking more like a thirty-year-old woman than one in her late forties. "Ginny will love that. I'll get her pills ready for the morning so you can take them with you."

"What pills?" Mia asked, concerned. All medications and care plans had to be approved through Mia, as she was Ginny's legal guardian. Ginny was, overall, a healthy, almost seventeen-year-old girl.

Karen skimmed through the medication binder on the white Formica counter to check. To calm herself, Mia stared at the white oak cabinets and the stenciled acrylic apples dotting the front. "She's on a multivitamin and a cranberry concentrate organic substitute."

"Oh," Mia said through a sigh. The thought of someone

unnecessarily medicating Ginny, and behind her back to boot, made her sick. The vitamin was standard and the cranberry pill was to help ward off Ginny's frequent urinary infections. "Yes, please have them ready. I'll bring her back after lunch tomorrow."

Karen nodded. "How's the new job?"

She almost laughed. "It's temporary. I'm really just helping out an old . . . friend. I feel bad being so far away."

"Ginny's doing really well, so don't worry."

"Thanks. That makes me feel a bit better. She had her physical yesterday, didn't she? How did it go?"

"Mary took her to the appointment. Let me see." Karen paged through another binder and read off the sheet. "Vitals: BP was 114/84, pulse 78, and temp 98.9. Sounds good. PAP results should be back this week."

"Good." Because she had Down syndrome, Ginny's heart had to be monitored just to make sure there were no irregularities. So far in her young life, she'd been okay. Mia felt a twinge of guilt for not being able to take Ginny herself. "Well, I'll go get her then," Mia said, taking the small envelope with the vitamins from Karen.

Ginny was waiting with her bag on the bed when Mia reentered her bedroom. "All set?"

"Yeah!"

Mia glanced at the bag and then her sister. "Why don't you say good-bye to your friends? I'll carry the bag to the car."

"Okay."

Mia waited until she left the room before opening the bag to check the contents. Inside were two teddy bears and a candy bar. Laughing, Mia walked to the dresser and pulled out a nightgown, underwear, and change of clothes. Bag in hand, she met Ginny at the car.

Once they were on the road, it occurred to Mia that she

hadn't been back to the apartment in more than a week. When she'd left for Wilmington, her fridge and cabinets were bare. "How 'bout we stop at the store for some snacks?" *And breakfast food, milk, lunch meat, bread . . .*

"Yeah! Can we make popscorn?"

Mia grinned and turned left at the next intersection, flipping on her headlights in the near dark. Popcorn was still one of those words Ginny had trouble pronouncing. "Sure. With extra butter." Except her air popper had broken two months back and she didn't have the money to buy a new one. She'd just pick up microwave popcorn and hope Ginny didn't mind.

"Can we go see Mama?"

Mia's hands tightened on the wheel. Though they'd buried her two years ago, Ginny still had the notion Mama would come back. "Mama died, honey. Remember? We can't see her." Mia glanced at Ginny's profile, watching her lip quiver. At least Ginny had some fond memories of their mom, few and far between as they were. "Hey, pretty girl. We'll pick up some flowers and take them to the cemetery tomorrow. Does that sound like a good plan?"

Ginny nodded but said nothing. Mia sighed, wishing and praying things had been different. If there was one thing Mia needed right now with her emotions all over the crazy place, it was a mom. Someone to hold her and give advice. Someone who loved her no matter what. Instead, she had an empty apartment, bills up the wazoo, and a hole in her chest.

Steeling her resolve, she sucked in a breath. Ginny would have more. Ginny would have love, even if it was just from her. At least it was more than Mia ever had.

Cole crossed his ankles over the railing and relaxed in the rocking chair on the back porch. He stared down into the bowl of leftover spaghetti in his hands, letting the warm salt breeze ruffle his hair. Food didn't fill the emptiness inside. Setting the bowl down by his chair, he looked out over the horizon. Seagulls squawked overhead, circling the water and waiting for fish to surface. The sea grass swayed with the last gust of wind, brushing together to make a hushed, dry crackle in the dusk.

Two weeks ago, the sound brought only reminders of white radio noise. Two weeks ago he couldn't sit out here because the sound of the surf only reminded him of how he wished he was here while overseas. Two days ago he wouldn't have been able to eat spaghetti. His excuses to give up, his painful memories, had begun to be erased and replaced with Mia.

He swiped a hand over his face, over the shadow on his jaw, and wondered what in the hell he was doing thinking about Mia when he had no damn right. He imagined Karma was laughing her sweet ass off right about now. And he had little doubt Karma was a woman. A scorned one.

Not for the first time, he wondered what would've happened had he not forgotten his keys that night. Wondered what would've happened if he'd just thrown Ginny and Mia in the car and left. To hell with everything but young, true love. Dean would probably still be alive. But he didn't think he and Mia would've made it. They were fated to be a memory and nothing more. His mother would've found a way to destroy the beauty in how he loved Mia, in how she'd once loved him back.

Setting his feet down, he rose and headed toward the water, absently grabbing his thigh, though it didn't hurt much. If Mia was only meant to be a fated memory though, why did she come back? It felt like some higher power was rubbing his sins in his face. Bring back the only woman he ever loved, tease him with the possibility of sanity and healing, then take her away all over again.

Bending to pick up a shell, he tossed it, watching it skip across the waves before disappearing. His responsibilities to his parents no longer loomed overhead. He didn't owe them anything, and he didn't know if he ever really had. After he'd come into his trust, he'd become financially stable. More than stable, really. And even if he wasn't, he could fall back on his degree if he so desired, work like normal people did, like he had his first year after graduation. In those first few years after Dean died, Cole only made it home during Christmas. By choice. His parents were a nonentity in his life now. He didn't know if he'd ever return their calls, or if he'd ever speak to them again. They'd tried to visit him in the hospital, had attempted to come here to the house. Rose had changed the security code for the front gate at his request. They hadn't tried to call or visit again that he was aware of.

He should miss them. They were his parents after all.

He *did* miss Lacey. More, he missed Dean. He couldn't do anything about his brother, but he could with Lacey.

After Dean's death, Lacey felt even more obligated to their parents, becoming the poster child for a model daughter. Part of that was Cole's fault. Had he not spiraled out of control, isolated himself from the family, maybe the Covington future wouldn't rest on her. Lacey had given up her hopes and dreams, too. She used to paint lovely, idyllic scenes of the ocean. Cole wondered if she still had dreams or if she was just an empty shell going through the motions. Had she ever fallen in love? Perhaps, heaven forbid, with someone not her social equal?

Cole took his cell out of his pocket and palmed it. A couple days ago, Mia had returned his house phone to his bedroom and his cell to the bedside drawer, claiming she was confident he wouldn't call the National Guard to remove her from the premises. Smart woman.

He should call his sister. If not for Lacey's insistence, for her love he didn't deserve, Mia would still be gone, and he'd be wasting away upstairs, clothed in a dirty robe and regret. Well, he'd shed the robe. How did one start a conversation with someone who had saved his life? Mia had said to start with *hello.* He smiled, finding Lacey's number in his contacts and dialing to connect.

After hearing the ring, his gut turned to ice. He almost hung up, but Lacey answered on the second ring, her worried "hello" crossing the miles between them. Staring out over the water, he froze.

"Mia? Is that you? Is Cole all right?"

His fingers fisted the phone, his arm trembling with such force he thought he'd drop the thing. He opened his mouth, but nothing came out.

"Oh God. Why aren't you answering? Is this a bad connection? Maybe I should call the house." The last part was said quietly, as if talking to herself.

Dammit. "It's . . . me."

Silence. "What's wrong? I can be there in three hours. Two if I take the 'Vette and ignore the state police."

His throat clogged with emotion, but he willed it down and smiled. "You drive like a rabid squirrel as it is. I would advise against it."

More silence. "Cole?" she whispered, as if she couldn't believe her ears. He could hear the tears, her voice threatening to crack.

"Hell, Lacey. Don't cry."

"I'm sorry. It's just . . . you haven't called me since the day you returned from boot camp."

What a selfish prick he'd been. He cleared his raw

throat. "I was just sitting here on the beach, wondering if you paint anymore."

She must've realized the safety in the conversation change because her voice no longer held the weepy edge. "No, I don't paint anymore. I do organize charity art auctions from time to time."

Now that's a shame. Still under Mother's thumb. "Have you ever been in love?"

He could imagine her head rearing back in whiplash. "Uh. Have I . . . ? Cole, where's Mia?"

Shaking his head, he closed his eyes with a smile. "I haven't killed her and buried her under the porch, if that's what you're asking." Pause. "She's in Charlotte, visiting her sister."

"Right. It's Sunday," she mumbled.

"I'm not crazy, either. I was just wondering, is all."

A heavy sigh blanketed the line. "I guess not. I don't think I've ever been in love."

"You would know. Trust me." He debated whether or not to sit in the sand, then thought better of it and walked back to the porch to sit in the rocker.

"This is about Mia, isn't it? I didn't know who else to call. She'd be the only one . . ."

Her voice trailed off and he nodded as if she could see, understanding completely what his sister couldn't voice. Mia was the only one who could break through the depression to get to him and bring him back. "I haven't killed her and buried her under the porch," he said again.

Her laugh came out more like a relieved breath. "Things must be going okay then, if you're calling me from the beach."

Instead of answering, he shifted his gaze to the wild sea oats. "You should fall in love, Lacey. At least once."

She made a sound of frustrated concern. "Oh Cole. I'm coming up there tonight."

In an instant, he knew what she was thinking and felt like pond scum. "I'm not going to kill myself, Lacey. I would've done it by now." When she didn't say anything, he repeated the promise.

"I'm worried about you."

"Don't be. Besides, I'm the big brother. I'm supposed to be the one looking after you. I will from now on." Before she could say anything, he stood. "I have to go."

"Okay. Thanks . . . for calling. It was good to hear your voice."

"Yeah. Yours, too." He opened the back door. "Oh, and Lacey?"

"Yes?"

"Start painting again."

After spending most of Sunday feeling sorry for himself and all of Sunday night staring at a blank Word document in the library, Cole showered and shaved early Monday morning, wanting Mia to think he'd been fine in her absence. With a towel around his waist, he walked to the dresser and opened a drawer. He spent the next five minutes staring at the contents.

Before Mia's return, his wardrobe consisted of his bathrobe. Last week he'd ventured enough outside his comfort zone to don sweats and a tee. Pulling out a pair of jeans, he walked to the bed and yanked them on. The walk-in closet was full of suits and casual dress clothes he hadn't worn since before enlisting. Now, he didn't have anyone to wear them for and, frankly, no desire or need.

Yet he wanted to look good for her. A stupid notion, but there nonetheless.

Jeans were a minor upgrade. He grabbed a clean, fitted black tee. After shoving his feet into tennis shoes, he ventured downstairs to start a pot of coffee, amazed that he could take the stairs one step at a time and not hobble on one leg. At the bottom, he glanced up the staircase and grinned. The expression felt foreign and his jaw muscles protested.

He was starving, but he knew Rose was coming in for her shift soon, so instead of grabbing a bowl of cereal, he sat at the table with a cup of coffee. And waited. And waited. A trickle of fear zipped down his spine at the thought of Mia not returning. He took another sip of now cold coffee and forced the anxiety away. She said she'd come back. Promised him.

Keys jingled in the lock and his gaze darted to the door. His heart pounded so loud he heard nothing but the pulse in his ears. Rose opened the door and cast a glance his way. She looked down again and stepped over the threshold, only to double take and glare at him. Her jaw fell and her pocketbook dropped from her fingers, scattering the contents across the floor.

His eyebrows shot up, and he stood to help her retrieve the purse contents. Squatting proved too difficult. He bent at the waist and snatched her keys and wallet, then held them out for her. Obviously in some state of shock, she stood there. Shoving the items back in her pocketbook, he held that out for her instead. Something must've snapped her out of it because she finally held out her hand and took the purse.

She muttered something that sounded like a prayer and then made the sign of the cross. "Mister Cole, you're out of your bedroom."

Ah, okay then. She was shocked to find him still alive and in better condition than when she left. "Yes. And please don't call me *Mister Cole*."

Her head bobbed. "Sorry, sir. Mr. Covington."

He smiled, which apparently made her shock revert. "And definitely don't call me that. Just Cole is fine, Rose."

"Your hair," she mumbled, as if that was an appropriate response.

"Mia cut it."

"Your clothes."

"Mia burned the robe. Metaphorically speaking. I think she really just threw it out."

Her sharp, pointed gaze traveled down the length of him before returning to his face. She crossed herself again. "It's so good to have you back."

"Well, I'm cleaner at least."

He stepped back to let her enter the kitchen and walked to the counter to pour another cup of coffee. He held the pot up in question, silently asking if she wanted some. She shook her head. Returning to the table, he sat and watched Rose expectantly.

"What would you like for breakfast, Mr. . . .uh, Cole."

Just saying his name, without the proper address, obviously made her uncomfortable. Years in maid service under his parents had drilled her to be invisible and polite. Knowing her place. He wasn't his parents.

"Rose, I appreciate everything you've done for my family through the years."

Shock returned. "Well, it's my pleasure."

"I doubt that. In any event," he continued, "if you feel the need to cut back your hours, please do so. And the guesthouse is yours for as long as you'd like, including after you retire."

She did a sort of tilt on her feet and Cole felt an immediate alarm before she righted herself. "But, why?"

Because you took care of Mia and Ginny when no one else did and not because you had to.

He thought over a more appropriate response and shrugged. "What am I going to use it for? Besides, anyone who put up with my mother for thirty years deserves a medal. Or rent-free living. The only condition is you call me Cole. Just Cole." He thought about the series of robot staff his family had employed through the years and shook his head. "Okay, two conditions. You have to make yourself at home, be comfortable, friendly, and . . . yourself."

The way she looked at him—like he'd sprouted wings and was singing a poor rendition of "Kumbaya"—was quite endearing. After several attempts to speak, she slowly nodded her head and glanced around the kitchen.

"What would you like for breakfast? I'll make you anything you want."

Cole grinned. "Pancakes." Mia would have a fit.

Rose nodded and began pulling out the necessary ingredients. Cole sat back in his chair watching, pretending not to stare at the door every few seconds for Mia. Nine-fifteen, no Mia. At nine-twenty Rose poured batter into the skillet. It smelled heavenly.

"Watchin' the door ain't gonna get her here any faster, Mister Cole."

Caught. He ran a hand down his face.

"She'll come." Rose flipped the first batch of pancakes. Cole listened to the sizzle and stared at the door.

At nine-thirty Mia walked in, wearing a fitted pair of jeans and a yellow blouse that showed off curves she hadn't had in her youth. His heart started beating again. Rose set the pancakes on a plate.

Mia eyed the two of them and smiled. "Someone got dressed without me threatening him. How nice."

Cole narrowed his eyes, more in an attempt to hide his pleasure than irritation. "Rose is making me pancakes. You never made me pancakes."

She made a noncommittal sound and walked to the counter to pour coffee. After adding cream and sugar, she sat down across from him and took a sip. Her full, red mouth pursed. "I see Rose didn't make the coffee today. Oh, this is terrible."

Trying not to stare at her mouth, he muttered, "It's caffeine. Just drink it."

She stared at the cup as if contemplating. "I'm on coffee duty from now on. In fact, you should be arrested for crimes against breakfast blend." She stood and went to the sink, pouring out her cup. She dumped out the rest of the pot and started over.

When she thought he wasn't looking, Rose grabbed Mia's sleeve. "You see that, Miss Mia?" she whispered, jerking her head toward Cole. "You did that. I told you you'd help." He couldn't see Mia's reaction with her back turned. Rose peeled a banana and sliced it over the pancakes, then walked over to the table to set the plate down.

Cole waited until she brought over the syrup and dumped half the bottle on the pancakes. He took a huge bite and groaned. "Oh, so good. No one makes pancakes like you, Rose."

Mia cleared her throat.

Cole put up his hand. "No, don't even say a thing. You'll ruin this moment."

Rose laughed. "You can have 'em every morning if you react like that."

"Oh no, he can't," Mia argued, snatching a pancake from the platter.

She sat down at the table and reached for the syrup. He hugged the bottle to his chest. Shaking her head, she laughed so loud he stopped chewing. She took his pause for granted and stole the maple syrup. He swallowed and looked at Rose to avoid watching Mia eat. It was too arousing.

"Hm," Rose mumbled. She leaned against the island and set her chin in her palm, staring at the two of them.

Mia pretended not to notice, but her cheeks flamed. "Cole's on a new diet, Rose. High protein and vitamin C. If you wouldn't mind adjusting."

Cole groaned but Rose agreed. "Surely."

"You can prepare the same meals, of course, just focusing more on lean meats, fruits, and vegetables."

Cole groaned again, but this time Rose laughed. "Worry not, Mister Cole. I'll make you good food."

"I hope so. This one here tried to starve me last week."

"Excuse me?" Mia retorted, indignantly.

"You're no Rose in the kitchen. Sorry." He was pretty damn sure he didn't look sorry. He shoved more pancake in his mouth and smiled.

Mia's eyes narrowed, but her grin was wicked. "Rose," she addressed his housekeeper, staring straight at him. "I think tofu and whole grains would be a great addition to his diet, too, don't you think? I mean, that way Mister Cole can have pancakes *every* morning. Whole wheat pancakes with ground tofu and turkey bacon on the side."

Even Rose looked horrified.

"You wouldn't."

Her stare dared him to challenge her, but then her features softened into a smile and his innards danced at the sight.

"Even I'm not that cruel." She stood and set her plate in the sink. "But be nice to me, I could change my mind." She kissed Rose on the cheek. "The pancakes were delicious. Cole, let your food settle for twenty minutes. I'll meet you in the gym. We can go an extra ten minutes to work that off."

Cole watched her exit the room, a bounce in her step and hips swaying under the denim. He stared at his half-finished meal. "She ruined breakfast, Rose."

Rose barked out a laugh. "Yep. Good to have Miss Mia back, I'd say."

chapter
nine

"Looks like a storm is coming," Mia said as she slipped her feet into her flip-flops.

The guest bed was still rumpled from their lovemaking, something he wanted to do again. Soon. Once just wasn't enough. But it was getting late and he needed to get her home.

He patted his pockets. "I left my keys up at the house." He glanced out the bedroom window. "Why don't you head out the back and meet me at the gate? I'll go out front and get my keys from the main house."

"Okay," she agreed and stood, looking uncertain.

Her face was still flushed, her hair a tangled knot from the number of times he'd had his fingers clenched between the strands. Damn, she was the most beautiful thing he'd ever seen. And she was his. They'd worked out a plan and for the next two years they'd stick to that plan, until they were in a better position to obtain what they wanted.

What they wanted—*needed*—was a life together. He didn't know why he'd fought it for so long. They were young, but they'd work it out. Of that he was certain. He had a connection with her, like he had with no one else. Without words, without actions, she somehow saw through his facade to the real person he'd learned to hide away. It wasn't just her beauty that drew him, nor her sweet nature. Mia had the innate capability for true empathy, and a childlike view of the world that made even his cynical self believe in happiness.

Smoothing back her hair, he planted a kiss on her forehead, the only thing he could do to show just how much she moved him. "I'll meet you at the gate in five minutes."

He waited until the back door closed before stripping the bed. He checked the small guesthouse for any other sign they'd been there, and was satisfied everything was as it had been before. Bunching the sheets in his hands, he ran out the front door and tossed the linens in the dumpster near the garage. He strode through the front door, past the entry and stairs, to the small table where he'd set his keys earlier. Backtracking, he headed for the door again when his mother called his name from the sitting room.

Ignoring her, he marched past the room to the entry.

"Colton, a word please."

He sighed. It was never just a word when it concerned Mother. And he made no mistake in knowing she wasn't requesting, she was ordering. As he stepped into the sitting room and looked around, his mother glanced up lazily from her magazine. Father was in the corner chair, swirling a glass of single malt scotch in his hand.

"Make it quick, Mother. I'm on my way out."

Meticulously, she set the magazine aside and reached for her brandy on the coffee table. "Yes, must hurry to get your harlot home."

He turned to leave.

She rose with all the grace of a swan. She spoke with the sharp bite of a raven. "Let me make myself quite clear, Colton. You are to end this . . . *affair* now." The disdain dripped from her mouth, her disgust apparent.

Closing his eyes, he sucked in a breath, not even bothering to wonder how she knew. "I will do no such thing. Last I checked, Mia and I were consenting adults."

"And what if she gets pregnant? You'll embarrass your good name and taint your father's upcoming election—"

"I don't give a damn." He turned again, but his mother's cold, calm voice brought him whirling back.

"I can cut you off. No more cars or Harvard or trust fund."

It took only the blink of an eye to think that over. "Then I'll just have to make my own way, won't I?"

The only sign of her surprise was the tightening of her fingers around the crystal snifter. "You forget what influence I have in the great state of North Carolina." Her surgically arched brows rose. "I can see to it that no college accepts her."

A slow, grinding headache formed between his temples as his blood pressure no doubt soared. Worse, this was so much worse—fear settled into his chest.

"That's right, Colton. I'll pull every contact I have and make her life miserable. I'll fire her worthless mother, leaving them destitute. How long do you think it would take that woman to find another job?"

Cole tried and failed to swallow. Through the wedge in his throat, he muttered, "Why are you doing this?"

She sat back down on the edge of the davenport, her painfully erect posture in place, satisfied that he would no doubt comply with her demands. She waved her hand dismissively. "Why? My reasons should be obvious to you. The bigger question is why you let it go this far."

The keys dug into his palm with the pressure of his fist. In the length of time it took him to stand there, he reasoned out several ways this could go. He and Mia could continue their relationship behind closed doors until he graduated and let his mother believe they'd ended it. Though he hated the idea, they could put their plans on hold until graduation and not see each other at all. What was two more years, really? Or . . . he could walk out the door right now and they'd find a way to get by. They'd have only each other, without a penny to their names, but what choice was there?

Cole didn't have a single doubt that his mother would follow through on her threats. A bead of cold sweat trailed down his back. She'd make their lives hell. Mia deserved better.

He glanced at his father, who, as always, had removed himself from the argument. For a future politician, he avoided conflict too well to succeed. He had the charming, snake-like smile and the drive, but Cole didn't think he had the heart.

Mother smoothed out her silk robe with a stiff hand, drawing his attention back to her. When she looked at him, there wasn't an ounce of love or compassion in her gaze. Not for her son, or his feelings. He supposed it shouldn't surprise him, yet the blow was astonishing. He deflated with the realization. She had never loved him. Never would. He wasn't Dean. He was merely the insufferable black sheep who brought dissatisfaction and humiliation. Someone to tolerate out of duty.

"Colton, I hope you'll finally see reason."

"There is no reason in any of this." His voice, barely audible, cracked.

She sniffed. "Apparently you're not taking this seriously enough." Thunder boomed overhead and lightning split the sky. "How is Mia's little sister doing?"

His gaze flew from the window to his mother with dizzying speed. She wasn't asking about Ginny out of politeness. Oh, no, no. Mother had more cards to throw on the table. One by one his senses shut down, until the room became a void.

"I wonder what would happen to that poor, disabled girl if someone were to call social services? Foster care, I assume, right, Cole? Years and years in the system, no place to call home. I can only imagine how strangers would take care of the poor girl. They wouldn't let Mia see her, of course, and if she were to try to get custody, the courts would refuse. No judge *I* know would allow guardianship."

Whatever air remained in his lungs seeped out. He'd go penniless for Mia. He'd turn his back on his fortune, his family, on everything he'd ever known if it meant a lifetime with her. But he wouldn't do this. He wouldn't risk Mia or Ginny. And his mother knew it.

Maybe he was his mother's son after all, because ice water slowly crystallized, began flowing through his veins. A defense mechanism, no doubt, but effective. "You have no heart inside your chest. No soul for the devil to take when you die."

His father finally spoke up, only to crush whatever hope lay withering inside. "Just do as your mother says." He didn't even glance up, couldn't even look his son in the eye while delivering the death blow.

Cole stared at the floor, trying to fit the puzzle pieces

together in his mind to make this work, find a solution. Tremors shot through his limbs when no answer came. He'd have to give her up. Forever. To save her. To keep Ginny and Mia safe.

Without any knowledge as to how he got there, he stood in the front doorway staring out into the rain, which was now pouring down in earnest as gusts took the drenching from vertical to horizontal. Leaving the door wide open, he strode down the porch steps and past the fountain. Every step down the long driveway matched the beat of his heart as rain slapped his face, until he finally reached a shivering Mia at the gate.

"Wh-what took so long?" she muttered through blue-tinted lips. Even after he left her waiting in the pouring rain, her voice held no trace of irritation.

Oh, my dear Mia.

Cole took one long last look at her, at this girl he loved with his whole damn worthless heart. Ebony hair matted to her pale face, deep blue eyes staring back at him with trust, her small-framed body trembling in the downpour. Interlaced rain and tears blurred his vision. With strength he'd never known, he reached over and hit the ten-digit key code on the stone pillar. The gate swung open with a creak.

"Go, Mia. Don't ask me any questions and don't come back."

Her mouth popped open, her face paler than a corpse. "What are you talking about, Cole? This doesn't make any sense. What do you mean *go*?"

He swiped a hand down his face, but more rain streamed down in its wake. She'd never go on her own. He should've known that. She'd ask him a thousand questions and see the truth in his eyes. And the damnedest part of all was, she'd try to fight.

They'd both lose. Against his mother, there was no competition.

He should've pulled his car up. He should drive her home and do this at the trailer. But she had too few good memories there. He didn't want her to have to look at the trailer every day and remember this moment. He needed the painful reminder to remain here, so she wouldn't return.

"It's over, Mia. We're done. Please, just go." His voice rasped out, razorblades searing his throat, tearing the flesh and muscle behind his ribcage. He wasn't even sure she heard the words spoken with no conviction.

"No, Cole." A plea, not defiance.

Her voice broke and so did his heart. He ground his teeth until his molars nearly cracked with the force, holding back tears until she left the property. She could never know the truth, would never know how bad this hurt.

She launched herself at him, clinging her petite curves to his hard muscle and grasping the material of his drenched shirt on his back. "No, Cole. You said you loved me. You said—"

"I lied," he yelled over her sobs, over the rain, prying her free and setting her away from him. "I got what I wanted from you. I waited a long time to get you in bed. A challenge I finally conquered. It's over. Go home, Mia."

If he wasn't hollow before, if everything he'd uttered wasn't a painful jolt he'd never recover from, then the look on her face would've done him in. Those gorgeous blue eyes rounded in pain, in disbelief. Her arms crossed over her middle, as if trying to hold herself together.

An agonizing cry moaned from her throat. "I—I don't believe you. You wouldn't do something like that. You're not this person."

"You don't know anything about me," he roared, lying

through his teeth. She was the only one who did know him and that made this so much more excruciating. "You saw what I wanted you to see." He had to get her to go, and the only way to do that was to kill any hope. *Dammit, do it! Save her! Do it, do it, do it.* "You mean nothing to me. I don't love you."

As if her legs could no longer hold her upright, she backed into the pillar and slumped. She stared at his chest, shaking her head with violent intensity. God, he wanted to tell her the truth, throw her in his car and get the hell out of here, to never look back. To spend the rest of his life making up for the cruel lies he just spewed.

Not possible.

After several minutes, she straightened, tugged her arms tighter to her chest, and stumbled toward the open gate. To her credit, and his relief, she didn't turn back. If she had, he may have finally lost it. Weakened. She faltered only once by the shoulder of the road and then kept going. He stared at her back, watching her go, until she crested the hill by the bridge and almost disappeared from view.

Headlights reflected over the iron gate, momentarily blinding him. Cole turned his head as Dean's car pulled into the edge of the drive next to where he stood. The driver's window slid down. "What's going on?" his brother yelled over the storm.

Cole glanced at Mia as she completely disappeared into the night, from his life. "Mind your own business."

"Where is she going?" Dean asked, ignoring him.

"Home."

"Home? She lives twenty miles away. It's pouring and dark!"

Cole said nothing.

"Go after her, dammit!"

He looked at his brother, at everything Cole would never be and said the only thing he could. "I can't."

Cole turned and headed for the house, drenched and bone-cold. Empty.

Dean got out of the car, the interior lights glowing in the night. "What is wrong with you?"

Cole kept going, forcing one foot in front of the other. At the fountain, he turned, surprised to find Dean still standing there by the open car door, staring at him from several yards away. Dean shook his head, climbed back in the car and spun out of the drive, racing down the soaked asphalt in the direction Mia had gone.

Cole teetered on his feet, fell to his knees and let loose a roar of pain so forceful his chest felt like it cracked open, his teeth vibrating. And then the tears came.

Present

Cole allowed Lacey to come visit and Mia was glad. He may not admit it outright, but Cole needed his sister. The three of them had just finished a nice lunch on the back porch and decided to try a movie. It was Wednesday, which meant the landscaper was on the property maintaining the grounds.

So while Cole fished through his Blu-ray collection in the sitting room, Lacey and Mia stood by the window staring at the landscaper. Tall, toned, and tan, the man went about his business shirtless. Muscles strained against his jeans, sweat slid deliciously down his pecs.

"Oh, he is so yummy," Lacey said.

"Yes, he is," Mia agreed. Cole made a sound of disgust behind them, making Mia smile. "Hey, Rose," she called. "Come here and enjoy the view!"

"He can probably hear you, you know," Cole muttered.

Rose walked in, drying her hands on a towel and stood next to Lacey. "Whatcha lookin' at?"

"Man candy," Lacey said. "Wherever did you find him, Rose?"

Rose directed her gaze out the window and smiled. "His daddy was your gardener for years, Miss Lacey. That's Gregory Winston's son, Jake."

Lacey looked at her with huge eyes. "No. That can't be little Jake." She looked at the man again. "He used to pick wildflowers and throw them in the pool. You remember that, Mia?"

"Yes. He's not so little anymore. He's our age, too, isn't he? Maybe a year younger. His older brother Alec is a horror writer in New York."

"He sure didn't act his age," Lacey said, her voice drifting. "If I'd known he'd grow up to look like *that*, I'd have been nicer to him. He used to put bullfrogs under the front porch swing when I sat there."

Mia laughed. "You should go talk to him. I'll bet he still has a crush on you."

"Crush? No. He was just a mean kid." She smiled. "I couldn't talk to him," she said seemingly to herself. Shaking her head, she turned to Cole. "What movie did you find?"

Cole held up two cases, *Dumb and Dumber* in one hand, and *Animal House* in the other. He shrugged.

Lacey rolled her eyes and walked to the shelf. "Your taste in movies is tragic, dear brother."

Mia knew why he'd picked the titles. They were brainless comedies that wouldn't make him slip. She had just opened her mouth to pick one of Cole's choices when Lacey whirled, her long, thick blonde hair swirling.

"*Casablanca*! Now that's a movie," Lacey announced.

The first time Mia saw the film was with Cole as a teen during one of their many rainy days together. "Here's lookin' at you, kid," she and Lacey said in unison. They laughed and looked at Cole. He seemed hesitant, but Lacey didn't notice. She turned and put the movie into the player.

"I'll go make y'all some popcorn," Rose said, leaving the room.

Cole stared at Mia with an unreadable expression. "It'll be okay," she mouthed.

He nodded and sat on the couch. Mia took the spot right next to him in case something happened and he regressed.

Lacey positioned herself on the other side of Mia and grabbed the remote. "Best movie ever."

"This movie is terrible," Cole argued. "They romanticize war and heartbreak. She ended up with the wrong guy!"

This was the most she'd heard Cole speak all afternoon. "Totally disagree," Mia said. "He loved Ilsa and let her go in order to save her."

Cole's expression fell as his gaze darted over her face. Intense, dark eyes bored into her, wreaking havoc inside her stomach. A familiar sadness and regret loomed in the space between them. Swallowing hard, she looked away.

Rose came in the room and set down a tray with a pitcher of lemonade and bowl of popcorn. As she straightened, she looked at the television longingly. Unsure of how Cole would feel about his housekeeper joining them, Mia stayed quiet waiting to see if anyone noticed her lingering.

"Why don't you join us, Rose?" Lacey asked.

Cole turned his head, as if just seeing Rose. "Have a seat," he said, pointing to an open chair.

Tears burned her eyes as Mia watched Rose's surprise and hesitation. In all her years of service, no one had probably ever asked for her company. She gingerly sat on the edge of the chair, as if ready to spring right back up. Rose, Lacey, and Cole's attention refocused on the movie. Mia watched Rose.

Cole's hand dropped beside Mia's on the cushion, his arm close enough to absorb her body heat. Mia reached over and covered his hand with hers, squeezing once. She jerked her head in Rose's direction as if to say, *You just did the nicest thing*, and then let her hand rest next to his again.

Two scenes later, his pinkie brushed hers, just slightly, but the feel of his skin, even miniscule as it was, had her mouth dry, her nerves on fire. She kept her eyes glued to the flat screen, while everything inside her went haywire. She didn't understand this. She should not still have feelings for this man. Cole should not still be able to affect her. Even if ten years hadn't gone by, he'd thrown her—and her love—away. He'd used her, lied to her, and walked away.

Yet, he carried your picture through the desert of Iraq.

Somehow, she'd find a way to ask him why. If she learned nothing else by helping him, she'd at least know the answer.

Halfway through the movie, with gunfire and airplane engines, Mia looked over at Cole, hoping he was okay. He hadn't moved a muscle in an hour. She tapped two fingers on top of his hand, just in case.

"I'm fine," he whispered quietly enough for only her to hear.

Relieved, she tuned back in to the classic movie, quoting all the great lines from the film in her head at the appropriate times. By the end of the movie, Lacey was weeping openly and Rose was wiping her eyes with a handkerchief.

"Well," Rose said as she stood, "I best be getting dinner on." She looked at Cole and her features smoothed in relaxation and sentiment. "Thank you."

Cole looked adorably flustered.

Lacey sighed. "And I have to get back to Charlotte."

"I'm going into the library," Cole announced.

Before he left the room, Lacey stopped him. "What's in the library?"

He looked at his sister. "Project Mia."

Mia laughed and poor Lacey looked confused. To Cole, she said, "I hope that's not what you're calling it." To Lacey, she said, "I'll explain later."

Still confused, Lacey nodded. "Can I give you a hug good-bye?" she asked Cole.

Mia's heart seesawed in her chest as she watched the two of them stare at each other and the years fall away. Cole had finally chosen to start writing his memoir, at this very second, which meant he was healing. He'd have a long, long road ahead, but he was trying. The happiness that brought couldn't be measured in words.

Finally, Cole nodded and Lacey stepped into his embrace. Over the top of his sister's head, he looked at Mia. A thousand expressions crossed his face before Lacey let go and he looked down at her. "I'll see you later," he said. "Can you . . . visit again next week?"

"Um . . ." Lacey looked at Mia as if she'd just been slapped. "Yes, of course. I'll come on Wednesday again, if that's all right?"

He frowned. "To gawk at the gardener."

"Incentive." Lacey collected her pocketbook with a smile. "Mia, walk me out?"

Cole headed for the library and shut the door. Mia met Lacey on the front porch. Before she knew what hit her, Lacey pulled Mia into a hug so fierce she lost air.

"You okay, Lace?"

Lacey pulled away and grabbed Mia's forearms. "I don't know how you did it, but thank you. He seems almost normal now. Not just his appearance, but . . . all of it. I should've called you sooner. I knew you'd get through to him. Rose was right."

Gone was the purebred Covington. Today Lacey had been the carefree teen that Mia remembered fondly before her mother got to her, before life and obligation made Lacey a society robot. "You should cry more often, Lace. You're entitled. And for God's sake, fight. *Laugh*."

Lacey drew in a deep breath and glanced away. "You don't understand, Mia."

"I do understand."

Lacey looked at her with eyes that mirrored Dean's, a frown on her mouth that resembled Cole's, and Mia realized Lacey was finally starting to see just how well Mia did understand. They may have come from vastly different classes and backgrounds, but they were more alike than they realized. Mia had spent her whole life devoted to her family, picking up the pieces and gluing the delicate fragments back together. Lacey had, too, and her punishment, her sentence for following the rules, was to have no life at all.

"Come," Lacey said, pulling her by the hand. "I want to show you something before I go."

Mia trailed across the driveway to the guesthouse, where Lacey opened the door and dropped her purse on a chair. She immediately walked to the short hallway near the bedroom and bathroom. Mia followed, wondering what she was doing. Lacey reached up to the ceiling and pulled a cord for the tiny attic storage space, where a wooden ladder dropped down.

"I've never shown this to anyone before, not even Cole." She climbed the ladder until the top half of her body disappeared. "When my parents put the house up for sale, I almost raced back here to collect them. But then I figured

I'd let the new owners find them instead. Maybe they'd make for a great story to someone else." She climbed back down with several unframed eight-by-ten canvases. Lacey stared at the top one with longing. "I imagined strangers looking at these, wondering who the people were and conjuring romantic tales."

She passed one canvas to Mia. Mia froze with recognition and memory. Lacey had painted Mia and Cole on the beach, wrapped in each other's arms, kissing, partially hidden by wild sea oats. In the distance, the ocean glittered in the sun, foam waves breaking the shore.

"I used to watch you two," Lacey admitted. "Spying was more like it. I watched your romance unfold, hoping one day to find a man who looked at me the way he used to look at you. I never found him."

Lacey handed over the other paintings. Mia took them with shaking hands. One painting showed a youthful Cole looking out his bedroom window, staring down at a much younger version of herself in the mimosa grove. Another had them standing outside this very guesthouse, his arms around her as they stared at the ocean. The last one had the two of them in the rain, standing by an open gate in the dark. Mia flipped through, but there were no more.

"I told your love story through paintings." Lacey shrugged. "I always wanted to do another after the rain one, but . . ."

As she trailed off, Mia felt tears welling. "But there was nothing to paint afterward."

"No happy ending. No ending at all."

"Yeah." Mia looked at the canvases again. Each painting held so much emotion. Each brushstroke made her feel the elation, the fear of first love again. "I never knew you were watching us."

"I'm watching now, too." Lacey's face was resolved, but

quizzical. "Maybe now I can finish the story. You can give me a final image to paint."

Mia swallowed, shaking her head. It was a nice story, sweet and sad, but there would be no happy ending this time either.

As Mia typed on the laptop at the kitchen table, Rose put the finishing touches on dinner while humming a soothing hymn. In her email to Dr. Melbourne, Mia updated Cole's physical and mental status and all the goals he'd mastered. She mentioned the movie, writing his memoir, calling and letting Lacey visit, and how he was able to walk almost without a limp due to the routine exercise. She did not, however, go into detail about the past or what Cole had said specifically. That was for Cole to tell the doctor if he chose. She did mention Cole not leaving the house, and her suspicion that this was because of his scars and not a fear of the outdoors, knowing Dr. Melbourne might diagnose agoraphobia. Cole wasn't afraid of public places or the outdoors, he was ashamed of his appearance.

"Do you think he's regressing, Miss Mia?"

Mia hit Send and looked at Rose. "What do you mean?"

Rose untied her apron and set in on the counter. "He hasn't come out of the library since Miss Lacey left. That was two days ago."

Without wanting to divulge too much, Mia thought over her response. "I think he's getting better, actually. I asked him to start a journal. That's what he's doing in there."

Rose nodded. "Mighty fine idea, child." She donned mitts and removed a pan of chicken from the oven, setting it on a cooling rack. "This is ready. I'll just go say good-bye to Mister Cole and be off."

"Have a great weekend, Rose."

After shutting down the laptop, Mia grabbed a plate from the cabinet and prepared Cole's dinner. The baked chicken smelled awesome. Rose must have used rosemary because the scent of it overpowered everything else. She spooned some boiled potatoes and fresh green beans next to the chicken and headed for the library.

Rose's voice drifted out into the hall. "I wanted to thank you for the offer to stay in the guesthouse, but I must decline." She paused and though Mia couldn't see them from the hallway, she imagined Rose wringing her hands together. "Mister Cole, I have to retire soon. I can finish out the year. My grandbaby is lookin' for work. She's a great girl. She could use the opportunity if you'll allow her to replace me."

After a long silence, a heavy sigh drifted from Cole. "All right, Rose. Why don't you bring her by in a couple weeks and she can train with you? Show her around."

"Yessir!"

"Don't call me sir." Though his words seemed rigid, humor laced his voice. Rose shuffled to the door. "And Rose?" Pause. "I'll . . . miss you."

Nothing happened for several minutes. Mia stared at the plate, wondering if it was okay to go in. Then Rose said, "I'll be here a few more months, Mister Cole. Dontcha worry."

Mia stepped back as the library door opened and Rose emerged. Rose lifted her gaze to Mia, nodded once and walked away. Mia watched her retreat down the hall and stood there until the back door closed.

Rose was going to retire. Mia didn't know Rose's grand-daughter, but if she was anything like Rose, Cole would be in good hands. But would it be enough? After all Mia's effort, what would happen to him when her time here was over? He still hadn't left the house and aside from Lacey, no one visited.

She tapped on the door with her free hand and walked in. Cole was sitting at the computer. He quickly minimized the screen before turning.

"Dinner," she announced.

He muttered a thanks, but stared at his steepled fingers.

"What's wrong?"

"Nothing."

She wasn't going to play this game. It was up to him whether he wanted to talk to her or not.

When she was halfway to the door he said, "Rose wants to retire."

"The nerve of her. Should we have her drawn and quartered?"

He swiveled around in his chair to look at her, something very close to a smile tracing his lips. Time for some tough love. Or . . . medicine. Yes, tough medicine.

"Rose is the hired help, not a friend. So am I. You knew we weren't permanent."

Not so much as a tick from him. "When are you leaving?" His voice was unnervingly flat.

"I said I'd stay until you're better."

His hands dropped to the arms of the chair. "What constitutes 'better'?"

Drawing in a breath, she said as she exhaled, "I'll let you know."

Back in the kitchen, she began cleaning up dinner. He followed and lingered in the doorway. She didn't know where the anger came from, but a bitter taste lingered in her mouth and she couldn't get rid of it. "Out with it, Cole."

"You're . . ." He sighed. "You're not the hired help.

You're more than that. And I pay Rose to do a job, but I don't treat her poorly."

She leaned against the counter and closed her eyes. He was right. He was totally right. She'd never seen him raise his voice to Rose or bark orders or ignore her. And the sweet thing he did by asking her to watch that movie with them proved he wasn't his parents.

"We were . . . hell, we used to be friends, Mia."

Oh God. He was going there. "I don't remember it that way."

"I do."

Anger flared anew. "You know what I remember, Cole? I remember you ignoring me at a bonfire while your friends made fun of me. I remember you taking my virginity and throwing me out like trash. I don't remember you ever acknowledging me in public or taking me places outside of this estate where people knew you."

Oh hell. She shouldn't have opened her mouth. Ten years of resentment had just landed at his feet like a gauntlet.

"I don't know what to say, Mia." He stared over her shoulder as if he wasn't even in the same room anymore. More than anything, he just appeared shell-shocked. He shouldn't be. They were his memories, too. "I remember . . . hating the way others treated you and wanting to shelter you from that. I remember opening up to you in a way I have yet to do with anyone else. I remember the freedom you gave me, even if it was only an illusion."

If he'd punched her in the face she wouldn't have been more surprised. "What?"

He stared at her feet. Swallowed. "You never knew how special you were. It kills me to know that after all these years you still don't. I thought . . . I *tried* to show you. Up until this very moment, every memory of you but one is a beautiful one."

Her skin prickled as if dropped in a vat of ice water. Her breathing grew more and more shallow. Could it be even remotely possible she'd had it wrong all these years? She didn't think so. He had stood right in front of her that day in the rain and said he didn't love her. Said she meant nothing to him.

"What does that mean, Cole?" Her voice shook as the words breathed out. She grabbed the counter behind her to keep upright.

He looked at her, straight in her eyes, and held the gaze. "It means I may only be closure to you, but you mean the world to me."

She uttered a strangled gasp. She was suddenly foreign in her own body. She watched him leave the room out of her peripheral vision. Her grip on the counter slipped and she sank to the floor.

chapter
ten

Summer's End: Ten Years Before

Cole slowly lifted his head as the sunrise emerged over the water, sand plastered to his cheek. His clothes were still wet from the rain the night before, suctioned to his body like a desperate woman. He'd never made it back inside the house, couldn't bring himself to walk through the door and see the satisfaction on his mother's face. He remembered staggering to the beach, chest aching from sobbing, and collapsing onto the sand.

The pain hadn't subsided with the morning tide. Not one iota.

With profuse effort, he rose, brushed the sand from his face and stretched. The hollow space where Mia should be was a nagging reminder even before he took a step toward the house. She was gone. And her tear-streaked face was the only thing he saw as he climbed the dunes.

Rounding the property, he stepped onto the driveway and directed his gaze to the gate. A Wilmington Beach squad car was pulling out onto the road where he had ripped out Mia's heart the night before. He watched the vehicle until it turned and then he glanced at the house. Wouldn't it be just like his mother to call the cops on him for not returning in a timely manner.

Anger was so much easier than pain. There was no guilt in anger. Anger was relief from the bone-jarring intensity of how much he hurt. Taking the steps two at a time, he flung the front door open and stalked to the sitting room, knowing just where his damn mother would be at this time of morning.

Before he could get one word out, Lacey launched herself off the davenport and into his arms. Reflexively, he caught her and wrapped his arms around her. Her chest shook, her tears dampened his neck.

"Oh, Cole," she wailed. "Dean's dead! I can't believe it!"

What? He blinked. If this was some fucked up joke to teach him a lesson . . .

He looked over Lacey's head to his father, who stared out the window as if waiting on someone. His mother dabbed her cheeks with a lace handkerchief, gaze drilling Cole in place.

Anger drained so fast he barely had time to register the loss. It was replaced by the numb, terrible anguish of shock.

Cole pulled his sister away and held her at arm's length. "What are you talking about, Lace?"

"He . . . he was driving last night," she blubbered, "and his car ran off the road. They said because of the rain. The roads were slick. He hit a tree. He's . . . *dead*!"

She collapsed against his chest, making the most god-awful shrieks. Cole held her close to him as his own knees threatened to give out. The cloud in his brain began to clear. Dean had taken off after Mia last night because Cole couldn't stand to look at Mia's grief-stricken face. Because Cole was too weak to fight his mother, too weak to spend one more second with Mia after he'd said the most indescribable things.

And now, because of him . . .

"No," he heard himself say. "*No.*"

Lacey bobbed her head.

Cole fell to his knees, taking Lacey with him. Clutching his sister, the room spun around him.

Dean. Drove. Mia. Home.

"Was he alone in the car?" Cole whispered, barely able to force the words out.

"Yes," Lacey muttered, face still pressed to Cole's chest, fingers digging into his biceps. "He died all alone!"

Before his muddled brain could process that, before relief had crept its way in, his mother did the unimaginable. She rose, walked past her two sobbing, wrecked children who were still alive, and left the room without a word. Father shook his head, still looking out the window as if expecting Dean to drive up, and pressed his palm to the window pane.

Cole almost retched, but he held the reflex down long enough to rise, still holding Lacey in his arms. He ascended the stairs carrying his sister, and out of sheer instinct, he walked into Lacey's bedroom and to the patio doors, where he collapsed on the balcony. Lacey curled into a tight ball in his lap and wailed as he smoothed her long, silky blonde hair with his palm.

He'd killed his brother. He. Killed. Dean.

Hot, searing tears streamed down his face as he blankly stared out over the horizon, stroking Lacey's hair. "I'm sorry, Lacey. I'm so, so sorry," he muttered, over and over and over again, until his voice was hoarse and barren and he couldn't do anything but merely think the words.

Present

That was the last thing I ever said to my brother. "I can't."

And three days later at Dean Allan Covington's funeral, packed with grieving mourners, Mia Galdon bravely walked over to our family wearing a simple black dress just one shade lighter than her ebony hair. I stood back as my mother said to her in a grated, harsh whisper, "You have some nerve showing up here. My Dean is in the ground because of you, you gold-digging tramp."

With that, my mother sniffed and smiled weakly at the next attendee in line. She never shed a tear that day, not in public anyhow. To her credit and my astonishment, I heard her crying later that night while alone in her bedroom. It was the first and only time in my memory that she seemed human.

And the last thing I ever said to beautiful, kind, and devoted Mia? "I never want to see you again."

Through the years, those two phrases, "I can't" and "I don't ever want to see you again" merged into one phrase meant for both of them. I pleaded with God to let them hear my words. The first part, said to Dean, fused with the last, said to Mia. "I can't . . . ever see you again."

I can't ever see you again, Dean, because you're dead. I killed you.

> I can't ever see you again, Mia, because we were
> never meant to be. Because I'd slowly kill you day by
> day until there was nothing left of you.

Cole's jaw trembled as he stared at the computer screen, fingers hovering over the keyboard, shaking violently. He glanced down to the lower right-hand side of the screen.

August 28. 12:40 a.m.

Dean had died at 10 p.m. on August 28, ten years ago.

Cole flew from his chair, careening it backward and crashing it to the hardwood floor with a resounding thud in the otherwise quiet room. A raw, deep burning ravaged his chest, clawed up his throat. He hadn't cried since Dean's funeral, wouldn't allow himself the privilege. But tears formed behind his lids and he fisted his hands for the strength to block them. He glared around the library, looking for something, anything to . . .

There. He strode two steps to a table and palmed a lead crystal vase. Without hesitation, he launched it across the room where it shattered against the wall, the fragments catching the lamplight. His breath soughed in and out.

Footsteps pounded down the stairs outside the library. Damn it. He'd woken Mia.

Not now, not now, not now. Not like this.

The door banged open and she flew over the threshold, skidding to a stop ten feet from where he stood. Her blue moon-print pajamas were rumpled from sleep. Her widened gaze darted around the room before landing on the broken vase. Her shoulders sagged as she looked at him.

The ache returned. Or maybe it had never left. He whirled around so she couldn't see him. "I'm fine. Please, just go back to bed."

She didn't say anything and she didn't leave.

"Mia," he ground out, dangerously close to losing it irrevocably. God help them both if he did. "Just go."

He jolted when she came up beside him. From the corner of his eye he saw her head turn toward the computer and then over to him. She hadn't looked long enough to read anything, and he was too intent on holding it together to care if she had. She saved the document and shut down the computer.

"Let go of the anger, Cole."

No. Letting the anger go would lead to greater, devastating pain. That day so long ago had been replaying in his head for the past ten years. Mia. Dean. Mia. Dean. His chest shook. *No.* He gripped the edge of the desk and hunched over, bowing his head as if there was anywhere to hide.

A delicate, warm hand settled between his shoulder blades, rubbed small circles against his bare skin. He'd forgotten he had no shirt on, just plaid pajama bottoms. Exposed. He thought he'd be alone in the library for the night. She stepped closer, her breast brushing his shoulder.

"Cole." That was it. Just his name.

And the dam broke.

Repressed tears flooded out, soaking his face. Agony razed his chest. His head felt like it had split wide freaking open. And what did she do? Hell, she wrapped her arms around him, offering comfort he didn't deserve. He tried to shove her off. She came right back, her arms pinning his. The sounds coming from inside himself sounded more animal than human, but he couldn't hold on anymore. Control was gone.

His legs gave out and Mia went down to her knees with him. Her fingers didn't brush away the tears, her mouth didn't tell him it was okay, and her understanding gaze never left his face. Clutching her shirt, he dropped his head to her chest.

"*I* should've driven you home."

She stilled, but only for a moment, as if finally realizing his tears had nothing to do with war. *If only.* Her hands fisted in his hair and she tugged him closer. With her silent encouragement, they adjusted positions and she sat between his legs. She wrapped her legs around his hips, bringing them closer than they'd been in way too long. Closer than they'd ever been, it seemed.

He'd always seen himself as weak, but losing it in front of her was a whole new realm of pathetic. Damn if he couldn't stop crying though. Damn if she wasn't the only thing he wanted to hold on to.

Mia said nothing, did nothing but ride it out.

Time passed. What felt like an eternity of days. Eventually the pressure eased and he went limp against her. Spent, he buried his face in her nightshirt so she couldn't see. So mortifying that she was the stronger of the two. He was so freaking worthless that he couldn't hold it together even after all these years. What she must think of him.

Her swallow clicked, her breath hot against his ear as she spoke. "Dean had an appointment on my side of town that night," she whispered. "The apartment complexes across the street from the trailer park were up for sale. Dean was thinking of buying them. He wanted to fix them for low-income families, wanted to use one of the buildings as a community center. The owner worked and couldn't meet during regular business hours. When Dean stopped back here that night, it was to pick up the property files. Instead, he picked me up on the road."

Cole lifted his head and her gaze roamed his face. She

sighed. "Because he drove me home and sat with me in the car talking, he was late for the appointment. If I hadn't gotten in the car, he'd be alive."

Cole opened his mouth to argue, but she put a finger to his lips and shook her head.

"If he hadn't spent an hour calming me down in the car, he'd be alive." She looked away. "Those are the things I told myself after he died." She looked back at him, her gaze so direct he couldn't even swallow. "It could have been any rain-soaked road, in any part of town, on any given night. He would've died anyway. Not because you didn't drive me home, or because he tried to comfort me, or because he missed the appointment. It was his time to go. God called him home, Cole."

Moisture coated his eyes again, but not like the ravaging tears from before. She didn't blame herself or him. Mia saw Dean's death as a work of fate, an act of God. Cole tried to wrap his mind around that as he stared at her. Cole didn't know anything about Dean's plans for the apartment complexes and he was pretty sure Father didn't either. Buying that property wouldn't be much of an investment, but more of a community project. And it was just like Dean to want to do something like that, not for the perfect image, but because he truly wanted to do good.

"It's time for you to stop blaming yourself." He looked at her, at the truth he knew she felt in her heart. "Time to move on, Cole. Dean was a good man, but he's gone. You're still here. Lacey is still here." She pressed a hand to his cheek and he leaned into the caress. "You're a good man, too. I wish you could see that."

Only Mia could look at someone like him through the rose-colored glasses of innocence and affection. No one, not his family, friends, or even he himself had ever seen him as anything more than the spoiled rich kid with no direction. His chest constricted.

Her smile was weak. "You know what Dean said to me after I got out of the car?"

Cole shook his head.

"He said, 'I'm sure Cole had his reasons for what he did tonight and the intention was probably admirable.'"

That sucked the air right out of him. Dean was angry with him that night for not going after Mia himself. Like his parents, Dean always appeared disappointed in Cole. Unlike his parents, though, Dean seemed to look past the obvious. Cole pictured that irritating, knowing smile on his brother's face now.

Mia let out a shuddering breath, drawing Cole's attention back to her. Their faces were so close he could count the little gray flecks in her bright blue irises, the long black lashes framing her beautiful eyes. How those eyes haunted him. Her jasmine scent rose up, making him fully aware of her. An inch, maybe two, and his lips could be over hers again. He could be home again.

He closed his eyes, closed his ears to his conscience roaring at him to stop, and closed the short distance between them. A gentle brush at first, but then her lips parted and he took what he'd wanted for ten years. It seemed he was always taking something from her. But she softened. Gave back.

Not recognizing the sensation in the pit of his stomach, he wrapped his arms around her and drew her against his chest. Her soft to his hard. Seeking more, her body beneath his, her tight heat, he laid her back on the floor without breaking the kiss. His hands slid under her pajama top, fingers spreading over the smooth, taut skin of her belly, and their kiss became a demand.

Missed. Her.

As the pressure in his gut intensified, he moved his mouth to the soft crevice near her neck and kissed the rapid pulse beating there. She grabbed his arms, not to pull away, but to encourage, and the strain in his stomach became unbearable. Then he recognized it.

Guilt. Shame.

He pushed off the floor and onto his knees. She cried out in protest. Or surprise. His breath heaved in and out. He watched the rise and fall of her breasts as hers did, too. Her red, full mouth was swollen from his assault.

He couldn't do this to her again.

Standing, he swiped a hand down his face and stepped back. Toward the door. Out. "It's getting harder and harder to fight this, Mia. I'm not strong enough."

She sat up, then stood, wringing her hands together now that there was nothing in them.

Hell.

He exited the room, and left her standing there.

Over the next couple weeks, Mia spoke very little to Cole and vice versa. They ate in silence, did his therapy in silence, and passed each other in the halls in silence. The silence was keeping him awake at night. An invisible, impenetrable wall had grown between them since he'd kissed her, and Cole wasn't so sure he should tear it down, or even if he could.

The doorbell rang, indicating Lacey's arrival for their Wednesday visit. He rose from the couch in the sitting room to answer it.

Rose's granddaughter was here this week, training for when Rose retired. A wispy twenty-year-old, Bea was polite and quiet. She seemed afraid of Cole and he had no idea how to break her of the habit. Cole was trying to be more independent, letting Rose show Bea around and get settled in.

He opened the door for Lacey and, after a brief pause, she issued a relieved smile. It appeared that every time his sister visited—she expected to find him dead. That was Cole's fault, for all the heartache he had caused Lacey, and he was trying his hardest to rectify that, too. Lacey deserved to be happy. If worrying about him less was the first step, then by all means, he'd sure as hell comply.

"Morning," he said in greeting. He was pretty sure his smile fell flat.

Lacey stepped inside. "Where's Mia? Her car's not here."

"Shopping. Rose is training a new maid, so Mia offered to do the grocery run."

"Oh, okay. No gardener today?"

Cole shook his head, grinning. "Jake has come and gone. He got an early start today."

A pout protruded from her bottom lip. "Bummer. How's the new maid?"

Cole closed the door and gestured toward the hall. "Petrified. Come meet her?"

He headed toward the kitchen with Lacey in his wake. Bea was just pulling a batch of oatmeal raisin cookies from the oven, the scents of brown sugar and sweet cream butter wafting through the room. Rose was by her side.

"Bea, this is my sister, Lacey. Lacey, Bea."

Bea straightened as if she'd just been caught with the family jewels and wiped her hands on her apron. She looked much younger than twenty standing there before them. She was a hundred pounds, if that, with cafe-colored skin as dark as Rose's. Thick black hair trailed down her back in a low ponytail. Bowing her head, she said, "Nice to meet you, Miss Covington."

Lacey eyed Cole, shaking her head as if to say, *What did you do to her*? Lacey looked back at Bea with a painted, soothing smile. "Just Lacey is fine. Or if you must be formal like Rose here, Miss Lacey."

Bea nodded without looking up at her.

Lacey fisted her hands on her hips, reminding Cole of her once-youthful defiance. "I see my brother's reputation precedes him. He doesn't bite, Bea. Neither do I."

"Yes, ma'am."

Lacey studied her. "Oh, Lord. Am I old enough to be a ma'am?"

Rose chuckled as she placed some cookies on a plate at the kitchen island.

Cole grinned as Bea's gaze darted between Cole and Lacey. He tried for humor. "You *are* a spinster, Lacey."

Bea laughed, then immediately slapped a hand over her mouth. Cole shook his head, hoping one day soon Rose's granddaughter would realize he wasn't going to string her by her toes from the shower rod.

Cole snatched the plate of cookies and walked to the kitchen door. "Come on, Lacey."

"Nice to meet you, Bea." Lacey looked at Rose in a silent plea, then met Cole at the open door.

They settled into the Adirondack chairs on the white-washed back porch with the plate of cookies between them. The early fall air was cooling, but still held enough humidity to make breathing an effort. The salty breeze swept over them as the waves pounded the sand.

"Have you been painting again, Lacey?"

She cleared her throat. "No. Mother never liked when I dabbled with that."

Disappointment weighed in his mind. "I don't consider your talent 'dabbling.' And who cares what Mother thinks?"

Her fingers wove together in her lap. "Easy for you to say. You don't have to see her every day." Quiet settled between them until she said softly, "She asked about you the other day."

Cole didn't answer, didn't care to. He had no will or initiative to see either of his parents yet, if ever. Too much damage had been done and they couldn't, *wouldn't*, understand why. Made no acknowledgements as to their part of what had happened.

"I've been thinking about finally getting my own place," she said, staring at the water. "I stayed in that house so long because I thought they needed me." She shook her head miserably. "I contacted a real estate agent, but when we sat down to discuss what I was looking for, I had no clue. Isn't that sad?" Cole said nothing because he knew she wasn't seeking an answer. "Maybe I should look for a house in Wilmington instead of Charlotte. I could be closer to you then."

Farther away from Mother and Father. "I'd like that, Lacey."

She looked at him, a childlike smile appearing faintly. "What would I do with myself?"

His gaze returned to the ocean. "Anything you want, Lace. Anything you want." The comfortable silence that followed his statement seemed to be filled with meaning. Cole's attention wandered to the conversation he'd had with Mia a couple weeks ago in the library. "I want you to look into something for me."

Lacey took a cookie and bit into it. "What would you like me to look into?"

"There are some apartment complexes in West Wilmington, on Birmingham Road. Find out who owns them and what state they're in."

She swallowed the cookie. "Why? That's not a great area of town, Cole."

He nodded. "I know." Folding his arms over his chest, he debated how much to tell her. On the spot, he decided to have no more secrets from Lacey. She was his sister and he loved her dearly. She didn't make demands of him or push him. She loved him back, without hesitation or agenda. He braced himself for her reaction. "According to Mia, Dean was thinking of buying the complex and repairing the site for a community center. If it's still there, that would be an area in desperate need of help."

Lacey's eyes opened wider, her mouth trembled. "I didn't know that."

"Me neither, until Mia told me."

Lost in thought, Lacey looked at the porch railing in front of her while Cole waited for her to process the information. "So . . . you want to buy the property? Follow through on what Dean had in mind?"

"Right now I'm just thinking. I don't know what kind of shape the buildings are in or if it's even possible. I have a lot of money left from my trust, but not enough for a project like that."

"I do," she whispered. "I have the money. We could get investors, if needed."

Cole looked at her, but she seemed to be talking to herself. "*We?*"

Flinching, she looked over at him. "It would give me something to focus on if I moved to Wilmington. If the project is even doable. But if you don't want my help—"

"I *do* want your help. This isn't about you or me. We'll do it for Dean. Together."

"Yes," she said, eyes welling. A tear slipped out and trailed down her pale cheek. "I'll look into the property and ownership. Maybe send an inspector out."

Satisfied, Cole nodded. "Thank you."

She wiped the tear away and sniffed. "I miss him. It's so hard to believe it's been ten years."

Cole leaned forward and gripped her hand in his. The contact felt foreign after not having much interaction with his sister. Except for Mia, he couldn't remember the last time someone had touched him. "I miss him, too, but I'm glad you're here."

She choked on a sob. "I'm going to hug you," she warned, but gave no time for a reply. She was off her chair and leaning over his before his brain caught up.

He stood, cradling her in his arms and tightening the hug until her feet dangled an inch above the ground. Their parents were never much for displays of affection, private or public, although even as a child Lacey had seemed to need it. Both Dean and Cole had hugged her often, stroked her hair or patted her shoulder, letting her know they loved her, giving her the reassuring contact she craved. How long had she gone since Dean's death without this comfort? Probably too long.

And it had probably been ages since she heard, "I love you, Lace."

chapter
eleven

From the couch in the sitting room, Mia stared at the news report with the remote clutched tightly in her hand. Rose sat on one side and Bea on the other, both also fixated on the news. They were saying the tropical storm was due to hit the Carolina coast three days from now. Initial reports announced the storm didn't have much power, but updates claimed it had quickly gained momentum. Though not strong enough to list as a category hurricane, the tropical storm could do damage. A lot of damage.

When Cole walked into the room to see what was happening, Bea stood like a shot of lightning.

"Sit, Bea," Mia directed. "You're not in trouble."

Cole glanced at the television. "When?" was all he said.

"A couple days," Mia answered. "They're suggesting an evacuation for everyone directly on the coast, for us to head inland."

Cole looked at her, jaw tense. He shook his head slowly.

She closed her eyes and swallowed. Cole wasn't going to leave the house.

"Rose, Bea, could you start lunch? Cole and I need to discuss what to do."

She waited until they both left the room before opening her mouth, but Cole raised a hand to stop her.

"I can't. I'm not leaving."

"Cole, we can go to a hotel inland. If they're booked, we can make the drive to Charlotte. No one will see you at my apartment. You'll have to slum it."

With pursed lips, he shook his head. "No. You go back to Charlotte until it blows through. I'll send Bea and Rose home until it's safe to return."

"You're being unreasonable," she ground out.

A slow, lazy blink. A deep breath in and out. Silence. "This house was built with an iron foundation. The windows are double-paned. The patio doors are bulletproof glass. The shutters are heavy aluminum and so is the roof. The house has withstood more than a hurricane or two, Mia."

The best money could buy. She knew that, but . . . "And what if something happens to you? You'll be alone."

"Nothing will happen to me."

The storm was due to hit the coast sometime Thursday. If it blew through quickly enough, she could maybe still make it on Sunday to visit Ginny. That is, if the roads were clear and they survived. "I'll stay with you. Stubborn jerk."

His head reared back. "You will not. You're leaving. Tonight."

"You have two choices, Cole. You go with me or I stay."

"I will not put you at risk—"

She crossed her arms. "You just said nothing would happen."

His eyes narrowed.

"Choose. Me here or you there."

He said nothing, so she left the room and walked down the hall. Once inside the kitchen, Mia addressed Rose. "Both of you finish up here and go home until I call for you after the storm. Do you have a safe place to stay?"

Bea looked at Rose. "My aunt has a place in Columbia. We went there during Hurricane Floyd and Irene."

"Okay, go there. I have to run to the store to get supplies—"

Cole filled the doorway. "You're not staying, Mia."

"Do you have flashlights or a generator?" she asked instead of responding. She was not having this argument with him in front of others.

He placed his hands above his head on either side of the doorway, something he used to do when they were young but she hadn't seen him do since. His biceps strained against the blue T-shirt. She swallowed hard, trying not to let her attraction flare in her face.

The first time he'd kissed her in his bedroom, she'd barely had time to acknowledge what was happening before he broke away. She had chalked that up to his nightmare, thinking he didn't realize what he was doing. But that kiss in the library was deliberate. They'd almost crossed the line and she didn't stop it—*he* did.

And if the past and the way he'd treated her weren't enough of a deterrent, the life she'd worked so hard for should be. She didn't belong in his world any more than he belonged in hers. They had their own lives, separate lives, and she had to remember that. Had to remember he'd thrown her away once and would again. People like Mia were dispensable to the Covingtons.

Cole looked at his maids and then at her, obviously not liking her argument to stay through the storm. "What about Ginny?" he said quietly, worry lacing his tone.

Her heart tripped mid-beat before righting. God, he'd thought of Ginny. "She's safe at the group home inland. If the roads aren't clear by Sunday, I'll go when they are. I'll call the staff to inform them and speak to Ginny before the storm comes." It's all she could do. She couldn't leave him here alone.

His arms dropped to his sides, resigned. "The back porch closet has a generator, but I don't know if it works. There're battery-powered lanterns and flashlights on the shelf above."

She nodded. "I'll check out the closet. Bea, can you bring in all the planters, chairs, and anything else that can easily fly away? Rose, please make a bunch of sandwiches and find the cooler just in case. I'm heading to the store to get supplies before it gets crazy."

As they got to work, she looked at Cole before leaving. "You sure you want to stay?"

His brow wrinkled. "Please go home to Ginny."

Fine. That was that. They were both staying.

The roads were nuts, partly due to rush hour and partly due to the storm coming. People were trying to evacuate inland. The smart ones anyway. She sighed and pulled into the packed Walmart parking lot. At least it was just a tropical storm. If it was a hurricane coming, she might just have to drug Cole and drive him to Charlotte.

As if she could lift him into the car.

Elbowing her way inside, she grabbed one of the last carts and headed for the grocery aisle. She'd give the chain store this, they were prepared. Skids of bottled water sat between the aisles. She lugged three cases of twenty-four bottles to her cart, one by one. To be safe, she grabbed a few gallons of water, too. She made her way down the aisles, tossing cans of soup and nonperishables into the cart. When she got to the flashlights, there were slim pickings. Cole had three. That would have to be enough. She'd leave what was left for others in need. She was able to snatch a large pack of C and one small pack of AA batteries. They'd have to make do. Cole's closet had three battery-powered LED camping lanterns and a box of wide pillar candles also.

Satisfied, she headed to check out and spent the next thirty minutes in line waiting. Finally back at her car, she loaded the items and relaxed behind the wheel. She should call Ginny now while she was alone. She debated going back to Charlotte yet again, but Ginny was safe where she was. It was Cole who needed her help now. And Cole was right, the house had been built with hurricanes in mind. It was a solid structure.

Pulling out her cell, she dialed the home and explained the situation to the group home manager, Karen. "If there's a problem and you can't reach me, call . . ." Mia cut herself off. Who could they call? Ginny and Mia had no one but each other. "I guess you could call Rose." Mia rattled off her number. She thought over what to say then. "As a last resort, call Lacey Covington." Mia gave Karen that number, too, hoping this wasn't a mistake.

"Got it," Karen said. "No worries. You just take care of y'all, now, you hear?"

"Thank you. Can I talk to Ginny, please?"

Mia stared at the customers in the parking lot while she waited for Ginny. When her time in Wilmington was over, Mia was going to move Ginny out of the group home and back in with her at the apartment. They'd spent too much time apart. At the time, Ginny had needed the structure and Mia's hours were unstable. The bills were piling up and

Mia had had to do what was best. In exchange for helping Cole, Lacey had paid off Ginny's tuition. They'd just have to make the commute. It was a blessed new beginning.

"Hello?"

Mia smiled. "Hey, pretty girl. What are you up to?"

"Nothin'. We made cupcakes today."

"Aw, sounds yummy. How's school?"

"Good."

Mia shook her head. Without prodding, she wouldn't get much more than that. "So, listen, Ginny. There's a storm coming in and I might not make it there on Sunday. I'm going to try real hard, but just in case I can't, I promise to make it up to you, okay? We'll have a big sleepover the next weekend and we can go wherever you want for dinner."

"Okay." That was it. No disappointment, no guilty words.

It broke Mia's heart more than she cared to admit. Ginny had been disappointed a lot in her life, even though she may not have realized it. Mia did her best to make up for Mama's shortcomings. Ginny was almost resigned to what she had. "I'm sorry, Ginny."

"Okay." Pause. "Is it a bad storm?"

Ah, so that's what her sister was focused on. "Yes, but we're prepared. I'll be okay. And the storm is pretty far from you, so you're safe, too. I promise. I'll see you . . . soon."

"Okay."

"I love you . . ." she tried to say, but as usual, Ginny hung up prematurely.

After staring at the cell screen for several minutes, she dialed Lacey's number to inform her of the plan. Though concerned, Lacey thanked Mia for staying with Cole. Mia bit her lip before telling Lacey the other reason for her call.

"I told Ginny's group home to call Rose if I wasn't

available. I hope it's okay, but I gave them your number as a secondary emergency contact."

"Of course it's okay!"

Mia breathed in relief. "I have to get back. Thanks, Lace."

Mia turned over the ignition, then made her way to the road, deciding to get gas before heading to the house. Best to have a full tank just in case. The gas station was busy, but she was in and out in fifteen minutes.

For the first time since hearing about the storm, Mia realized what was about to happen. She was about to be isolated in a house with Cole Covington for God knew how long. Alone. Just the two of them.

She could only pray the storm blew through quickly. Still, her stomach rolled with anxiety.

Cole stood next to Mia in the front doorway as she said good-bye to Rose and Bea.

"Call me when you get to Columbia, please. Let me know you're okay."

Rose nodded once and patted Mia's cheek. "We'll be fine, child. You just worry about closing up the house. I want to hear from you as soon as you can." Rose stared Cole down. "You take care, Mister Cole."

Cole attempted a smile, watching as they descended the porch steps and climbed into Rose's car. Once they were out of sight, he blew out a breath. "You still have time to head to Charlotte," he said.

"Pack a bag. Let's go."

And she called him stubborn.

The smart thing to do was leave. The house had survived three hurricanes and several tropical storms since it was built, but never with someone inside. The Covingtons had off-season staff who knew the procedure for closing the house to the elements. Before he owned the house, the family only stayed here during the summer months.

Cole couldn't explain it, but the thought of leaving the property caused his heart to pound and a cold sweat to break out over his entire body. He'd seen the way others stared at his limp, his scars rising over the neckline of his shirt. It wasn't just the physical scars though. He didn't know how to be around people anymore.

Mia shook her head and walked inside. Cole followed and shut the door. He met up with her in the kitchen where she was key-coding the front gate to lock from the wall-mounted box. She stared out the kitchen window when she was finished, her arms crossed, her body tense.

"We should go out and take a walk while we can," Cole said. "Tomorrow we'll need to batten down the hatches."

She looked over her shoulder at him and nodded, so he held the door open for her. They stepped onto the sand and over the dunes to get closer to the water. The waning sun blazed the sky in deep purple and pink, the ocean nearly black over the horizon. Cole could feel the storm coming. His arm and leg were tight and the air had a heavy, still quality.

They walked in silence for a while until she stopped and faced the water. "You're going to have to leave the house sometime, Cole. I'd like to help you, if you'll let me."

"I know," he said, standing next to her and crossing his arms. "And I appreciate all you've done."

Something awkward settled between them and he didn't like it. She was growing even more distant from him, as if preparing herself to leave. He should let that go, knew he had to let *her* go eventually. But not yet. *Please, not yet.*

"Mia, what's wrong?"

Her smile was forced. "Nothing, I guess. Just . . . worried."

"We'll be fine. We've survived worse storms than this." Her smile fell and he realized the implication in what he'd said.

Her gaze followed a seagull circling the water. "You use the term *we* a lot."

Did he? Guess he was more delusional than he thought. "My apologies."

Turning fully to face him, her head tilted as she studied him. She must have worked out whatever problem weighed on her because she nodded. "How are the nightmares? The flashbacks?"

He tried to think of the last time he'd had one of either. "Gone."

"And how are you handling the memoir?"

Yes, the memoir. It ripped his soul out with every word he typed. Yet, since he'd cried with her that night in the library, a weight had seemed to lift. He'd spent the last ten years feeling like he was hauling a mountain inside him, intense and heavy. There was this pain in his gut, which never let up, until that night. Oddly, all he could feel now was empty. Lighter, but empty.

"Writing the memoir is helping. I never would have thought of doing something like that without your sugges-tion." For that, she smiled, and he wasn't so empty after all.

"Forced you, you mean?"

He didn't realize he was grinning back until he wiped a hand over his jaw. "Correction. Until you *forced* me. Thank you, by the way."

"A smile looks good on you, Cole."

"Then I'll try to oblige and do it more often." She

looked away, the worried expression returning. "What's with all the questions, Mia?"

Tilting her head down the beach, she indicated she wanted to head back. "I don't think you need me here anymore."

His steps faltered, but he corrected himself before she noticed. He knew this was coming, knew she had a life without him to get back to, but the thought of his house without her in it made his throat raw. They climbed the porch steps, but before they could go into the house she blocked the doorway. Hesitantly, she took his hand and sandwiched it between hers. So warm. The touch of her could warm him even on the coldest of nights.

She looked at their joined hands. "If your flashbacks and nightmares are gone, you're able to control the memories. You're eating, sleeping, and dressing without me making you. Physically, you're strong again. And after you cried in the library . . ."

He pulled his hand away and stepped back, the embarrassment evident by the way his face heated. But damn her, she cradled his face in her hands, forced his gaze down on her.

"Crying means you're dealing with Dean's death. You shouldn't be ashamed. Tears are normal. You have every right to shed them."

"Jesus, Mia." He swallowed.

Who would help him deal with her loss? Who would fill this gap she left in his heart? He'd had women since her. Many women. None of them were her. None smelled like jasmine or tasted like honey or could talk his ear off without saying a thing. Somehow, he could only be himself around her. He only existed in her presence. Time hadn't changed a thing. His feelings for her had only grown from young infatuation and interest to true, deep . . . love.

"You don't need me anymore," she whispered.

The hell he didn't. She was the only thing he did need.

Removing her hands from his cheeks, he squeezed them before letting go completely. How crazy it was he'd never been able to let her go. "You've changed."

Her hand darted to her short, pixie hair.

"I don't mean the hair. I like it short though."

"I've been thinking of growing it out again."

"I liked it long, too." Now they were discussing her hair to avoid the serious conversation. They'd never shied away from telling each other everything when they were young, and lately they'd gotten back into their old feeling of comfort. "You've changed in other ways. You grew a backbone, for one."

"I didn't have much choice," she said. "Life forced me to toughen up."

"I'm sorry about why, but I'm glad for how. I like this new, bossy Mia."

A breathy laugh. "You've changed, too. I don't mean the broody, dark Cole either. You're not spending your life trying to make others happy and you're not taking those close to you for granted anymore. I like the new Cole."

No one liked the new Cole. No one liked the *old* Cole.

"That means a lot coming from you."

She looked over his shoulder at the sky before her gaze landed on his chest. Her long, dark lashes created shadows on her cheekbones. "I'll stay on through the rest of September."

He stared at the top of her head, watched the breeze ruffle the soft, black strands, which had grown a couple inches since she'd arrived. "I don't know how to say goodbye to you." He meant to think that in his head, not say it aloud, but now that he had, he finished his thought. "I . . .

never knew how to say good-bye to you, Mia. In my own mind, I figured I'd see you again and get it right the next time around. But . . ." He trailed off, knowing full well he wasn't getting it right now either.

Her shoulders straightened. "I'm here a few more weeks. No need for that now. Besides, who says we need to say good-bye at all? We could all use a few more friends around."

Friends. That might be worse than never seeing her again. She'd visit once in a while and he'd count the days until she returned. And then on one faraway day, she'd knock on his door with a ring on her finger, claiming she'd met someone who made her happy in all the ways he couldn't.

"I'd like to stay friends, yes," he mumbled, forcing the inevitable future aside.

She opened the door and he followed her inside, hating the person who coined the phrase, *Let's just be friends.*

"Why don't you get some writing done while we still have power? I'll go check the weather report and make us a quick dinner."

In "Project Mia," Cole was in that tenuous part of the story after he'd gotten injured in Iraq and was being sent home from the German hospital. Fun times. Thing was, he didn't know what to write about after that.

Mia walked to the kitchen sink and washed her hands. He watched her, like he always did, the fading sunlight bathing her skin while she did this mundane task, and knew there wouldn't be many more days he could do this. Soon, she'd be gone.

Cole pivoted and headed toward the library. At least now he knew what to write about.

chapter
twelve

"What can I do?" Cole asked, watching Mia run in and out of the sitting room. She was bringing pillows and comforters downstairs in case they needed to sleep on the main floor.

"I need to pull my car into the garage. Is there room?"

"Yes. I have my Jeep and the Boxster in the garage. There's room for two more vehicles."

"I'll be right back. Can you close all the fireplace flues? We can start on the shutters when I get back inside."

She grabbed her keys off the table and ran out the front door without waiting for his answer. He shook his head and walked to the fireplace in the sitting room. Mia was in full action mode since watching the weather report earlier that morning. The tropical storm was coming in later that afternoon, which was almost a full day earlier than predicted. He closed the flue in the fireplace and headed upstairs to get the one in his bedroom. This house only had the two chimneys.

He turned when he heard her feet padding up the stairs. "Done," he said.

"Okay," she huffed. "Let's start on the shutters. Do we need to go out and get a ladder?"

"They close from the inside," he said calmly, amused at how flustered Mia had become. Quite adorable, actually. He walked to the window in his bedroom and unlocked the pane. Sliding the glass up, he waved her over. She stuck her head out. "Heavy aluminum, like I said." He unlatched the shutter from the stone exterior and swung the left side until it closed in and covered the glass. He did the same with the other side before demonstrating how to hook the shutters together. "Okay?"

"Yep. You finish your room and Lacey's. I'll get mine and the guest rooms. Don't forget the bathrooms."

He watched the doorway long after she disappeared, listening to her going about her task in the other rooms. Once he finished, he met her downstairs. "The living room and kitchen shutters latch from the outside because the bay windows are too big to open."

"I'll do it." Out she went.

Cole thought he may need to tie her down later to get her to stop moving at this warp speed. Liking the image, he closed the shutters in the dining room, library, and gym. She came in the kitchen door with her hair standing on end. Cole glanced out the door, noting that the wind had picked up considerably since this morning.

"The patio doors?" she asked.

"Bulletproof glass, remember? I shut the drapes, just in case."

"Okay," she said through a sigh, plopping down on a

kitchen chair. "The generator is ready. Rose said it's only enough to power the kitchen."

"If it works, that's all we'll need it for."

She nodded, staring off into the distance, as if not listening. "There's a lantern in here, in your room, and in the sitting room. I have a flashlight in my bedroom. We need to shut off the water main." She rose, ready to set off in a flurry again.

"Done, Mia. Sit back down." To demonstrate, he sat in a chair next to hers. "I went on the back porch to cut the main earlier."

"Right. Okay. I'm acting like a spaz, aren't I?"

He laughed. "It's kinda cute."

Her eyes narrowed, but she said nothing. After a few minutes, she glanced around the very dim room. In an hour, it would be completely dark, forcing them to rely on the lanterns and candles if the storm was bad enough. At the moment, they had power. He stood and turned on the light. She blinked rapidly as her eyes adjusted.

"Why don't we watch a movie?" he suggested.

"Or the weather."

Cole made his way out of the kitchen and down the hall. "Or the weather," he mimicked.

After turning on both the lamps, Cole flopped on the couch and propped his feet on the coffee table. Seconds later, Mia walked in and sat on the other side of the couch. She glanced at his feet with raised brows.

Cole shrugged. "Always wanted to do that."

Mia grinned. "If your mother could see you now."

Yeah. If.

But she couldn't. "Know what else I always wanted to do?" he asked. She looked at him like she didn't want to know. Cole set his feet down and stood. Grabbing the back of the couch for balance, he stepped onto the cushion and straightened to full height. "Feet on the furniture." He twisted and pivoted into place to make his point.

She threw her head back and laughed. "Too bad it's your furniture now."

"Way to ruin the mood," he said, but he kept his smile in place to show he wasn't annoyed. Sitting back down, he flicked on the television with the remote, already set to Mia's weather station.

After several minutes, she looked over. "You could stand on your mother's furniture if you visited her."

Mia, Mia, Mia. She'd found a clever way to hint that he should reach out to his parents, try to bridge the gap. Probably a therapy technique for healing, in her mind. And of all the people who should be bitter toward the Covington patriarchs, Mia was the most justified. Her attitude toward them now was proof she'd been the better person all along. Too good for the likes of him.

She was right though. Eventually he'd have to call his parents, have to see them again. But not now. Now he was locked in the house with Mia for at least the next few days.

"The look on her face would be worth it," he said.

Mia handed a plate of chicken salad on rye toast to Cole and sat on the couch with her own dinner. The wind howled and screeched outside, rattling the shutters. She wondered if the banging and pounding reminded him of gunfire. He seemed unfazed as he took a bite, watching the radar.

"I'm fine, Mia. Eat."

Smiling, she took a bite and focused on the television. The tropical storm had hit the Carolina coast about an hour ago, but the worst was yet to come. They weren't anywhere near the center of its path, yet. Honestly, she was shocked they still had power, considering the way the storm raged outside.

Some of the idiot reporters on the TV were shown near the coast from earlier in the day, when the winds first started to gust. Rain pelted horizontally, flushing a woman's cheeks a bright red. Another reporter lost his umbrella midsentence.

Cole leaned forward and set his empty plate down on the table. "I can't watch this crap anymore. Can I turn on something else?"

Mia figured they weren't going to learn anything new anyway, so she shrugged. "Sure. It's your house."

He flipped channels, each a second blur before the next. News. News. *Twilight. Law & Order.* More news. *Ghost Hunters.*

Mia picked up their plates and rose. "You want a bottle of water?"

"Sure," he mumbled absently. "Wait. Do we have any beer?"

She paused in the doorway. "You can't drink on your medication."

"You mean the medication I'm not taking?"

She spun around. "What do you mean, Cole? I give you the pills every morning."

He looked at her. "You give them to me, but I don't take them."

Walking back to the couch, she set the plates down and sat. Her nursing training had taught her better than to not watch patients swallow their pills and do a mouth check. She guessed her problem was she didn't see Cole as a patient, didn't see this as a job. She trusted him. "Why aren't you taking them?"

He shrugged. "I didn't take them before you got here. After you made me start therapy, I felt fine. Didn't think I needed them."

"Huh," she muttered. "Those are antidepressants. I'll have to let Dr. Melbourne know about this."

"The guy at the Charlotte VA? You're reporting to him?" He didn't look happy.

"Yes," she said tentatively. "I told you I got a treatment plan from him. We email once a week. I send him updates on you—"

Cole stood so fast her neck hurt following his movement. "So let me get this straight. You tell him the things we talked about? My family, *our* past. I thought those things were between us, Mia!"

God, now what? She stood. "They are just between us."

"You said you report everything to him! Jesus, Mia! I trusted you!"

"I don't report everything. And you *can* trust me, Cole."

He paced away, back again, his hands fisting in his hair. "Do you have any idea what someone can do with that information? I'm hounded enough by the press since my father's election. Why do you think my number's unlisted?"

"A doctor cannot divulge patient information. It's against HIPAA health code privacy policy."

He whirled, hands fisted. "As if that's stopped them before." He ran a hand down his face. "After my injuries, reporters showed up at the hospital. They find out things, Mia."

"That wasn't from me. That could have come from anyone." It wouldn't surprise her if his own parents had fed the press that information to draw attention to his father's campaign. Rally the people to back the man who'd fathered a hero war vet.

"I *trusted* you!"

"And you can trust me now, Cole!" She raised her voice, nearly shouted to break through his anger. Finally, he turned his heated gaze to her, breath heaving in and out. "Never have I given you any cause to think I would betray that trust," she said, "even when I could have. I did not, nor would I ever discuss your family. What we talked about was between us. Just us. I report to Dr. Melbourne on your physical status. Your overall mood, how you are socially, whether you're eating or sleeping. Those medical necessities." Winded, hurt, she sat back down. "I would never hurt you," she said quietly. "I thought you knew me better than that."

A very, very long pause. "Mia . . ." A soft, apologetic voice.

She shook her head and waved him off, unable to look at him. "He's the primary doctor and you're under his care. I had to report to him. There was a possibility they'd try to initiate your power of attorney. Take your independence away."

His breathing grew harsh. "I'm . . ."

Finally, emotions under control, she looked at him. He was staring at her with that wretched shame on his face. The same expression he got every time she found him in a vulnerable moment. Like when she saw him without his shirt, crying in the library, trying to explain his feelings . . .

He swallowed hard, stared at her feet. "My family always demanded a confidentiality contract with the staff. I have my help sign them, too, just in case. You never signed one, even when you filled in for your mother that summer—"

"I didn't think I needed one."

"I know." He ran a hand through his hair. "That came out wrong."

"Give me one now. I'll sign it. Where are they?" she asked, standing. "In the library?"

"No, Mia . . ." Weaving around the table, he grabbed her arm, grinding her to a halt. "God. I know you don't need to sign it."

"Obviously you don't. If you need a piece of paper, then by all means, let's do it." She didn't know what was worse, the pain in her chest because he thought this little of her, or the look on his face as he tried to amend his own words. "Come on, Cole."

"You're one of only two people I trust on this earth, Mia!" His voice, louder than the raging storm, reverberated off the walls. He dropped her arm and stepped away, as if afraid he'd hurt her. "I'm sorry. I don't . . . know what else to say. I was stupid. You and Lacey, I trust you both." His voice was pleading, his eyes pained beyond words. "I'm sorry," he whispered.

When tears threatened again, she swallowed and looked away. He apologized, but the words couldn't be taken back. What a shame his life had come down to this. That he had to question even her.

My, how the night had turned. It had started out pleasant enough, storm aside. Now the air in the room was so heavy she couldn't breathe.

She tried to focus on what had started all this in the first place. "If you're doing well off the medication, there's no need for Dr. Melbourne to keep you on it. Which is a good sign." A great sign actually. It meant Cole was doing all this on his own, without chemicals or dependence. "I'll print out the emails I sent to him so you can read them, keep them for your records."

"You don't need to. Mia, honestly, you don't."

Her glance darted around the room, landing on the

plates. She walked over and grabbed them. "I'll see if there's any beer in the fridge."

She thought he'd follow her to the kitchen, but was relieved when he stayed put. She needed the few seconds alone to cope with what had just happened. She had no doubt he was sorry, had more doubt he didn't mean it, but God . . . the betrayal cut. Cole could do that to her, time and time again. He was one of only a few people who could get to her like this, make her feel small and unworthy.

Like that night Dean died, ten years ago. The things Cole had said. How he'd thrown her away as if their time together meant nothing.

She opened the fridge as a gust slammed the shutters against the bay window, making a whistling sound from the air trapped between the glass and the aluminum. The house seemed like it was shaking on its very foundation. The floor vibrated with intensity.

She drew in a deep breath and reminded herself the house was secure. As she bent over to check the fridge for beer, the power cut out, cloaking the room in total darkness.

"Mia?"

Cole scanned the black room, waiting for his eyes to adjust before standing to see if she was all right in the kitchen.

"Hold on," she called from the hallway. An eerie blue glow preceded her into the room—she was holding the camping lantern. She reached over and switched on the other one on the coffee table.

Cole sighed. Her spine was still rigid, her movements forced.

He felt like an ass. He *was* an ass for what he'd said to her.

Trust was a thin line between them already and he was afraid he'd just severed it with the accusation about divulging family secrets. He knew better, knew Mia would never do such a thing. She didn't want to hear his apologies though.

"Want to play poker?" he asked, hoping to do something in the silence, keep their minds off the storm. For the first time in a very long time, he hated the isolation.

A corner of her mouth quirked as she set a bottle of Corona in front of him. "Do you still cheat?"

Mock offense. "I never cheated. You just suck."

As she made a sound of disbelief, he rose to get a deck of cards from the entertainment cabinet. He set them on the couch cushion between them and turned to face her. "You deal."

"What are we playing?"

Strip poker sounded excellent. "Texas Hold 'em?"

Without a word, she removed the cards from the sleeve, shuffled, and dealt. Crossing her legs underneath her, she sat sideways on the couch to face him. She examined her hand in the dim light, her eyes reflecting off the lantern, almost seeming to glow. She had a terrible poker face, which is why he always used to beat her. Cheating had nothing to do with it. He could tell she had a great hand before the flop by her faint, knowing smile.

He decided to bait her. "I bet fifty."

Her brows rose. She held out her hand, palm up, as if to ask for the money.

"I bet fifty hypothetically," he amended.

She shook her head. "Cents or dollars?"

He laughed. "Thousand."

Her jaw dropped, and he resisted the very strong urge to reach over and close her mouth with his own.

"Fine. Since this is hypothetical, I call."

She dealt the three flop cards, an ace of spades, two of hearts, and four of diamonds. How sad. He had a pair of twos. If her grin was any indication, she had an ace in her hand.

"Check," he said.

"Seventy-five," she announced her bet.

"Seventy-five thousand, huh?"

Her smug expression was cute as hell. "Million."

He laughed so hard he had to grip his side to stop it from splitting open. "Oh, you are terrible at this. You need to learn how to bet, Mia."

She shrugged. "Call or fold."

Sobering, he shrugged, too. "All right, I fold. But show me your hand."

She turned over her cards and he did a double take. A seven of clubs and a nine of spades.

"You *played* me."

She grinned.

"My view of everything right and wrong in the world just imploded."

She laughed and he stopped cold while she collected the cards. She held them out for him and when he took them, their fingers brushed. He almost tossed the cards over his shoulder and laid her back on the couch. Almost.

He missed that laugh.

He dealt and won the next hand with a full house, kings over jacks. Cole watched her long, elegant fingers as she shuffled, wondering how many others she'd touched with those hands of hers. How many men in the past ten years had the damn pleasure of visiting heaven because of her touch. Clearing his throat, he looked down at his hand without seeing anything.

"So, what was college like?" he asked, suddenly wanting

to know what she'd done in their time apart. "Did you party hard? Have twenty boyfriends to string along?" Christ, he almost winced at his brilliance.

She made a noise teetering between a groan and laugh. "Hardly. I didn't have time to party. After class I worked full time at a diner near the campus. On weekends I drove from Charlotte to Wilmington to take care of things at the trailer. Someone had to pay the bills and keep an eye on Ginny. I'm so glad I had Rose right next door. She helped out during the week."

Wow. Didn't he feel like an idiot. She'd spent her whole teen years being the adult, when she should've been out with friends and going to proms and dating a high school football star. Cole had hoped her college years had been kinder. Guess not.

"Didn't you have any fun, Mia? Date at least?"

Why all the dating questions, man? You really want to know?

"There were a couple of guys, I guess. No one serious. College boys weren't really into long term and I didn't have the luxury of pretending I could offer anything remotely close to a good time."

Her tone wasn't bitter or sad. She didn't look anything but stoic. Accepting of the figurative hand she was dealt. Speaking of . . . "Pair of sixes."

"Flush. I win."

He didn't care. He wanted to find out more. *God, please tell me she had some joy in her life.* "What about after college?" he asked, trying to keep his tone unaffected.

"I moved Ginny to Charlotte to live with me. We had a small one bedroom, but she loved it. There was a nice gay couple who lived across the hall who watched Ginny after school until my shift was over. I dated a radiologist for a while, but it didn't work out." She looked at him. "I got nothin'."

It sure seemed that way, but she meant the card game. "Straight." He shuffled and dealt. "Why didn't it work out?"

She shrugged and, again, he admired her strength. "Not many guys want to marry a woman with full custody of a disabled sister. I was still struggling to get her decent therapy in the state programs. Ginny's better now that she's at St. Ambrose, but it took a lot of years to get there."

Cole remembered the spirited girl. Ginny had a great smile, but was prone to temper tantrums. Best he could recall, she didn't talk much either. Mia seemed to be the only one who could calm her down. She used to sing to Ginny, her voice soothing and lilting, washing over him like a warm breeze.

"What about you? What was the military like?"

Not the escape he'd thought it would be. And it didn't take away the horrible memories or the guilt, just compounded them. "Boot camp wasn't so bad, once I realized my money didn't matter there. I was a no one, just like everyone else. Once I was deployed, the men spent a lot of down time talking about women. It was childish really, everyone trying to one-up each other. I used to look forward to calling in air strikes or locating an enemy insurgent group just to have something to do besides listen to the inane chatter. But we always had each other's backs. Not for a second did I ever worry about trusting them."

He stared at his hand. Pair of queens. "We discussed, in detail, what we wanted to do when we got back home. Those were the best conversations. Some guys would talk about marrying a special girl, others about what they wanted in a career. I used to fall asleep to the sound of their voices. They were normal, and I never got to be normal."

"Sounds like you made a lot of friends."

Damnedest part was, he hadn't talked to one guy since returning. "Not really. I mean, I liked the guys well enough, but I was too different from them. Almost like a dad. They felt more like children to me than friends."

She smiled and it reached her eyes. "Cole Covington, the mature one."

"Hard to believe, I know."

He folded his hand. She reshuffled and dealt.

"What about when you went home on leave or were discharged?"

"I hated being on leave. Spending time with the vapid and shallow parental units wasn't an option. I'd spend a couple days here alone and go back." He swallowed, realizing that talking about this wasn't as hard as he thought. "They don't prepare you for what it's like to return. Most Americans don't support the war, they just want revenge for 9/11. They fly their flags and say things like 'Support Our Troops,' but they don't get it. Trust is a big issue. It's difficult going from a war zone, thinking every second is your last, knowing the guys you're with have your back no matter what, to civilian life, where the stakes are so much lower. Most people seem undisciplined compared to the men who serve." He shrugged. "Most of the other guys were angry after coming back from leave. Some even said the country wasn't worth fighting for when civilians cared so little about life. All the crimes and murders in the States were an insult. The protesters were the worst."

He folded his hand and looked up at her. She studied him with focused intent. "What?" he asked.

"That's more than you've said to me in the two months I've been here."

"You asked."

"And I'm not complaining. Are you writing all this down in your memoir?"

He couldn't read her expression. "Yes."

Her gaze dropped to her hands, then the window rattled as a gust blew hard. "Don't get mad, but you should consider publishing it. I think others can benefit from your experience. What you just said will affect how I treat injured vets, will help me understand some of what they're feeling."

The thought of anyone with a credit card in a bookstore knowing his whole sordid tale made him shudder. He took a drink from the Corona and said nothing.

She had that look again, like she wanted to say something but was too damn scared of his reaction. He'd give anything, *anything* to see something besides fear on her face. "Say it."

Her gaze flew to his. "Say what?"

"Whatever it is you're thinking. Whatever it is you want to ask. I know you, there's something."

She blew out a breath and glanced away, uncertain. He waited her out. After several minutes, her gaze fell to his chest with a faraway look in her eyes.

"When I agreed to help you, I was given a copy of your medical file. In it was a picture of me. They said you had it on you when you got injured."

That stopped him cold. Froze his heart, his limbs, and the room around him. Suspended time in a vacuum.

He'd spent every night pulling out her picture to stare at it. Every waking second reliving that night he'd sent her away, broken her heart, and, ultimately, caused Dean's death. Working in New York at the literary agency hadn't taken the memory away. Going halfway across the world to the desert of Iraq hadn't either. Nothing had.

And she wanted an explanation. There wasn't one.

"I don't understand, Cole. You said I meant nothing, that you never wanted to see me again. So why then carry a picture of me—"

He surged off the couch, scattering the deck of cards across the floor. He paced away from her, trying to calm his heart rate so the organ wouldn't explode in his chest. While overseas, he'd made a deal with God that if he survived he would find her. He would tell her the truth of that night so in case she had held on to his words all these years, she would know they were lies. He couldn't bear to think of her going the rest of her life thinking those lies were true.

But then he'd returned to this house, the house where it had begun and ended, and locked himself away. Hiding. Seeing her again that first time brought back that vow to God. An opportunity. A disaster. He'd been here with her, had chance after chance to tell her the ugly truth, but hadn't.

The shadows in the room deepened, closed in on him. The walls quaked with the storm raging outside, the floor vibrating beneath his feet. How easy it would be to open the door and step outside, let the winds carry him into oblivion. But then she'd never know the reality of what had happened that day.

Cole thought about Mia's life since, about what she just told him tonight. She hadn't fallen in love, nor formed any lasting attachments to another soul. Had not moved on.

Cole turned, saw her on her knees, picking up the deck of cards off the floor, and knew he had to finally move on, too.

So much easier said than done. They were both broken.

"Mia, have you ever told a lie so big it changed your life?"

Her head lifted, her gaze quizzical. She set the cards on the table and stood, the coffee table and ten long years between them.

"I have," he said, forcing the words out through a gravelly voice. "After we made love in the guesthouse—"

"No," she said with vigor, cutting him off. "Don't do this, Cole. That's over and done with."

"I went back into the main house to get my keys. You remember?" As if either had forgotten.

She turned away, denial evident in her tense stride. "Cole, please."

He flinched at her plea, remembering how she'd said the same thing when he'd tried to send her away that night. "Mother and Father were sitting right here in this room. My mother ordered me to end our relationship."

Her head whipped around. Oh, those big, endless blue eyes. "What?"

"When I refused, she threatened you. Said she would get them to drop your acceptance to UNC, would make sure no college took you. She threatened to call the authorities and have Ginny taken away if I didn't comply."

Her jaw quivered. She looked like she was trying to form words, but nothing escaped. She grabbed the neckline of her tee and bunched it in her fist.

"Mia, she had the clout and connections to do it. I couldn't let her. You would have lost everything. So I did the only thing I could. I lied."

A ragged breath escaped her perfect red mouth. Her gaze landed over his shoulder, but she wasn't in the room anymore. She was standing at the front gate in the rain, reliving. Watching her killed him dead inside.

"I didn't mean any of it, Mia," he whispered, unable to put any force behind the words. He was too tired of fighting, too tired of pretenses. "I couldn't go on with the rest of my life knowing you thought you were everything they said about you. You're special. You're important. You're beautiful and kind and better than the life you were given."

A crash boomed from outside. One of the property trees coming down, most likely. Mia didn't seem to notice. She stood stock-still for so long Cole began to worry.

Slowly, her watery gaze drifted to him. "You did it to protect me. You . . . protected *Ginny*." Her fingertips pressed against her mouth.

The way she made it seem, that what he did was admirable, nearly had him on his knees. It wasn't admirable, it was cowardice. And she acted like she couldn't allow herself to believe him.

Cole cleared his raw throat. "You were worth losing everything for."

Truth. Finally.

Her hand fell away. Something close to a whimper filled the quiet, a sound from deep inside her and so wretched with pain it nailed his heart from clear across the room.

They stared at each other for long minutes. Cole was unable to look away.

Without taking her gaze from him, she side-stepped the table and walked to him. He had less than three seconds to evaluate her expression.

Anger. Remorse. Doubt. Fear. Lust. Pain. All etched on her face, in her eyes.

He braced himself for the harsh sting of her hand across his cheek that he knew must be coming.

Instead, she rose on her toes and crashed her mouth to his.

Stunned into immobility, he hesitated, until her hand cupped the back of his head and her chest molded to his torso, snapping him out of the shock.

And for the first time in what seemed like an eternity, he was whole again.

He angled his head to deepen the kiss, slid his tongue against hers in the most sensual dance. There were no lies between them now, no past to shatter the memory. Without even being aware of it, Cole released the guilt and sought her.

Only Mia.

They came to an abrupt halt against the doorframe, having blindly backed themselves against the wall. Cole broke the kiss as Mia slid her hands under his shirt and tugged it over his head.

"Wait," he muttered when she brought her mouth back over his. Her fingers glided down his chest, causing his stomach to draw inward. "Mia, wait." He pressed his palms to the wall on either side of her head. "Be sure," he whispered. Daring to lose everything a second time, he looked into her eyes. *"Be sure."*

"I'm sure."

Her lack of hesitation did him in. He stared at her a second more before turning away to grab the lantern from the table. She deserved more than being laid out on the hard wood floor. They both did. He took her hand firmly in his and wove their fingers together.

"Upstairs."

thirteen

Mia swallowed hard as she walked up the stairs, hand in hand with Cole, the dim lantern fisted in his other hand lighting their way. Her stomach fluttered nervously.

The things he'd said downstairs . . .

Mia had gotten her answers. The events were clicking into place, making sense now, where before there were only nagging questions. Doubts.

The sacrifice Cole had made for her and Ginny had her reeling. Quaking. All these years she'd held on to that pain, that hate, just to survive. For nothing. She wanted to lash out at his mother, for everything she had put them all through. But there was no room for anger tonight. There couldn't be. Tonight was about her and Cole. The time wasted and the space between them became a blur. She wasn't wasting a minute more.

At the top of the stairs he paused. She looked at him,

thinking maybe he was holding on to regret. But he handed her the lantern and swept an arm under her legs, lifting her from the ground and cradling her to his bare chest.

"Cole, your leg."

His forehead dropped to hers. "I've had ten years to think up a million ways to make love to you, Mia. Let me."

Oh God. Oh wow. She nodded, unable to speak.

He strode into his bedroom and set her on her feet next to the bed. She placed the lantern on the nightstand, the faint glow barely illuminating a portion of the mattress. He walked away to close the door before returning to her. As if suddenly shy, he ran his shaking hands up and down her arms.

She shivered, anticipation and anxiety filling her, but she reached for the hem of her tee. His hands closed over hers, and he shook his head. With deliberate ease, he removed her shirt. His dark eyes took their fill, his fingers tracing the outline of her bra over the rise of her breast. With his other hand, he reached behind her back and unclasped her bra. It slid from her shoulders to the floor. Her yoga pants and panties soon followed.

His hands fell to her hips. His fingers dug into her flesh. "Beautiful," he murmured.

Her face heated with desire, with want. They weren't teenagers with a time restriction anymore. There was no one here to threaten them into obedience.

Just the two of them.

Needing to touch him, she laid her palms on his chest, splaying her fingers and running them down over the corded muscles of his abs. He drew in a sharp breath but didn't try to stop her. The button on his jeans popped when she tugged, the zipper creating an echoing sound in the lull of the storm. His erection strained against his briefs and she remembered what he'd felt like inside her. Stretching, filling, completing. She dipped her fingers into the waistband and urged them down.

Down, down.

Mia followed the path, kneeling in front of him, until he stepped out of the jeans and briefs. Her hands slid up his legs, brushing the coarse, sandy blond hair and finding the scar on his left thigh. From the floor, she looked up at him, but his eyes were pinched tightly closed. Wrapping both hands around the firm thigh, she pressed a kiss to the scar. He expelled an uneven breath and wove his fingers through her hair.

Keeping her touch light, she stood and moved to his side. One hand on his back, the other on his abs, she kissed the scar on his shoulder. When she traced the scar up his neck with the kiss, her hand dipped lower to his erection, closing her fingers around the thickness.

"Mia," he groaned. "Please, don't . . . stop."

His breaths were shallow, panting in and out, and she loved that he was as affected as she was. His hands fisted at his side, his eyes still sealed shut.

"God, don't . . . You have to *stop*." He whirled to face her, dislodging her grasp and trapping her arms between their bodies. His muscles tightened with a loud swallow. "It's been quite some time since I've done this. This is too important."

She pressed her cheek to his collarbone, slowing down their tempo for just a bit. "It's been a while for me, too." She waited several beats. Lifting her head, she cupped his jaw and ran her thumb over the stubble, listening to the rasp. He gazed down his nose at her, jaw clenched. "We have all the time we need tonight."

His head lowered, pinned their gazes. "Yes," he murmured, his hot breath mingling with hers. "Yes."

And then he closed his mouth over hers, kissing her into oblivion until she couldn't stand of her own accord and her world teetered off its axis. They staggered to the bed, fell together, while their tongues tangled. Each stroke of his tongue matched the rhythm of her heart. His hand came up to cup one breast, kneading until the ache mingled with the one between her thighs. She arched up off the bed.

"Shit." He suddenly broke away, dropping his forehead between her breasts. "I don't have . . . I'm not prepared. I wasn't expecting to . . ." His very large hands clutched her sides. "Not for a long time anyway."

And then she figured out what he was trying to say. No condom. "I'm on the pill."

He froze.

"It's okay. I'm on the pill, Cole." He still didn't move. She looked down at the top of his head. "Cole?"

"There is a God."

He rose over her, crushed his mouth to hers, and kissed her senseless again. Desperation and relief poured off him in waves. The emotions filled her.

She wrapped her legs around his hips, needing him inside her more than air in her lungs. It had always been like this with him, even before they'd made love that one time. The fact that time hadn't changed this urgency, this need, should've given her pause. Should've scared the very life out of her.

It didn't.

"Mia, slow down." He cupped her bottom with both hands, drawing her hips up to a grind, belying his words. "Give me time to get you . . . ready."

Oh, she was ready. So, so ready.

But how sweet of him to take care of her, wanting her to go over that edge first and prepare her body for him. She was already wet, already so taut she felt like she'd snap. She wanted to do this *with* him.

"Together," she said. She grabbed his hips, aligned their bodies for that ultimate connection.

Yet he didn't move. His face hovered near hers, gaze roaming over her hair, her face, before lingering on her mouth, as if trying to memorize every feature. When he finally seemed satisfied, found whatever it was he sought, he entered her with one hard thrust.

She gasped in sheer pleasure. He stilled, gaze boring into her, giving her time to adjust to his size. She realized he was still shaking, either from trying to hold out for her or because his emotions were as wild and frantic as hers.

"Mia. I . . ." He closed his eyes, buried his face in her hair and chanted her name over and over, as if he thought he was dreaming.

"I'm here," she said. "Right here, Cole."

He pulsed inside her. She nudged her hips, drawing him deeper, until they were fused together so intimately that she entered paradise.

That seemed to break the thin tether of his control. He eased out and drove back inside, sending her shattered nerves spiraling. Each determined, quick thrust tore her apart, sent her closer and closer to the brink of insanity. She grabbed his shoulders to hold on, but her fingers wouldn't clasp. They dove into his hair, fisting, needing something to ground her.

One of his hands reached up and gripped the pillow by her head. "Can't hold on . . . much longer, Mia."

But she was already there, clutching him like a vice as

the orgasm quaked. Ravaged. Cole immediately followed and when he cried out into her hair as he climaxed, she nearly wept at how much she cherished the sound.

Cole reached over and clicked off the lantern on the night-stand. With the shutters and drapes closed because of the raging storm, there was an immediate and sudden black-ness. After draping the blankets over himself and Mia, he spooned her back and linked their fingers over her chest.

Cole fumbled for something to say, but nothing came. He'd never even dared to dream that being with her again was possible. Sure, he'd had fantasy after fantasy to get him through the lonely nights. But he wasn't so far gone that he'd allow himself the privilege to believe the fantasy.

Yet, here she was.

Being intimate with her again tore his heart right out of his chest. It moved him to tears and, even now, twenty minutes later, he fought them back. How badly he wanted to tell her he loved her. That his love, it seemed, hadn't faded over time. Cole didn't think Mia was ready to hear that though.

"Are you sleeping?" he asked quietly.

She kissed his hand in answer, brushing her lips over his knuckles with a gentleness that had more tears lodging in his throat. "Nine hundred and ninety-nine thousand more to go."

He inhaled the scent of her hair. "What?"

"A million ways to make love to me. That's what you said."

He smiled against the back of her head. "Nine hundred and ninety-nine thousand, nine hundred and ninety-nine. Technically. You missed a few in there."

She laughed. "My mistake." She rolled over in his arms and pressed a kiss to his throat. "Was it everything you hoped it would be when you dreamed about it?"

It humbled him that she wondered if she was a good lover. She may have grown tougher through the years, but it seemed she still needed reassurance now and again. Still his Mia inside. He rested his chin on top of her head, wishing he could see her through the darkness engulfing them. Wished he could see her eyes when he said, "No dream could ever match having the real you."

She grew silent, but he knew by her erratic breathing that she wasn't sleeping. "I'm sorry I wasn't more gentle," he said.

Hell, he'd barely held out. His own insecurity had seeped through. It had been too long since he'd been with a woman. The last was some random female he met in a bar on leave almost two years ago. He couldn't even recall what she looked like, never mind her name.

"I'm not complaining," she mumbled, sleepiness in her voice.

But she surprised him when she nipped his throat. Not hard, but playfully. It had his libido stirring again. When they'd slowly undressed each other earlier, she'd been so careful in how she focused on his injuries. Kissing the scars as if she could kiss away the memory. Endearing. Yet she didn't treat him as if the scars mattered at all. Mia gave in to her passion same as Cole did. Fast, hard, without regret.

He slid his hand down her back, wanting to go slower with her the second time. Savor each moment, take his time pleasuring her. In the absolute dark, they'd only have the touch of each other. Feel. And now he was completely turned on, nearly to the point of pain.

Mia draped a leg over his waist and slid over him, forcing

him to lay back on the mattress with her on top. With their
sight gone, all his other senses kicked into high gear. She
smelled like a mix between his scent and hers. Her slim,
warm body stretched over the length of him, heating his
skin with desire. He felt her mouth over his, the gentle press
of her lips, and he changed the velocity. Swallowed her
whole in the kiss, thrusting his tongue against hers like he
craved thrusting inside her heat. Her hands slid down his
arms, linking their fingers together, which she directed to
the pillow behind his head, holding them there.

"Is this okay?" she whispered against his mouth.

Hell. "Yes."

"I'm not hurting you?"

His dick throbbed, but they'd fix that soon enough. "No."

Blindly, he lifted his head to seek her kiss again, but her
warm, slick tongue slid over his nipple instead. Her hair
feathered his skin. His head slammed back.

"Sweet Jesus, Mia."

She smiled against his skin as she moved to the other
nipple. He reared up, sliding his erection against her belly.
She traced a path with her mouth to his neck, where she
licked circle patterns that almost had him begging. *Begging.* His hands gripped hers tight, all but lost circulation
when she made her way to his ear. She took the lobe
between her teeth, bit, then sucked the throb away.

Now he did beg. Repeatedly.

There was something so utterly arousing about releasing control over to her. About submitting willingly, blindly,
to whatever she wanted to do to his body. He realized with
surprise that he'd never let a woman take the reins. He'd
never trusted a woman enough.

"Cole." Her breath fanned his neck.

Oh holy hell. The way she said his name.

She rose up, but before he could whimper a protest at the loss, she came back down with him inside her.

Screw control. Screw slow. They could try slow later.

He shot off the bed to sit, taking her with him, keeping them joined. Her hands fisted in his hair, pulling the strands, her mouth raining kisses over his face. Her breasts rocked against his chest, the peaks erect. His arms closed around her as she rode him.

Cole held on for all he was worth. To her. To sanity.

His leg started to protest, a slow ache at first, but then painfully cramped. He grabbed her ass and flipped her to her back and the pressure eased.

Tiny mewling sounds panted from her mouth, then a strangled gasp as she climaxed, her muscles clamping around him like a tight fist with the orgasm.

He came hard, swift, offering one long last thrust before he collapsed on top of her.

He heaved in air. Expelled the gust. Guess he was still alive. Sure felt like she killed him. He needed to move, knew that somewhere in the back of his mind. He allowed several beats to pass to collect strength before he made a move to get up. She pressed a hand to the small of his back to pull him back down.

"I like your weight on me," she mumbled in a voice illustrating her exhaustion.

He laughed and slid to her side, still half-smothering her but allowing her some room to breathe. Grabbing the blankets, he covered them and draped his arm over her.

The last thing he remembered before sleep kicked in was their legs tangling and her soft caress roaming up and down his spine.

chapter
fourteen

Mia processed her surroundings before even opening her eyes. Her right arm was completely numb. She attributed that to the fact that Cole was still sprawled across her. She smiled. He didn't quite snore, but there was a loud rattle to his inhalation that she found intimately sweet. Aside from his breathing, the room was quiet. No gusts pummeling the shutters. The floor didn't seem to be vibrating at all beneath his bed.

Slowly, she opened her eyes and blinked, taking in the dim room. The artistic black and white photos of European cities were still hanging on the walls. There were no cracks in the eggshell blue–painted drywall. His king-sized bed was still in one piece as they lay sprawled on top. It seemed they'd survived their first tropical storm together. Inside and outside. She smiled again and stared down at the top of his head.

The night before came rushing back. How he'd told her

the truth from all those years before. How her first response had been to go to him.

They were adults now. Cole was independent from his parents. There wasn't anything to stop them from coming together now.

Except . . .

Well, except themselves.

She wondered what last night meant for them. She had Ginny to take care of. Had a life in Charlotte. Sort of. Cole was trying to get his life back in order here in Wilmington. She didn't think he was ready for a relationship right now. He needed to focus on getting well. Healing. She needed to focus on finding another job soon and preparing her apartment for Ginny to move in.

She looked down at the top of his head again. His sandy blond hair had grown too long since she'd cut it last and was curling over his nape. Maybe this was how it was meant to be. Maybe this was the closure they both sought. Cole finally able to move on from Dean's death and find solace in revealing the truth of that night, Mia finally able to let go of all that pain and humiliation she'd suffered at the Covington hand. Replace the bad memories with good ones.

They were free now.

Her chest began to ache. She didn't want to be free. Like the scared, insecure teen she used to be, she just wanted Cole.

And just like before, that didn't seem possible. There were too many obstacles between them to make it work. Regardless of how he felt, he was still a Covington and she still didn't belong in his world. No matter how she felt, Ginny had to come first. Ginny was all that mattered. Cole possibly still had feelings for Mia, apparent by the things he'd said and done last night, but Ginny was a part of her package. Not even Cole could take on baggage that size. He shouldn't have to.

Perhaps their coming together last night was because Cole's hand was forced back then and they'd never gotten to play out how their relationship could've been. Maybe it was just the romance of being isolated together, the rest of the world shut out.

But the real world was still out there, lying in wait to take everything away again. Inevitable. A hard, bitter pill to swallow. And Cole had already proven he didn't take pills well.

They didn't even know each other anymore. Yeah, they'd proven the passion was still there, maybe a thin shred of the friendship, but ten years was a long time.

She blew out an uneven breath, fighting tears. Reality sucked big time. The warm glow from the night before faded, replaced with a gaping hole she knew she'd never fill again. Such was life.

Such was *her* life.

Cole stirred and moaned. "Please don't wake me," he mumbled.

She matched his quiet tone. "I was trying not to."

He lifted his head and set his chin on her bare breast. A slow, sleepy smile crossed his face. "Not dreaming."

It had been so long since she'd seen this relaxed, happy side of Cole. Something inside her snapped. Cracked her chest wide open with a ragged claw. "No, you're not dreaming."

But she was.

He slid his body up the length of her and nuzzled her neck. "Could've sworn I was. I think I am still dreaming. Don't wake me up, Mia."

And because she didn't want to wake up either, because the pain of that would be far too great, she slid her arms under his and around his back. Just once more, she'd let the future wait and give in to the passion he invoked deep inside her.

His hands drifted from her breasts to hold her hips as he made his way down her body with open kisses. She opened for him, throwing her head back as he flicked his tongue over her wetness, bringing her close to the edge and back again, never quite allowing her to release. She clutched the sheet beside her until her fingers ached.

Just when she thought she was going to die from his touch, from the mounting tension, he rose over her. Was inside her. Tears welled behind her closed lids, lodged in her throat. She could feel his gaze on her as he pulled out, pushed back in with deliberate and unhurried ease. Her moans sounded like a plea, even to her own ears. He was making love to her with all the gentleness and slow grace they hadn't been patient enough to exhibit last night.

"Look at me," he said. "I want to see your eyes."

She forced her lids open, hoped there were no tears spilling for him to see. His gaze was determined and focused as he slowly thrust again. And again. And again.

Keeping one arm braced to bear his weight, he lifted his hand to cup her cheek. The pad of his thumb brushed over her bottom lip. A crease lined his forehead. "Waited so damn long," he said. Another thrust, this time so deep she felt him in her soul. "God, how I missed you."

Her orgasm came without any warning. So shocking. So profound.

Shudders wracked her body. She felt her tears spill. His arms snaked under her back, cradled her head and pressed her face into his neck. His breath skated over her ear, driving her over another edge. Before she even had time to come down, he tensed in release. She held on with whatever she had left.

"You're crying," he said into her hair.

"I know." *Damn it!* She couldn't seem to stop.

"Did I hurt you?"

She shook her head.

"Then what's wrong, Mia?" He lifted his head to look down at her, still holding her tight, and wiped the tears from her cheeks. More poured out in their wake, making his efforts fruitless. "I'm at a loss here. I've never had a woman cry during sex." His gaze intensified, hardened. Fear edged his eyes. "God, Mia. Please talk to me. What's wrong?"

The pressure from holding back was too much. She sobbed openly, despising herself. She couldn't remember the last time she'd cried. She'd never been one to hold back her emotions, but she preferred to cry alone. And not often. Giving in to tears meant giving in to the despair she carried with her always.

Cole sat up, taking her with him and setting her in his lap. She tried to push away and get up, but he held firm. "No, let me hold you. You held me when I let go. Let me do the same."

Oh man. Oh God. Cole still had that undeniable sweet side that could make her melt in seconds. Somehow, it got to her again. Past her resolve and armored walls. What she tried so hard to deny. What her damn shields kept her safe from.

Love.

He turned her face to his, letting her cry but not letting her off the hook. "No secrets, Mia. Tell me what you're thinking."

"I . . ." She blew out a watery breath. And then she let loose. To hell with it.

"Where is this going, this thing with us? What does it all mean? You're reconnecting with Lacey and getting over Dean and healing from your injuries. You haven't talked to your parents, who probably still hate me. They did all this to us. To you. They ruined everything, but they're still your parents and you won't talk to them. I have Ginny to think about. I live there and you live here and we haven't been friends in years. We don't know each other anymore, so how can this work?"

Spent, she stared at him warily and swallowed. God, she never could keep her mouth shut around him. Cole had this way of coaxing her innermost secrets out to dissect and examine. Always trying to fix what was broken. Find a way.

Fix this one, Cole. Come on.

"Yeah," was all he said.

She blinked, waiting for more. For some brilliant Cole Covington insight.

His gaze traveled over her face, but he didn't seem to see her. His expression was skilled carefully blank, his thoughts withdrawn and hidden away.

And there she had it. The answer. There was no answer.

"Yeah," she said, too, through a bitter sigh.

She climbed off his lap. He made no attempt to stop her. Her chest ached with more tears, but she did her damnedest to push them down. Looking around for her clothes, she spotted them on the floor near his side of the bed.

Without another word, she dressed and left the room.

Cole stared at the bedroom door Mia had just exited through, gripping the edge of the mattress, as his hope spiraled and crashed down with an unceremonious puff of smoke.

This was not how this was supposed to go. Not this time around.

Her words rolled through his mind, one at a time, as he tried like hell to process.

Ginny. Yes, Ginny was everything to her. He knew that. Would never try to take that connection away. Why would she think he would?

Lacey. Dean. They were everything to him. But Dean was gone and Cole was trying to move past the guilt to accept that fact. And having Lacey in his life again was helping. Lacey wouldn't get in the way of their relationship.

His parents. Damn them. Not even in his life anymore but still causing heartache. Still wedging between him and Mia. They shouldn't matter to her though. What part could they possibly play in the here and now?

What else had she said? Something about her living in Charlotte and he in Wilmington. Really, did that matter in the long run? Mia had told him she was between jobs when she agreed to come here. What was holding her there? Three hours distance should not be a factor either. And she also said something about their friendship. Cole had been under the impression they had mended things between them. Hadn't he told her she meant the world to him? Hell, he had opened up to her. Bared every piece of his soul.

But . . . Mia hadn't.

Cole stood up, needing to talk to her. This was not going to end like this. He loved her. Plain and simple. There was no stronger driving force than that.

He found his clothes and dressed. Reaching for his watch on the dresser, he checked the time and reared back. Nearly noon. They'd spent half the day in bed. The entire night.

Cole glanced around, suddenly noticing the lack of sound. The storm had passed.

He walked to the French doors and drew the drapes. The beach below was strewn with debris. Driftwood. Garbage. Dead fish. Branches. Hell of a cleanup they'd need to do. The sky was dull and gray, the waves higher than normal as they pounded the sand. He unlocked and opened the doors, the salty breeze making its way over him and into the room.

He spotted Mia down on the beach, wearing faded jeans and a white sweater. Her arms were crossed as she stared at the water. As badly as they needed to talk, she needed time. So he'd give it to her.

He made his way through the second floor, opening the drapes, unlatching the shutters, and checking for damage before going downstairs and doing the same routine on the main floor. Everything appeared fine. Cole didn't find any massive damage. Seemed they were still out of power, and he knew it could take weeks to get it restored depending on how badly other areas were hit. They'd live.

The kitchen had no power either, which meant the generator didn't work as they'd hoped. It didn't surprise Cole. The generator had been in that back porch closet since his parents owned the place.

He opened the kitchen door and stepped on the porch. It was cool out, easily sixty degrees, but the wind made it feel colder. From halfway down the beach, Mia looked over her shoulder as he approached.

He shoved his hands in his pockets and rocked back on his heels. "I refuse to feel guilty about last night. Or this morning."

Her gaze returned to the water as she nodded. Her profile gave nothing away as to what she was feeling. "I wouldn't want you to feel guilty. I don't. No regrets, right?"

"Then why all the doubt, Mia?"

She closed her eyes briefly, as if struggling for patience. "Oh, Cole. I wish things could be different."

"They can be." They *had* to be.

She dropped her chin, staring at her bare feet. Her toe-nails were painted a cherry red, damn near close to the same shade as her mouth.

"I thought you hated me," she whispered. "All this time I thought you hated me. I didn't know why. It never made sense." She sighed heavily and looked at the wild sea oats. "Now I know what really happened. It makes me ache inside, knowing you blamed yourself. None of this was your fault, Cole." She looked at him with fierce eyes. "None of it. There is no blame to pass."

He started to panic, could feel it rising behind his rib-cage. "I'm not asking you to leave this time, Mia. I'm ask-ing you to stay." Begging, if he was being honest. "Ginny can stay here with you. *With us*. We'll make up one of the guest rooms for her. I'll get her private tutors—"

"No, Cole. I can't stay."

"Why?" he pushed.

She studied the debris littering the beach before answer-ing. "Even if our lives weren't in the way, even if there were no other boundaries or hurdles to climb, there will always be your mother."

He tried to object.

She shook her head. "She will never approve. Even Lacey knew that when she asked me to help you. She said your parents don't know I'm here and that we needed to keep it that way. You know why, Cole?"

Fuck if he knew. Fuck if he cared. But Mia was going to tell him anyway and something told him no matter what she said, it would stop any argument he had dead.

"Because she can still hurt us. She can hurt you because you never got from her what Dean did. In a way, you've been seeking her love and acceptance your whole life. And she can hurt me through my sister." She turned to face him. "Ginny is still a minor and will be for another year. Your mother's on the board at St. Ambrose and after school, Ginny will need constant care and supervision, for her whole life. A guardian. Me, Cole. *Me*. Which means no matter where I go, what I do, I'll be looking over my shoulder, waiting for your mother to take that all away."

He ground his molars to dust. Damn it all to hell, 'cause that's exactly where this was going.

Cole couldn't argue with her. And just like before, he couldn't risk Ginny being taken away from Mia. They were almost in a worse position now because his parents had even more influence with his father's office in government.

Mia took his hands in hers, so warm compared to the bitter cold inside his body. "Look at me," she said in that voice that haunted him still. "You cannot let this stop you from moving on. I'll leave here with better memories. The best memories. And one day, this won't hurt so bad, for both of us."

"Mia, you're killing me."

She held firm. "I forgive you," she said, her voice cracking, as if knowing those were the exact words he'd needed to hear all these years.

Damn, he nearly cracked, too.

"Forgive yourself," she added.

Never. He'd never forgive himself for anything that had happened. At least, that's what he always thought.

Yet, Mia had somehow managed to lift that weight from deep within him. Dean's accident and the terrible things he'd said to Mia weren't banging around in his head anymore. Neither were the men he'd served with, who'd died too young. Cole was pretty sure he *had* forgiven himself or, at least, that he was on his way.

But she was leaving. Again. So what difference did it

make if he forgave himself or not? She'd still be gone and he'd still be here missing her.

"I love you," he said before he could retract the thought. But she needed to know. Needed to know *someone* loved her. "Just . . . know that much is true."

She nodded as if this wasn't news to her, her Mediterranean eyes clear. God had created that color blue so Cole could find his way out of hell. He was sure of it.

"And I love you," she said, squeezing his hands in hers once more before letting them drop. "But we have a little more time together. We won't waste it."

He didn't know what to say past the new grief, so he just watched her while she glanced around the beach, committing this grown-up Mia to memory. After several minutes, she turned to him with a gentle smile that didn't reach her eyes.

"We should start cleaning up. My phone has Internet. I'll check the power company's website to see when the electricity might be restored. And the newspaper to see how bad the area's damage is. Maybe they'll have an update on the roads."

This mundane conversation made him sick. "Okay."

"Why don't you call Lacey and Rose to let them know we're all right? I'll call Ginny's group home and do the same."

He nodded, glancing at the water. Definitely making him sick. "Fine."

She turned to head back to the house. He plopped down on the sand, drawing his knees up and resting his arms on top.

Two more weeks was all he had with her. If Mia followed the same plan she'd mentioned before, by September's end, she'd be gone.

chapter
fifteen

The electricity was restored within a week. It took Mia and Cole nearly that entire time to clean up after the storm. They'd found some damage to the front porch and repaired the railing in two spots. The fountain wasn't so lucky. The crash Cole heard that night was, in fact, a massive willow tree that had been split clean in half by lightning. It had missed the house by inches, but took out the fountain. He hated the fountain anyway. Jake, his landscaper, had been nice enough to remove the remnants of the monstrosity and the tree. The debris on the beach was tedious to pick up, but they'd gotten it done.

Cole sat on the front porch, waiting for Lacey to arrive. The roads leading to their clandestine area of the beach were deemed clear yesterday. Lacey wasted no time in announcing a visit. He didn't mind.

What he did mind was Mia's cute rear end a few yards away, in the spot where the fountain used to be. She'd had the brilliant idea—her words, not Cole's—to plant a little perennial garden there. The area was eighteen feet in circumference. She had her work cut out for her. She insisted she wanted no help. Best Cole could tell, she planned on putting a decent-sized lilac bush in the center, as Jake had dropped one off for her yesterday. Mia had the hole dug and was struggling to get the bush in place. The thing was twice her size in height and width.

Cole shook his head and rose to his feet. Nudging her aside, he grabbed the thickest part of the stem and hauled it over to the hole.

"Thanks," she muttered, wiping her brow. "Now go away. I told you I was doing this."

The sun was out, but the air was cool. Fall was beginning to settle in, bringing biting winds and the smell of smoke from faraway neighbors burning leaves. She was dressed in jeans that had more rips than fabric and a pink hoodie two sizes too big. So cute. He smiled without saying a word and moved back to the white rocker on the porch.

Lacey pulled in a few minutes later just as Mia had replaced the dirt around the lilac bush. Mia straightened and shaded her eyes as Lacey emerged from the car. Cole watched the two embrace in a quick hug, feeling a warm sensation in his chest. Lacey needed more friends. Friends who weren't on social committees and who didn't consider the latest fall designer clothing trends the most important topic of current events. He hoped that after Mia returned to Charlotte the two of them stayed in contact.

That brought a pang behind his ribs that he absently tried to rub away. The days were counting down till she left.

Lacey was holding something, what looked to be a twenty by twenty canvas wrapped in brown paper. She walked up the porch steps and leaned over to brush a kiss on his cheek.

"I brought you something," she said.

Cole smiled. She had started painting again. "What did you bring me?"

Mia jogged up the steps, removing her gardening gloves, and leaned against the porch rail.

Lacey bit her bottom lip, an old nervous habit Mother never broke her of. "You might not like it. I mean, it's . . ." She broke off, biting her lip again. "It's different from my old stuff."

Though there was nothing wrong with her old paintings, she had Cole curious. He reached for the package Lacey tentatively handed him. He tore into the brown paper, giving the wrapping to Mia when she offered to take it and stared at Lacey's work.

His heart stopped dead.

In the painting, Cole sat on the beach with Lacey in his arms in front of him,. Dean was crouched next to them, an arm slung over Cole's shoulder, wearing the massive, charming grin he'd been known for. Behind them, the sun was setting in deep purple hues and the waves crashed the shore in late tide. She'd painted them all at the age they were when Dean died.

"Dear God, Lace," he forced out.

"Oh no," she worried. "You don't like it. It's too soon . . ."

Mia walked to him and glanced over his shoulder at the painting. She gasped, her hand falling to her chest. "Lacey, it's beautiful." Mia made a choking sound as if holding back tears.

Cole was having a hard time himself. "I love it."

"Really?"

He looked at his sister, shook his head to clear it. "I know exactly where I'll put it, too. This is . . . amazing, Lace. Truly."

Lacey let out a relieved breath.

"I'll leave you two alone," Mia said. Before walking down the steps, she grabbed Lacey's hand and nodded once. Cole watched her until she returned to her work on the perennial garden.

Cole stood and wrapped an arm around Lacey's waist. "Come on, let's go inside and hang it."

"I was worried you would hate it," she said once inside.

"Never."

Cole strode into the sitting room and set the painting to lean against the couch. He removed the oil painting of an old lighthouse in Ireland from above the heavy mantel and hung Lacey's painting there instead. The colors brightened the space against the white wainscoting, but most of all, it looked at home there.

Cole hadn't hung any family pictures when he'd bought the house. He'd redecorated and remodeled, adding his own personal touches here and there, but there was nothing inside the house that made it unique to him. Seeing the painting there made him want to rectify that decision. For the first time in years, maybe ever, the house felt like home.

"It looks good there," Lacey said from the doorway.

"Yeah," Cole said, gaze darting between her and the mantel.

"I brought my camera, too. Could we take a picture together? I don't have a recent one of us."

Cole grinned because their thoughts were in sync. But then he looked at her, prim in a calf-length emerald green sundress, and then down at himself in a pair of jeans and old T-shirt.

"I'll need to change."

Lacey waved her hand. "We can do it after lunch. It'll give Mia a chance to clean up. I'd . . . like a few of her, too."

Cole nodded and glanced away. He didn't have the heart to tell his sister that Mia was leaving soon. Hell, he didn't have the heart to think about it. He'd been trying his damnedest not to.

"I have some information about that property you wanted me to look into."

Dean's project. With everything that'd happened, Cole almost forgot. "Let's go sit on the back porch. You can tell me about it."

They settled into their chairs out back with a glass of sweet tea, listening to the seagulls squawk overhead.

Cole looked at Lacey. "So, what did you learn?"

She set her tea down on the table between them. "I have the portfolio in my car. Essentially, the property went into foreclosure about eight years ago. We're talking about twenty acres, including the land with the old apartment buildings. The bank owns it, but the repairs weren't worth the cost effort. It's pretty much abandoned. The guy I spoke with said it's been commissioned for condemnation. There're some homeless people residing there, illegally, of course."

Cole thought that over. "What are they asking for it?"

"That's the crazy thing. It would actually cost more to level the buildings than to buy the lot. The offer is that low."

Interesting. Maybe they could do something after all and without having to find investors. Cole looked at Lacey. She was biting her lip again. "What?"

"Ever since you brought it up, I've been doing nothing but thinking about this. I spoke to someone with the Wilmington Park Commission. With the board's approval, they'd be willing to put in a park, resources and all, if we paid for the lot and demolition. In addition, we'd have permission to build a community center run by their volunteers."

Wow. This was way better than what he had in mind,

especially with the park commission on board. They had better resources for maintaining the grounds. Turning the decomposing property into a park and community center would help the neighborhood, too. Help keep kids off the streets and give them a safe place to play.

"I told them we had conditions," Lacey said.

He looked at her, wondering what she could possibly consider a condition to this. He and Lacey would pay for the demolition of the apartments and the building of the center, and the park commission would maintain the grounds and the future center. It was perfect, or close to it. Dean's project could finally come to fruition.

"I told them the community center had to be named Covington Center and the park named Dean Allan Memorial Park."

Cole sucked in a breath. Held it. Damn, Lacey was full of surprises today. "What did they say?"

"The board meets in one month. My contact, Dale, will broach the idea to them and let me know." She grinned. "He sounded very interested."

Cole laughed. "Good for you. You did good, kid."

A memorial park in his brother's honor. And the community center his brother had wanted to build before he died. A perfect tribute to Dean.

"We'll make it happen, Lace." Cole would do anything in his power to make sure of it.

The only shadow over the idea was how long it took to get there.

After taking several pictures together at Lacey's request, Cole's sister headed back to Charlotte. Mia sat at the kitchen table, cradling a cup of hot tea in her hands. She couldn't get warm. Even with the high humidity, the temperature outside had subtly dropped, but Mia suspected this bone-deep cold was a result of her emotions and not the weather.

It seemed particularly unfair, after getting Cole back in her life, to have him taken away again. She'd thought about every possible solution, but there just wasn't one to be found. Ginny came first and she and Cole had separate lives. Mia supposed she could visit, but the idea made her ache. How could she look at him again, knowing how much she loved him, and that she couldn't have him?

Cole walked into the room and sat down across from her. "Alone at last."

She smiled. "You love Lacey's visits, so be quiet."

"I do," he admitted, leaning back in his chair and stretching his legs out. "I'm tired though. Glad she cut out early."

"I'll make you some dinner so you can rest."

She stood, but he gripped her hand and tugged her back into her chair. "There's no rush, Mia." His thumb traced circles over the pulse in her wrist.

The unspoken words between them hovered. Mia couldn't take it. "Did you get to see the new perennial garden when you walked Lacey out?"

"No, I didn't. Let's go have a look, shall we?"

Nervous, she walked with him to the front door. She wasn't sure how Cole would react to her idea for the garden, but if his response to Lacey's painting was any indication, he'd like it.

She waited on the porch while Cole stopped at the garden. She'd planted the lilac bush in the center of the circle with Calla lilies around the base. In the spring they'd pop, along with the tulips and snowdrops—all considered peace-bringing plants. Cole's gardener, Jake, had found a small bench to add. It was really only long enough to seat two people, but the wrought iron beauty would withstand the elements. Next to the bench though, was what worried Mia—a personalized engraved garden stone that said: *If tears could build a stairway, and memories a lane, I'd walk right up to heaven, and bring you home again.* On the other side of the bench, the other stone said: *Good-byes are not forever. Good-byes are not the end. They simply mean I'll miss you, until we'll meet again.*

Dean had been buried in Charlotte at the family's cemetery plot. She was certain Cole had never visited the grave. Mia wanted Cole to have a place not only to mourn, but to remember Dean fondly. Now that he was dealing with the tremendous loss, this wouldn't be an angry and bitter hole inside him. The second stone made her think of her and Cole more than Dean. Perhaps he'd look down on the stones in some faraway day and think of both Dean and her.

His gaze moved from one stone to the next. Several beats passed before he slowly turned his head. Tears shimmered in his eyes, but didn't fall. He looked back at the garden. Mia walked inside the house to leave him alone for a while, knowing he needed the time.

In the kitchen, she seasoned two chicken breasts and put them in the oven. She had half the veggies for their salad chopped when he strode into the room. She set the knife down, her heart tripping at his purposeful stride. In one fluid, swift motion, he cupped her cheeks, pressed her against the counter and crushed his mouth over hers. Her bones liquefied.

Cole tilted her head, directing the kiss deeper, and his moan rumbled from his chest to hers. No man had ever made her feel this passionately, this deeply. Not that she had a lot of experience with men, but with Cole, it came instinctively. Effortlessly.

He eased back and rested his forehead to hers. "I . . . I can't do this without you, Mia. I can't."

She swallowed hard, pulling him into a hug. "You can and you will. I promise."

He shook his head, buried his face in her neck. "There's no way to thank you for everything you've done. No kinder person on earth than you."

Again with the sweet words, shredding her heart. "Said the man who refused help and kicked me out of the house."

That got the desired response from him. He laughed and looked down at her. "*Tried* to kick you out. You ignored me."

"Yeah, I should get a medal. You're not easy to ignore." She sighed. "Go sit down. I'll finish dinner." His reluctant arms fell to his sides and he sat down at the table. "You better keep to the diet after I leave, Cole Covington."

He made an unlikely noise of noncommittal. She smiled and chopped the carrots for their salad. Silence stretched between them.

"I will wait forever for you if I have to, Mia."

The knife slipped in her hand, slicing her palm deep. Blood dripped onto the cutting board with an alarming flow. "Damn," she muttered and held her hand over the sink, turning on the cold water.

Cole was at her side, handing her a clean dishtowel and trying to examine the cut. "It's fine," she said.

"It needs stitches," he countered, always with a ready argument, worry wrinkling his features.

She took her hand back and ran it under the water. "Go to my car and get the red bag out of my trunk, will you? I have a first aid kit and sutures."

His mouth thinned. "You are not stitching yourself. We'll go to the hospital."

Mia looked at him, hand forgotten. He just said *we*. In reference to leaving the property. She nearly did a happy jig, but shook her head. "There's nothing the ER can do that I can't do here. Just go get the kit. My purse is by the front door."

He stared at her for several beats, then finally walked out of the room. When he was gone, Mia looked more closely at the cut. It was deep, but only about an inch long. It had stopped bleeding already, so she turned the water off and pressed the towel to the cut until Cole returned.

He set the bag on the kitchen table and started tossing items out. Pediatric CPR mask. Gauze. BP cuff.

"Cole, move aside."

Mia hadn't realized his hands were shaking until he sat down. The sight of blood probably brought back painful memories of Iraq. Mia quickly pulled out the first aid kit and sat down. She readily cleaned the cut, allowed it a few seconds to dry, then put on a thin layer of liquid stitch to seal it closed. Finishing it off with a waterproof dressing, she looked over at a very pale Cole.

"All better."

He sighed heavily, still staring at her hand. "You sure? Will that glue stuff hold?"

"Yes," she assured, and rose to replace the supplies in her bag. "You handled that well." He looked at her in question. "Blood didn't make you regress."

He shook his head. "Just worried about you."

Mia cleaned off the cutting board and scrapped the bloodied carrots, remembering the words that caused her to cut herself. He'd said he'd wait for her forever. Mia didn't want that. She wanted him to live a full and happy life. The life he was meant to have.

"I want you to move on, Cole. Maybe not right away, but soon." It took all her effort to look at him. "Be happy."

He said nothing, not even to argue. She finished dinner and sat at the table with him to eat. About halfway through their meal, Cole looked at her.

"Tell me about your mom," he said.

What was there to tell that he didn't know?

"A couple years after I brought Ginny to Charlotte, Rose called to tell me Mama was in the hospital. Years of drinking had killed her liver. The cirrhosis was taking over pretty quickly. I'd seen the signs when we visited, but it still felt like a shock." Mia shook her head, remembering how quickly she'd had to scramble to make arrangements. How scared and alone she'd felt. "While Rose watched Ginny for me, I closed up the trailer and had Mama transported to a hospice in Charlotte. After that, it was a matter of months."

Cole set his fork down, a grim set to his mouth. "Did you forgive her like you did with me?"

"There wasn't anything to forgive."

"Jesus, Mia. Only you could . . ."

Mia adamantly shook her head. "Alcoholism is a disease and Mama did the best she could. I know she loved me in the only way she knew how. I forgave her long ago."

"What about your dad? I never heard you mention him."

Mia shrugged. "I never knew him. Ginny and I have different fathers. I didn't know hers either. I vaguely remember Mama dating someone, going out late at night. I never met him. And after Ginny was born, he never came around."

"So you did it all alone? The illness, Ginny, your mom's funeral?" He took her hand in his, offering the sympathy she would have given anything for back then.

"I had Rose and Ginny. We made it through."

And only three people came to Mama's funeral. That was it. Just the three of them.

"What will you do back in Charlotte?"

Mia looked at him, seeing the question for what it was. Cole wanted to know if she had anyone in her life now. Anyone to go back to. "I'll look for a job, have Ginny move back in with me. Probably marry the first doctor I meet and raise a litter of kids."

Cole didn't take her answer in stride as she had hoped. Dropping her hand, he sat back and closed his eyes. "Mia," he muttered.

Not knowing where to go from there, she stood and collected their dishes. She cleaned up the mess until the kitchen was spotless and there was nothing left to do to occupy herself. Cole was staring at her, his face blank.

"Next Friday will be my last day," she said. It was time to be realistic and lay it out there. The longer this stretched out, the harder it was going to be to leave. "Rose and Bea will be back that following Monday."

He stared at her. Through her. "Come upstairs with me."

"Did you hear me?"

"Yes. Come upstairs with me, Mia."

"Cole, I don't think that's a good idea."

It hadn't been a good idea the past couple weeks either, but they'd made love every night, sometimes with heat and urgency, sometimes with the sweet ease that had tears welling behind her lids.

"I don't care. I just want you."

"Still a bad idea."

He slowly rose from his chair and walked over to her. He pressed his hips against hers until she backed into the counter. His arms trapped her there as he ran kisses along her jaw, lower, to her neck. She closed her eyes, trying to retain everything about him to pull for memory later. His woodsy, sandalwood scent. The sound of his stubble when she ran her fingers over his jaw. The way his muscles corded and bunched when she touched him.

The hum he made when aroused.

They knew each other's bodies so well now. Knew how to touch and taste to bring one another pleasure.

"You're right," he said. She had no idea what she was right about, nor did she care as long as he kept kissing her this way. "We've been in my bed a lot. Let's try the kitchen. I've never made love to you in here."

Kitchen?

He grabbed her hips, lifted her onto the counter in front of him and continued his open-mouth assault. The straps of her sundress slid off her shoulders. He tugged the material down to bare her breasts. His mouth moved over each one with detail, and she held his head in place as she wrapped her legs around his waist. His hands dove under her dress to the junction of her thighs, where his fingers flicked over her wetness through her panties.

She moaned deep in her throat, nudging closer to get more. He withdrew.

In a blur, her panties were removed, his jeans unbuttoned and shoved down his hips, and he was inside her.

Filling. Completing.

He moved within her, driving in and out, his thighs banging the cupboard with each thrust. She tried to bring them closer, held on to him like it would be the last time, as her mind blew clean out of her head. He cupped the back of her neck and drew her head in for a kiss. The thrusts of his tongue matched those of his hips.

The climax built until she shattered. He followed right after and she knew that the sound he made when he came was something that would stay with her always. A cross between desperate and relieved. Between shock and awe.

He brushed the damp hair away from her temple and smiled. "Kitchen down, three more rooms to go."

"Thought a lot about this, have you?"

His expression grew serious. "I think of little else than making love to you."

There was nothing she could rationally say to that, so she swallowed. "What other rooms?"

"The sitting room, by the fire. The weight room, with you in my lap on the rowing machine. And the library, on my computer desk."

My, he had thought a lot about it. She laughed, struck by how open they were with each other now. Not just the friendship and conversation, but sexually, too. "Not the shower, huh?"

He appeared to think that over. "I like your thinking. We'll finish off in the shower. Must wash all that sand off."

"Sand?"

He kissed his way down her neck, making her body hum again. "I want to be deep inside you on the beach. The sun on your face and the saltwater lapping your back."

Oh wow. Yeah, beach first. Right now, preferably. "Good thing you had your protein today."

chapter
sixteen

Cole stroked Mia's back as they lay in his bed, his gaze fixated on the stars shining outside his patio doors. She was leaving the day after tomorrow. He tried not to think about it, but like a festering wound, he kept picking at it in his mind. He'd tried bargaining with God, tried every conceivable way around this.

She had to go.

Mia couldn't possibly know, as his answering machine was in the library, but his mother had called several times in the past week, demanding to see him. He'd deleted each message, just as he'd tried to delete her from his life. The woman who'd given birth to him was a constant reminder of why Mia had to go.

He'd also finished "Project Mia." The ending was bittersweet and heartbreaking. He so desperately wanted a very different ending, one that involved Mia in his arms, just like this. Forever. But their life wasn't a fairy tale.

And even though no one would ever read the memoir, he couldn't bring himself to change the ending. A happily-ever-after on paper was no victory.

"I've been thinking," Mia said sleepily.

He groaned. "No good can come from starting a conversation that way." He kissed the top of her head. "You think too much."

She laughed and raised her head, resting her chin on his chest. "Seriously, Cole. What will you do after I leave? I'm worried if you spend too much time alone you'll fall into depression again."

"Don't worry about me. I'll be fine." But he should've known she wouldn't be satisfied with that placating answer.

She sat up, wrapping the sheet around herself, and stared down at him. "Maybe not right away, but eventually you do have to leave the property and go out into the real world. Find something you love to do and someone to do it with."

He was not going to lie here and listen to her demand he fall in love with someone else. That was a line he refused to cross. Cole got up and hunted for his briefs. Finding them near the dresser, he stepped into them and turned around. She hadn't moved. She looked like a pixie sitting on his bed, sheet wrapped around her middle and moonlight streaming over her, and he softened.

Another picture in his head.

He told her the truth because there could be no more lies between them. Never again. "I said I'd wait for you and I will. Even if we both die before that time comes."

She dropped her head, closed her eyes. "Then do it for me. I'm asking you not to wait. Don't torture yourself another ten years—"

"Time is irrelevant, Mia."

She must have sensed there was no valid argument with

him on this because she nodded, opened her eyes, and stared at her hands. After several moments, she looked up at him. "What about going back to work? Start your own agency from here, perhaps? Something to focus on, engage your mind."

That wasn't a bad idea. He was surprised he hadn't thought of it first. He loved books. Loved helping authors reach their publishing dreams. There was peace and calm in the written word, between the bindings of a book. And it would keep him just occupied enough not to go crazy after she'd gone.

"I'll consider it," he said passively, climbing back in bed to sit in front of her.

For now, he still had her. For now, he could pretend time wasn't ticking by.

He kissed her long and slow, waiting for her emotions to take over, for her to soften and lose her hold on reality. It didn't take long—it never did with Mia. She wore her feelings for everyone to see and felt everything she did in life with passion and purpose. Others could learn a thing or two from her. Cole already had.

He'd learned everything from Mia.

Cole ignored Mia when she asked if he wanted lunch, pretending instead to be focused on the movie. He tugged her closer to his side on the couch and ran his fingers up her arm. Panic rose up in his chest any time she got out of arm's reach. They'd skip lunch. He didn't give a damn.

In the movie, Hugh Grant was in a fistfight on a London street with Colin Firth over Renée Zellweger's honor. Cole should have such problems.

The doorbell rang and Cole was so unaccustomed to the sound that he looked at Mia in surprise.

She shrugged. "Jake probably needs something for the yard," she said. "Or instructions for the new garden. I'll get it."

He resisted the urge to pull her next to him again and turned back to the television as she went to get the door. Seconds later came Mia's startled gasp.

"Mr. and Mrs. Covington. What a . . . surprise."

Cole clicked off the television with a shaking hand. It took several ticks of the clock to fully register her words before terror had him on his feet and to the doorway.

No. *No, no, no.*

Yet, there were his parents, standing on the front porch, Father wearing an expensive three-piece charcoal suit and Mother in a mint green trouser ensemble. Father's hair had thinned since Cole had last seen him and was more salt and pepper than black. Mother's face had aged, as well, though much more gracefully, and more than likely with surgical help. She sported the same coiffed blonde bob she'd had the past twenty years, not a hair out of place.

"Don't just stand there," she demanded. "Invite us in. Where are your manners?"

Her voice still commanded respect and still grated his nerves. Cole opened his mouth to send them away, but Mia spoke up.

"Of course. Won't you please come in?" She opened the door wider to allow them through.

Mia. He'd forgotten she was standing there. Fear surged through his body as his mother cast a onceover in her direction. Mia, bless her damn beautiful heart, dropped her chin to avoid recognition. Or perhaps it was just too ingrained in her to avoid eye contact with someone of a higher social class.

Mother's hard glare turned on Cole. "For heaven's sake,

Colton, if you don't require your maids to wear a uniform, you should at least have them dress in suitable attire."

She thought Mia was the maid. Oh, thank God. They didn't recognize her. "She's not the maid, she's my private nurse, Mother."

Keep your mouth shut, idiot.

Mother sniffed, but didn't glance Mia's way again. "Very well. Get us something to drink then, while we catch up with our son."

Catch up? Her order to Mia had Cole's anger surging. "She does not work for you. She will do no such thing. You're not staying."

Father straightened and cleared his throat, looking weary and tired.

Crap. He had to get rid of Mia before his parents recognized her. Then he'd focus on getting rid of them.

"Mi—" Cole broke off with an internal curse. He'd almost called her by name. Damn, just having them in the house threw him off-kilter. "Miss, why don't you take a break in your room? We'll continue the exercises later."

Mia nodded, immediately understanding, and turned for the staircase.

"Hold it," his mother commanded.

Mia froze.

Mother assessed Cole from head to toe with a speculative glare, then turned her daggers to Mia's back. "Have I seen you somewhere before?"

Shit. No.

Mia turned and Cole nearly jumped in front of her to take the bullet. His body had become so numb he wasn't sure if his fingers were still attached. *Order her upstairs. Push Mother out the door. Fake pain to draw attention away.*

Jesus, Cole. Do something.

Recognition gradually dawned and Mother's jaw dropped before she had the good grace to snap it shut. "What is *she* doing here?"

Cole couldn't even swallow.

Mia spoke. "I only came to help, Mrs. Covington. Just to help."

"Help with what, exactly?"

Sweet Jesus, Mia looked way too calm. "With Cole's recovery."

Mother's gaze whipped to his, examining Cole as if trying to figure out with what, exactly, he needed help. "You let her back in my house, after all she's done?"

Those words penetrated, snapped Cole right out of his stunned stupor. "She has a name. You will address her as Mia or Miss Galdon. This is not your house, Mother. And she has done nothing wrong."

Father's quiet voice quickly cut in before Mother could retort. "Let's discuss this in the sitting room. Civilly."

Cole almost laughed. *Civilly.* The Covingtons were nothing if not civil. Always civil. To hell with civil.

His parents walked into the other room. Cole wasted no time and whirled to face Mia. Her tough facade had vanished and she trembled violently. Her wide blue eyes nearly popped from her skull.

"I'm going to fix this, Mia," he said under his breath. "I swear to you, they won't hurt you. Go upstairs. Stay there. I'll be up soon."

She nodded, looking like a bobblehead in a railcar, and rushed up the stairs.

Cole sucked in a breath and strode into the sitting room. One did not make the Covingtons wait, even if you were their son and they were in your house. His father stood by the window, his profile tight and tense. Mother sat perched on the end of the couch, staring at the mantel with hard, staid eyes. Cole followed her gaze. Lacey's painting.

"Lovely, isn't it, Mother? I think it's great Lacey's painting again."

Mother looked at him with a glare that could freeze the whole vicinity of hell in August. "What is that trash doing here, Colton?"

Cole wondered if a jury would let him off with a PTSD defense for killing his own mother. "Mia is not trash. And her reasons for being here are none of your business. You have no say in my life now. No part."

Mother rose. "Is this why you won't return a phone call? Why you have not offered to invite us for a visit? Because of *her*?"

Cole did laugh then, so hard he fought tears and he had to wheeze in air.

"Enough of this nonsense, Colton. It's time to stop acting like a child. Time you grew up."

Cole went from zero to crazy in three seconds flat. "Time?" he roared. "Don't speak to me about time. Time is all I have thanks to you!"

They didn't get it. They still didn't get it. Somehow, while being with Mia again, while growing and accepting, he had expected them to change as well. How foolish he'd been.

Cole tried for calm. They'd never change. Maybe they could understand him better though. "I loved her then and I love her now. I've loved her every second of every day in between. I gave up everything for you." Cole looked at his father, intently looking back at him. "For your political career." He looked at his mother, still derisive in her gall. "For you to save face. I lost Dean, lost Mia, and enlisted in the army. I watched men die just to forget it all. And I came back a monster!"

"You're being irrational," Mother admonished. "You don't know anything about love, about sacrifice."

Was she serious? She sounded serious. Then again, she always sounded serious. Cole stared at her, jaw dropped so far open it hurt. "I know you never loved me, Mother. So how was I supposed to learn about love if not from someone like Mia? Someone who loves others without an agenda or because she has to."

Strange how she didn't deny his accusation, just dismissed him as if brushing dirt from her shoe. After several elongated moments, she clasped her hands together and sat primly. "Dear Lord, Colton. Did you even stop to think what this could do to the family name? I'll bet you were too ignorant to have her sign a confidentiality contract. She could run her mouth to whoever offers the highest bid."

Just like that, like a slap upside the back of his head, Cole knew how to get Mia out from under Mother's thumb. Safe. Protected.

Why didn't he see this sooner?

"I didn't sign one either, Mother. In fact, I wrote a memoir detailing everything." Her gaze whipped to his and for the first time in his life, Cole saw fear in her cold, heartless eyes.

"I wrote about my life since the day I met Mia. About falling in love with her, the night of Dean's death, your ultimatum, my time overseas, and what has happened since." Cole crossed his arms. "There's irony for you, Mother. You spent all your efforts keeping me in line, keeping me from her, and *she* kept quiet. *She* kept your secrets. I won't be so generous. Mia never asked for anything from you, never did anything to you, and you hurt her anyway."

Slowly, deliberately, his mother rose to her feet, her gaze never wavering from Cole's. "I can and will make good on my threat, Colton. I will destroy her life—"

"No, you won't, Mother," he said just as calmly. He took one step toward her to make his point. "Because if you do, *I'll* ruin *you*. If I hear, anywhere down the road, that something happened to Mia or Ginny, if they so much as have a bad hair day, I'll publish the book. You *will* leave her alone."

"How *dare* you! We are your family and you're throwing all that away. For what? For a girl who'll spread her legs for your bank account?"

Cole knew he had her as soon as the crass words left his mother's mouth. "Mia never wanted my money. And we haven't been a family in a long time."

"He's right."

Both he and his mother turned to Father, who was still standing stoically by the window. Cole had forgotten he was there. Like always, the quiet man avoided confrontation, choosing instead to go along with what his wife wanted. Cole resented him for that. But when his father turned, looked at Cole with regret edging his eyes, Cole felt nothing but pity and sorrow for the man.

"You're right, Cole," his father said, crossing his arms and uncrossing them as if not knowing what to do with this newfound courage. "I never wanted any of this and I'm sorry, son."

"John, what are you saying?" His mother's voice rang out shrill.

His father didn't look at her, instead holding Cole's gaze. Cole couldn't breathe through the surprise to react.

"We haven't been a family since long before Dean died." He brushed a hand over his face as if that could magically erase the past. "I will formally announce my resignation on Monday. It's time I got back to the family business my father started, instead of letting my partners run the firm. I'm sick of . . . politics."

"John—"

"Be quiet, Kathryn. I'm speaking. For once, you will not interrupt."

Cole drew in air, watching his mother's face harden not with anger, but horror. No one ever dared to speak to her this way. Father just looked . . . relieved.

"I don't want a political career. I never did. Especially at this cost." Father shook his head, stared at the doorway like a lifeline. "You'll get no more interference from us, son. Come, Kathryn. We're leaving." Father took his mother's elbow and directed her toward the door.

She held firm. "Have you lost your mind, John?"

Cole couldn't fully hear his father's response, but it sounded somewhere along the lines of, "No, just lost my way."

The front door opened and closed. Seconds later, the car doors opened and closed in the driveway. He walked to the window and watched the taillights of his parents' Town Car get farther and farther away.

Cole sank on the couch when his legs threatened to give, replaying the conversation in his head with incredulity. His vision grayed, the room distorting out of focus. He ran a hand down his face. Pinched the bridge of his nose.

Did that just happen?

Free. He was . . . free. Mia was free.

Mia.

He ran from the room, taking the stairs two at a time and stopping inside her bedroom doorway. Not there. He rushed into his bedroom, beyond eager to deliver the news. After all these years, it didn't seem possible. They could be together. Finally. But she wasn't in his room either.

He turned to go back downstairs in search of her when something on the bed caught his eye. He walked over and looked down at several small canvases. Four paintings of

Mia and him when they were young. Recognizing Lacey's work, he flipped one over and, sure enough, his sister's signature was on the back. Wondering what they were doing here, he set them down and . . .

His breath caught.

The picture of Mia he had carried around in Iraq was lying next to the canvases. Those blue eyes and a whisper of a smile. He hadn't seen the thing since he'd been rescued. Thought he lost it. Cole knew every feature, had worn the edges to a fray with the number of times he'd held the picture. She was so damn beautiful it hurt. But even more so now.

Cole picked up the note that lay under the picture. Just a few words scrawled on the page.

Please, let me go, and I will do the same. I'll never forget. With love always, Mia.

Cole dropped to the bed, clutching the note in one hand and her picture in the other. She'd left. Fearing the worst, she had left. Cole couldn't blame her. There was no way she could've known how his parents' visit would turn out. He was still reeling and he knew them far better.

The immediate gut instinct was to go after her. She couldn't have gotten far. But he hadn't driven a car in more than a year. Hadn't left the property in the same time span. He didn't know where she lived or even if she was heading straight back to Charlotte.

Harder to admit was the fact that maybe he *shouldn't* go after her. His mother could change his father's mind. She was nothing if not persuasive. Yet his father seemed resolute to do just what he said. More determined than during all the political campaigns, more determined than through his silence over the years.

Cole could only pray that was truth.

Without his parents and the threat to take everything

away, there should be nothing keeping them apart. It was the very thing he'd wanted nearly his entire life. He'd dreamed about it, wished for it.

So why the hell couldn't he get up?

The doorbell rang. He looked out the bedroom doorway and down the stairs, instantly hopeful. Then the flitter of happiness dwindled. Mia never rang the bell. It wasn't her coming back to him.

Setting down the photo and note, he descended the stairs and opened the front door. Cole expected his gardener, Jake. Expected his father claiming a change of heart.

Instead, he found Lacey.

She wore no makeup. Her long, blonde hair was tied up in a haphazard ponytail. He couldn't ever remember his sister wearing jeans. Her face was a fallen wreck of apology. At her feet was a suitcase.

She'd finally left home. Left *them*

"Oh, Lace."

"They came, didn't they?"

Knowing she meant Mother and Father, he muttered, "Yeah."

Lacey nodded, staring at her feet. "Mia's gone, too?"

Hearing someone else say it brought pain unlike anything else. "Yeah."

A sob wretched out of her chest. "Cole, I'm so sorry."

He pulled her to him, cradling her head. "Not your fault, Lace. Not your fault." He held her tight, never wanting her to feel the kind of guilt he lived with. "What happened?"

"I . . . left." She blew out a breath as he let her go. "I guess I should've done it a long time ago, but . . ."

Yeah. *But.*

He knew that word well. He'd coined the singular term.

"Come in," he said. "You can stay as long as you need."

chapter seventeen

On her way out of town, Mia stopped by the old trailer park
where she'd once lived. From her car, she stared at the rows of
mobile homes, each in its own state of disrepair. She didn't
know why she came back here. Maybe part of her needed to
see how far she'd come since the scared little girl who'd once
called this place home. Maybe she needed the reminder of
what she had to go back to if she crossed the Covingtons.

Mia didn't know how she'd stood on her own two legs
when she'd opened Cole's door and saw his parents standing there. The past had roared back and everything she'd
worked for had ground to a halt.

It was weak, leaving Cole a note. But she was set to return
to Charlotte tomorrow anyway. Leaving this way avoided
tears and good-byes she didn't have the courage for. Hopefully Cole's family saw her leave of her own accord and realized she wasn't a threat to them. Hopefully they'd leave her
alone.

She feared for Ginny. They had no one but each other and the thought of them taking her sister away scared her to death.

A dog growled and barked from one of the trailer yards, making her jump. It must've seen her move in the car because it ran toward her, only to be brought up short by a chain. The pit bull was undeterred, snarling and snapping his teeth in her direction. The poor thing was skin and bones.

Rose's old trailer, once the nicest-looking of the lot, was in serious need of paint. The little front stoop was collapsed in on itself, now a pile of rotting lumber. The awning over the door was rusted through. Mia's old trailer, next to Rose's, was in even worse shape. The windows were boarded, there was no front door, and what looked like bullet holes riddled one side.

Mia shook her head. What was she doing here? This solved nothing.

With a heavy heart, she started the car and pulled away. Seeing the crumbling buildings made her think of Dean and what would've happened to the place had he lived.

Accelerating her speed to match traffic on the bypass, Mia settled in for the long three-hour drive. She'd managed to pack up her things and race out the back door of Cole's house without shedding any tears. Feeling them well up now, she pushed her emotions back with determination.

Get home, Mia. Just get home first.

Except it didn't feel like going home, it felt like *leaving* home.

Even without Cole's house, without the trailer park and her past, Wilmington would always feel like home to her. The soothing, rhythmic call of the ocean. The wide open beach and salty air. In Wilmington she didn't feel the claustrophobic despair. Didn't feel like the world was closing in with no way out. Didn't feel so alone.

But Cole was in Wilmington, and she couldn't have him. Her life, Ginny's life, was in Charlotte.

She drove on autopilot, her subconscious remembering the way from her many trips back and forth over the past few months. The pine trees, small lakes, and highway signs all sped past in a blur.

Happy her car had made it to Charlotte for the last time and that traffic was relatively light, Mia unlocked her apartment door and walked inside. It smelled the same, at least. Like aged pine and Windex, a smell she could never alleviate no matter what fragrance creations she purchased.

No one was there, of course. She lived alone. Soon, Ginny would move back in, but for now, the apartment was quiet. Empty.

Her duffle bag slid from her shoulder and fell to the floor by her feet. Mia swayed, overtaken by everything that had happened and exhausted from holding back her emotions. Her chest tightened. Her throat clogged. Hot, wet tears streamed down her face. Dropping to her knees, she gave in. Gave up.

For just a little while, she mourned what she couldn't have and how bad it hurt.

Shudder-breathing as the sobs subsided, she rested her head on the duffle bag and stared at the ceiling. A cobweb stirred near the light fixture, reminding her how long she'd been gone. She hadn't even made it past the short entry hall before losing it. She turned her head. From her vantage point, all she could see was one of her kitchen table legs and the hallway leading to the small two bedrooms and bath. The guest bedroom was the size of a walk-in closet.

Ginny would need more space than that. Spending the

night here once in a while was fine; the room served its purpose. But it wouldn't if her sister lived here permanently. Mia didn't need much space, really. And she didn't have near as many things as her teenage sister. Mia had made sure of that, made sure she gave Ginny everything she didn't have growing up.

Sitting, Mia began to find purpose. She'd move her own things into the guest room and set up her old bedroom for Ginny. Maybe even paint the room a bright yellow since it was Ginny's favorite color. Yes. And buy a pretty comforter set with matching curtains. Mia could afford the small splurge for Ginny's new room.

Happy for the distraction, *needing* the distraction, Mia stood and grabbed her pocketbook. After locking up, she went shopping.

That task done, Mia set her hands on her hips and surveyed the current guest room. A full-sized bed and dresser. There was no sense in switching out the furniture. The queen bed and two matching dressers wouldn't fit in this room.

Mia walked into her bedroom and started the long task of moving her clothes from this room to her new one. Once finished, she transferred her knickknacks, alarm clock, and lamp, and then stripped the bed.

The yellow paint she had bought was called Cheery Sunshine. Perfect for Ginny. Her sister was her only ray of sunshine.

She set about painting the room, humming as she went, until she realized even that reminded her of Cole. She used to hum to Cole to draw him out of a flashback. Mia swallowed and stared at the half-finished paint job. Again, tears streamed down her cheeks, absorbed by her cotton tee.

To hell with it. She was alone and she was sad. Crying

never solved anything. It never hurt anything, either. Through wet eyes, she could barely see what she was doing, but Mia painted the wall anyway.

It was long past midnight when she finished crying, and painting. Leaving the supplies in a tray on the floor, Mia ran some bathwater and stripped. Sinking into the hot water felt good, until she leaned back and the quiet returned. Memories of the time she'd showered with Cole after making love on the beach flooded her. His hands on her slick skin. The guttural sound of approval he made when they kissed.

Mia slapped her hands over her face as if that would stop the visions. God, would this ever end? This ragged pain ever go away?

It hadn't even been a day, she reminded herself. She'd gotten over him once, she'd do it again. She had to. Her sister depended on her. Becoming a depressed, useless life form wasn't an option. She just needed to stay busy.

After scrubbing the paint and dirt from her body, Mia dried off and slid into her pajamas. She walked past her new bedroom and into the living room. Trying to sleep now would surely prove disastrous. Instead, she booted up her computer and made a cup of tea.

She spent close to an hour updating her résumé and scrolling through the job posting websites before coming upon a nursing position at the VA clinic in Wilmington. After helping Cole, she really felt like helping vets was the field she wanted to get into. In a way, he'd helped her understand what returning soldiers were going through.

But Wilmington? No. Her life was here. She couldn't take Ginny out of St. Ambrose. Yet she stared at the screen and before she knew what she was doing, she had applied for the position.

She rubbed her eyes and trudged on, applying for several other jobs in Charlotte, all first-shift so she could attend to Ginny. One of the facilities was a nursing home two blocks from St. Ambrose.

Crossing her arms on the edge of the desk, Mia set her head down and closed her eyes. Though she immediately pictured Cole at his desk three hours away, she was so exhausted the tears didn't come.

Lacey bundled her sweater closed, fisting the material by her throat.

"You want to head back in?"

"No."

That's what his sister had said the last few times he'd asked. They walked the beach again, close to the surf, where the sand was firmer beneath their feet. Dusk was settling in, but it wasn't dark yet. They'd been walking for hours and Cole's leg was starting to stiffen, but he kept going. Lacey seemed to need the fresh air.

After a long silence, Lacey stopped and turned to face him. "What happened when Mother and Father came yesterday?"

Cole shook his head. He told Lacey what happened and then about the note Mia had left on his bed before taking off. He didn't know this until he and Lacey had headed outside, but Mia had also left the laptop Lacey had given her on the kitchen table. She'd printed out her emails to the VA shrink, Dr. Melbourne, too. That hurt. Cole had thought they were past all that.

"Wow," Lacey said at length. "I can't believe Daddy stood up to her."

Cole grunted, still surprised himself.

"Wait," she said, grabbing his arm. "You have to go after her, Cole. You have to go get Mia back."

Cole started walking again, staring down the beach toward home. He'd thought of little else since reading Mia's hasty note. "I have to do some things first, Lace. I may be better now, but I'm far from healed. She deserves a man without all this crap in his head." They'd waited ten years. What was a few weeks in comparison?

Lacey stared at him. "You still love her, Cole. I know that. She'd accept you the way you are."

Mia had accepted him. She'd accepted the arrogant kid he'd used to be and she'd accepted the broken man he'd become. It wasn't a matter of her accepting him, it was a matter of her choosing what she wanted.

"I've made decisions on her behalf nearly her whole life, Lacey, in one form or another. Devastating choices, some of them. In a twisted sort of way, I set this path for both of us. So Mia has to make the decision to come back. She has to decide if this is what she wants. If . . . I'm what she wants."

"Of course she wants you." Lacey's expression was fierce, making Cole want to smile. "But she doesn't know what happened with Father. She'll stay in Charlotte protecting Ginny."

They walked past the house and mimosa grove, stopping by the empty lot that sat beyond. Once upon a time, his parents talked about putting in a tennis court there. Dean was the only one who played tennis.

"I'll tell her, Lacey. When I'm ready."

Right now, he needed to survive on his own. Reconnect with Lacey and grieve for Dean. He needed to figure out who he was without all the guilt inside. If he and Mia rushed into things, they could set themselves up for failure. And failure was not an option in his mind. He would not fail her again. Too many people in her life had done that, himself included.

The wind blew his hair back as he stared at the lot. "That spot is big enough for a house."

Lacey looked at the open space and then at Cole, not following.

"You could build a house here, instead of buying one farther down the beach. Private here, too. That is, if you could stand living this close to your older brother."

Cole watched her profile, and his only thought was that Lacey herself had never lived. Never been on her own to do as she pleased.

"What do you say, Lacey? Want to be my neighbor? We can borrow eggs and sugar from each other. Or something."

Lacey laughed. Tears fell down her cheeks in tandem. "We don't know how to cook."

He shrugged. "We could learn."

She looked at him as if the thought had never occurred to her before. Bit her lip. "Yes," she said at length, nodding her head.

Cole didn't know if she had agreed to cooking lessons or building a house, but he felt better when she slung an arm around his waist and they walked back inside together.

"Want some hot cocoa?" he asked.

"Oh, yes. With whipped cream!" She sat down at the table. "You remember how Rose used to make us hot chocolate on rainy days? She'd put sprinkles on top of the cream."

"Yeah," he mumbled, staring at the package. Making hot chocolate couldn't be harder than making coffee. He set the kettle to boil, then dumped a package of cocoa each into two mugs. "I don't think I have whipped cream or sprinkles. Mia had me on this diet . . ."

He broke off, suddenly missing her again. He wondered

if the feeling would ever dissipate. Wondered if she would come back when he told her there was nothing to fear anymore.

The kettle screeched. He poured water into the cups and stirred. It looked drinkable. Well, at least he'd mastered hot chocolate. He brought the cups over to Lacey, sat down, and waited for her to take a sip.

"Aren't you going to drink yours?" she asked with raised brows.

"Just making sure you live first."

She laughed and the sound brought a warmth to his stomach that no hot chocolate ever could. She blew on her cup and looked at him over the rim. "So, you wrote a memoir?"

"Yeah. That's what Mia was talking about when you visited a while back. She hates that I called it 'Project Mia'." He took a sip from his cup and leaned back in his chair. "No one's read it."

Mia didn't know he'd renamed the memoir *The Weight of Weeping.* It had seemed appropriate, considering. Cole kept toying with the idea of getting it submission ready and sending it to one of the many editors he'd once worked with. It was a giant leap, one Mia had wanted him to make.

Cole looked at Lacey. "Do you want to read it?"

She blinked. "Seriously? You'd let me?"

"No, I'm offering," he said, realizing the honesty in the statement.

Lacey set a hand over his on the table. "I'd really like that, Cole."

He gestured at the cocoa with his chin. "Finish that and you can breeze through a couple chapters tonight."

Once they finished, Cole rinsed out their cups and led Lacey to the library. Though Lacey wouldn't judge him and she knew most of the stories he'd written about, he was still nervous as hell. Someone else would now know every detail of his life. At least, the parts that mattered.

He opened the document as Lacey settled at the desk to read. Cole pulled one of the Queen Anne chairs closer and sat as well. The screen was too far for him to read, but he knew every sentence by heart.

I was born on February 2—a cold, windy day for the likes of Charlotte, North Carolina. But my life really began sixteen years later, on the hottest June day on record. I had been swimming laps in the pool at my family's summer home in Wilmington when I emerged from the water to peer into the bluest eyes I'd ever seen, or would ever see again.

Lacey turned around to look at Cole. "That is so sweet."

Yeah, sweet. That was him. A weak opener for a book, he knew, but Mia had said to write what he felt and that was the brutal truth.

Lacey returned her gaze to the computer monitor, where she continued reading. And reading. And reading. Not so much as a word from her. He'd gotten up to pace the floor behind her chair twice and had gone into the living room to flip through the TV channels. Cole glanced at the grandfather clock in the corner. She'd been at it for hours.

"Lace, it's getting late."

"I'm not stopping."

Cole frowned. "But—"

"Not stopping. This is good, Cole."

He'd never considered his life or his story *good*. Tragic perhaps. Pathetic definitely. "Aren't you tired?"

"Not anymore. Could you make some coffee though. Please?"

Coffee. His sister wanted coffee.

Well, if she was this engrossed, maybe that would bode well for actually submitting the manuscript. He walked into the kitchen to start a fresh pot. He also assembled a couple of ham sandwiches to go with the coffee. Feeling proud of his sudden domesticity, he stared at the plate and realized he'd also absently added lettuce, tomato, and cucumber to the sandwiches.

Mia's influence. Even without her around she was in the house. His head.

Pouring two cups of coffee, he set them on a tray with the sandwiches and strode back into the library. He placed the tray by Lacey's elbow and noticed she was crying. Cole's gaze whipped to the screen. She was reading the part where Dean had gone after Mia in the rain. The night Cole had broken her heart. The night Dean died.

Lacey exhaled an uneven breath and looked at him. "It was all Mother's fault, wasn't it?"

Their mother was quick to blame Mia for Dean's death. Cole had blamed himself. Lacey blaming Mother would only spin them in the same circle.

"No," he said, sitting next to her and taking her hand, as much for emphasis as comfort. "It was no more Mother's fault for issuing the ultimatum than it was mine for not driving her home or Mia's fault for Dean missing the appointment."

It could have been any rain-soaked road, in any part of town, on any given night. He would've died anyway. God called him home.

Lacey would read the words Mia had said to him soon enough.

Cole sat back in his chair and grabbed one of the sandwiches, gesturing for Lacey to follow suit. She did and returned her focus to the monitor.

Over the course of the next few hours, they'd finished the pot of coffee and left the library only to don pajamas and use the facilities. Lacey was intent on reading the whole damn manuscript. Nervous as he was, Cole couldn't keep his eyes open anymore. He walked to the settee and stretched out, flopping his good arm over his face, listening to the mouse click as Lacey turned the pages.

The next thing he knew, Lacey was sitting by his hip, shaking him awake. Sunlight streamed through the window.

"You have to go get her, Cole. You *have* to."

She was crying again. Or still. Cole sat up and glanced at the computer monitor, noting she'd finished. Her eyes were red-rimmed, as if she'd spent the better part of the night crying. Cole's heart squeezed.

"Lacey—"

"No. No excuses. You have to go get Mia. And you have to publish this book. Don't think about Mother and Father or anyone else. You do this for you." Lacey wiped her cheeks.

Cole nodded, running a hand down her soft, blonde hair. "Okay, Lace."

"I mean it."

He laughed, touched by her tears and bossiness. "I will, I promise. You have to understand though, she has to come to me. In order for that to happen, I need to set things in motion. Give me time."

Cole rose to his feet, stretching his leg when it protested the uncomfortable position he had slept in. He needed a shower and fifteen minutes in the gym before he did anything.

Lacey stood, too. "I'll go make us some breakfast."

Cole stared at her. "Um . . . don't burn the house down. I'm rather fond of it."

She pursed her lips. "How hard can it be to make a simple breakfast?"

He thought about the hot chocolate the night before. "Maybe just a bowl of cereal?"

Lacey walked off muttering something about no faith in her, and Cole headed to the gym. He pounded through a brief workout and emerged, pleased to find no smoke billowing from the kitchen. He looked through the kitchen door. Lacey was on the back porch, watching the waves and eating . . . a bowl of cereal. She'd left the cereal box and an empty bowl on the table for him.

He grinned and headed upstairs to shower. Letting the hot water pound his muscles invigorated him and allowed him some time to think up a plan. He dried off, quickly dressed, and was about to head back downstairs when Lacey's laughter resonated.

It sounded like it came from the front yard.

He walked across the hall into Lacey's bedroom and looked out the open window. Near Mia's perennial garden in the circular drive, Lacey was talking to his gardener, Jake Winston. Man candy, Lacey had called him once before. Every time Cole tried to get his sister to talk to the man, she clammed up and shook her head.

He couldn't hear what they were saying, but Jake had a shit-eating grin on his face and with every second that passed, he leaned in closer and closer to his sister. Lacey was waving her hands as if deep in a story, Jake hanging on every word.

Most spectacular was that Lacey hadn't gotten dressed yet. Still wearing her pink silk pajamas, her hair tied in a knot on her head and with no makeup, she stood there *flirting* with his gardener. No pretenses. Not caring what others may think.

Well damn. If that wasn't the best thing he'd seen in a long time.

Cole headed downstairs to fetch his digital phone book from the computer. He scrolled through all the professional contacts from his agent days, stopping at one in particular.

Mary Clements. He'd sold quite a few memoirs to her publisher in the past. Hell, she'd even come on to him at a conference once. She'd remember him.

He got up to close the library door as he dialed Mary's office number. She picked up after two rings.

"Mary, it's Cole Covington."

"Well, I'll be. How the heck are you? What's it been, like five years?"

"About," he said, sitting in his desk chair. "Listen, I've got a memoir manuscript. You taking submissions right now?"

"I thought you were out of the business."

So did he. "I'm back."

"Well," she said, her voice flirty and loud, "I just cleared my desk because I'm going on vacation next week. You caught me at a good time. Who's the author?" He could hear her clicking a pen in the background, a habit that drove Cole nuts.

He sucked in a breath. "Me."

She paused. "Are you acting as your own agent?" He made some sound of agreement and she paused again. "You know the bigwigs upstairs don't like that. But hey, email it over. I'll take a look before I head out of town. No promises."

Breathing a sigh of relief, he issued his thanks and hung up.

He scrubbed a hand down his face and stared at the computer. He took twenty minutes going through the file to make sure it was submission ready, then typed Mary's address into an email.

Now or never.

chapter
eighteen

A little less than a week later, Cole got a call back from Mary Clements regarding his memoir submission. She wanted it. His book, his life story, was going to be published for the whole freakin' world to see. He just had to sign the contract, which the publisher's legal team was drafting, and which Mary would snail mail to him when she returned from vacation.

It happened way too fast. Typically submissions could sit in review queue for as long as six months to a year. He'd bypassed that by calling Mary directly and catching her at the right time. Cole knew the manuscript was decent. He also knew Mary had probably accepted the manuscript more because of his name than the content. This business sometimes was all about who you knew.

So that was that.

In honesty, he didn't care who knew anymore. Didn't

care how many people bought the book. He only cared about one person and her reaction.

Mia.

So he'd successfully made the first step in his plan, and now he needed to get the rest going. From there, it was up to Mia. God, he could only pray she'd come back, because he didn't know what he'd do if she didn't. Without her, he would never have found peace or moved on or dared to live again. Without her there was no hope.

Lacey was in her bedroom on her cell phone when he walked by. He waited outside the door for her to finish the call and then stepped in.

Her grin was huge. "That was Dale, with the Wilmington Park Commission. The board bought the idea for Dean's project."

A laugh of relief and triumph escaped. "That is great news. When can we get started?"

"Spring," she said with a pout. "They're suggesting we buy the property now and condemn the buildings before winter sets in. The park and community center can't go up until spring."

Cole nodded. "Spring it is. What's wrong?"

She shook her head, bit her lip. "The contractor I met with can't start building my house until spring either." She shrugged. "At least I'll have time to design what I want, right?"

"Right," he agreed, not seeing why she was so nervous.

"That means staying here a lot longer. Maybe I should find an apartment? You need your space and I'm intruding."

He sat down beside her on the bed. "Lacey, you're not intruding. You can stay as long as you need to. Besides, I plan on putting you to work." He grinned to take the edge off her worry.

She eyed him speculatively. "I thought we were doing Dean's project together."

"We are," he said, standing. "What do you know about web design?"

Her confusion deepened. "Not a lot. I mean, I did some in college, but nothing since. Why?"

"I need to get a website up for my literary agency. I'm going to use my degree and work from home."

She stared at him so long *he* started to worry. Finally, she nodded. "Well, one of the girls I went to college with does web design. I can call her."

He walked to the door. "I'd appreciate that. Have her give you a quote and let me know."

"Sure," she mumbled.

He made it halfway down the stairs before she called his name. She met him at the top of the stairs.

"Have you seen this?" she asked, handing him her iPhone.

Cole looked at the screen. On it, a Charlotte newspaper article announced his father's withdrawal from the upcoming gubernatorial election and his plans to resign as senator after this term. The article went on to state his father's reason was to spend more time with his family, then proceeded to list the frontrunners to replace his father in office.

Cole looked away. Father had actually done it. He wondered how Mother was taking it, then realized he didn't give a crap. Cole handed the phone back to Lacey.

"Good for him," Cole said.

"I never thought I'd see the day."

Cole grunted in agreement.

"I have something for you," she said.

He followed her back into her bedroom and waited while she took a brown bag out of the closet.

"I had them framed yesterday while I was in town meeting the contractor." She was biting her lip again.

Cole took the bag and peered inside, finding a black-framed, matted picture of Dean, Cole, and Lacey in front of the Christmas tree as kids. His heart rate sped looking at how happy they were.

Realizing the brown bag still had weight, he pulled out two more pictures with the same framing and matting. One picture was Lacey and Cole on the back porch, taken by Mia a few days before she left. They were sitting on the steps, bare feet in the sand, hip to hip. It was the first photo he'd allowed of himself since the injuries. He was wearing a black turtleneck sweater that hid the scars, but the smile on his face surprised him.

The other picture was a black and white of him and Mia on the beach, taken by Lacey the same day. Mia wore the same yellow dress as she had the day she'd first arrived back here in Wilmington. He couldn't see the color in the dress, nor her blue eyes and red mouth, but his mind knew those features.

"Very nice of you, Lacey."

He'd hang the two family pictures in the downstairs hallway, but the one of him and Mia he'd keep in his room.

Silence hung between them as he tore his gaze away from the photo. "I've got some work to do. I'll see you closer to lunchtime."

"I'm heading into Charlotte tomorrow. Mother has her card club and Father will be at the office. I can pick up some more of my things at the house without them there." She paused, and Cole knew Lacey had more to say. He waited her out. "I'm going to visit Mia while I'm in town. So, if there's anything you want me to tell her . . ."

No, there was nothing he needed Lacey to relay to Mia

on his behalf. But there was something she could *give* to Mia for him. Because, hell . . . it was time.

Time to see if she would come back to him.

From Lacey's bedroom window, Cole listened to his sister's car drive off. All his hope depended on what Mia would do with the information Lacey was about to give her. Until Lacey had shown Cole the newspaper article, he hadn't been one hundred percent certain the threat from Mother was gone.

Mia needed to know that he wanted her, loved her, for herself and not because she helped in his recovery. And not because of what happened ten years before in some twisted form of guilt. It was never guilt or appreciation or gratitude that drew him to her. It was the woman herself. The woman who would risk everything, give up her own happiness, for others. Who would return to her own form of hell to help a man she thought hated her. Who raised her sister alone and worked every day of her life to be better than where she came from.

In addition, Cole had needed to get his life in order before he contacted Mia. She may have planted the idea in his head to start his own agency. Heck, she planted the idea to change his major in college from law to English literature. But it was time Cole started using that degree, time he lived in and contributed to the world instead of just existing.

He had to prove to her he was better. The book being published and starting his own agency wasn't enough to exhibit his recovery. So, while Lacey prepared to head back to Charlotte for the day, Cole had made calls.

And it was getting late. He needed to get a move on.

He walked across the hall to his bedroom and sifted through his closet, choosing a dark brown turtleneck sweater to hide his scars and a pair of black trousers. He showered, shaved, and dressed. It wasn't until he was behind the wheel of his Jeep that he paused.

He hadn't driven a car in so long, nor left the property. Aside from Mia and his staff, he hadn't been a part of society. Swallowing, he started the car and drove out of the garage slowly.

By the time he made it to the other side of town, because he drove like a blind eighty-year-old woman, the reporters were already swarming the grounds where the new park and community center were to be. Behind them, the decrepit buildings of the old apartments were barely standing. Cole took out his cell and texted Lacey.

When you see Mia, tell her to turn on the news tonight.

Cole set his phone on the passenger seat and climbed out of the car. Like vultures, the reporters swooped in, shoving mics and cameras in his face, rattling off questions. He held up his hand and demanded they back off. Christ, the press had always loved him. Pretty face, always willing to give them a quote, and just enough of a bad boy to give their story a little interest. He knew they'd come when he dangled the bait. After all, Cole Covington hadn't been seen in public in more than five years.

They followed him up to the entrance of one of the buildings, still bombarding him with questions. Rolling his eyes, he turned and raised his hand for quiet. Then he gave them the million-watt smile they loved.

"I'm going to make a brief statement and I won't be answering any questions at this time."

He waited for a few of the reporters to ready their mics and get cameras situated.

"Ten years ago, my brother, Dean, passed away in a tragic car accident. My sister, Lacey, and I recently found out that before he died, Dean had plans for this property. So, we are following through on those plans in his memory. By this time next year, Covington Center and Dean Allan Memorial Park will be erected in this spot. Dean felt, as do my sister and I, that giving children a safe place to play and keeping them off the streets is vital. It is our hope that this project will strengthen the community. We will keep you updated on the progress. That is all for now."

Of course, they weren't satisfied with just a statement. They shouted questions and followed him back to his Jeep.

How badly were you injured in Iraq? Where have you been all this time? What do you think of your father's resignation? Are the rumors of your engagement true?

Cole rolled his eyes at that last question. They'd always had such a fascination with his love life. He shoved inside the car, locked the door, and slowly drove away. He checked his rearview several times to make sure he wasn't followed. With little effort, they could find out where he lived, but the locked security gate and him staying out of the limelight would keep them at bay until they gave up and moved on to the next story.

That mini press conference had nothing to do with public image or shoving his face in the spotlight again. Mia would know exactly what he'd done and why if she caught the news. She would know that he'd left the grounds of his property for the first time in a year. She would know Cole had fully recovered.

Mission complete.

Damn, he hated the press. He took several gulps of air, needing the reminder to breathe. His arm started to ache and he realized how tight his grip was on the wheel. His first time back in public had gone okay, but it was not an experience he'd like to repeat soon.

When he drove through the gates of his estate, his parents' Town Car waited in the circular drive. His father stood by Mia's perennial garden. Cole's gut dropped like lead. A bead of cold sweat dripped down his spine as his hands fisted on the wheel again.

It took him several seconds to garner the courage to get out of the car and walk over. Father didn't look at him, his focus remaining on the garden. Cole shoved his hands in his pockets, an attempt at appearing casual.

Father pointed at the engraved stones. "This is very nice, son. When did you add this element?"

Cole rocked on his heels. "I didn't. Mia Galdon did. She thought it would be a nice memorial."

Father looked up, gaze scanning the yard. "I didn't have the pleasure of knowing this Mia girl very well. She seems lovely."

Uh . . . yeah. What the fuck was going on?

Cole said nothing, waiting on Father to announce what he was here for. *Correct me if I'm wrong, but Father did say they'd get no more interference from them.*

"How's your sister?"

Cole stared at his father's profile, for the first time seeing the deep lines around his eyes and mouth. He'd never seen the man look so worn. Weary. "Lacey is well. I'll tell her you asked."

"I filed for divorce this morning. I wanted to tell you before you heard it on the news."

Cole stilled. Even his heart refused to beat.

"Your mother's . . . angry."

"Mother's always angry." Kathryn Covington had two settings: Bitch and Super Bitch.

Father turned to face him, looked him in the eye with what Cole could only interpret as regret. "I moved out of the house and bought a condo. The decorator's doing her thing." He fished in his pocket and pulled out a business card, handing it to Cole. "My contact information."

Cole took the card without looking at it and asked the first thing that came to mind. "Are you okay?"

A trace of a smile curved his mouth. "I think I'm supposed to ask you that." He looked away, not answering. "I haven't been much of a father, I know that. You turned out well." He looked at Cole and the move seemed to take great effort. "I'm proud of you."

Cole clenched his jaw until it popped, trying to keep his emotions in check. His father never once complimented him. He didn't issue insults either, but hearing those words did something to Cole he couldn't explain. Filled him with such warmth he couldn't catch his breath.

"You're a stronger man than I ever was," Father went on.

Cole's eyes slammed closed. He'd always considered himself weak. To hear someone like his father contradict that tilted his world off its axis. "Thank you," he managed.

When he opened his eyes, Father was halfway to his car. "Please call. I'd like to see you and Lacey again." He fidgeted with his keys, looking at his hands. "I'd like to meet your Mia properly."

His Mia. He could only hope.

Cole nodded.

His father got behind the wheel and drove away.

Exhausted, Mia drove from the nursing home where she'd been working for the past month to Ginny's friend's house to pick her up. Mia had met a single mother whose daughter was in Ginny's class at St. Ambrose. The woman, Sheila, was nice enough to offer to watch Ginny for an hour after school until Mia got off work. They also lived right down the block from the school. Bonus.

She rang the bell and waited for them to answer the door. Days like today made her hate her decision to become a nurse. Alzheimer's was brutal. Worse yet were the hundreds of residents who were dumped at the home by a family unable or unwilling to care for them.

But the job paid well, worked with Mia's schedule, and was close to Ginny's school. It wasn't the job working with vets that she'd hoped for, but beggars couldn't be choosers.

The door opened to Ginny's smiling face and her tension dissolved. "Hey, pretty girl. You ready to head home?"

"Yeah," Ginny said over her shoulder, already halfway to the street where Mia had parked.

Mia thanked Sheila and walked to the car, taking a brief second to admire her new Honda before climbing behind the wheel. With Ginny's school tuition paid through the year and Mia caught up on bills, she could now afford a monthly car payment. Good thing, too, 'cause the miles she put on her previous car going to and from Wilmington had all but stuck a fork in the old vehicle.

Mia pulled out onto the road. "So how was school today?"

"Good."

"Learn anything new? Solve world hunger? Initiate world peace?"

Ginny smiled wide. "That's silly."

Mia smiled back, changing lanes and getting on the freeway to travel to their side of town. Bumper to bumper. Lovely.

"We wrote letters about family."

This was the first time Mia could recall Ginny initiating conversation about school. "Oh yeah? What kind of letters?"

"To moms and dads."

Mia's mood sank. "Oh Ginny, that must've been hard. But you've got me, pretty girl. Always."

Ginny unzipped her bag and pulled out a piece of lined paper. "Dear Sister Mia," she started.

Mia grinned at her word choice, but kept silent.

"Thank you for my new yellow bedroom. I like it. I like that you are my sister, too. I like it when you sing songs 'cause I'm not scared when you sing songs. I like it when you say nice things to me. You are nice to me. I love you. Pretty Ginny Girl."

Tears welled behind her lids, but she forced them back and was grateful for the traffic to collect herself. "You're so smart. Great job writing your family letter. I'm proud of you. I love you, too, so much."

When they eventually got back to the apartment, Ginny put her letter up on the fridge and went into her room. Mia allowed her an hour of television before dinner, which gave Mia a bit of quiet time.

The answering machine light was blinking. She hit Play before pulling out pork chops to stew for dinner.

"Miss Galdon, this is Frank Wheeler from the VA Center in Wilmington. We received your résumé and would like to set up an interview. Please call me back at . . ."

Mia hit Pause and stared at the machine. After a month without a call back, she figured they weren't interested. Not that she could take the job, but still . . .

Stop staring at the machine. You can't take the job.

Mia sighed and set out a pan for the chops. Adding seasoning and tomatoes, she set the heat at medium, covered the pan, and opened a can of green beans. Just as she drained the can, the doorbell rang.

What the . . . ?

Mia wiped her hands on a towel and answered the door.

Lacey stood there, looking fresh in a pair of khakis and a violet sweater. Mia looked down at herself, still in scrubs and . . . was that tomato sauce? Great.

What was Lacey doing here? Was Cole okay?

"I'm sorry to stop by without calling. I was in the neighborhood."

Mia doubted that, but she breathed easier and gestured her inside. "How are you?"

Lacey laughed. "I have so much to tell you. And I miss you, Mia."

Mia felt emotion squeeze her chest. She missed Lacey like crazy, too. "Have a seat. Would you like something to drink?"

Mia tried to think of what she even had to offer when Lacey politely declined.

"I can't stay long."

Ginny ran into the room to see who rang the bell, as it was a rare occurrence.

"Ginny, do you remember my friend, Lacey? Lacey, this is Ginny."

"I remember you," Lacey said, taking her sister's hands. "I haven't seen you since you were a bitty girl. Look at you, all grown up now."

Ginny smiled, obviously liking Lacey and finding her within her comfort level. "You live in the big house with the ocean."

It never failed to surprise Mia how good Ginny's memory was. She had to have been about seven the last time she was at the Covington estate.

Lacey nodded. "My brother Cole, lives there now." Lacey looked at Mia. "Which reminds me. I'm building a house of my own on the edge of the property in spring."

Mia ran through the grounds in her head. "By the tennis court that never was?"

Lacey laughed. "Yes. Can we talk?"

Mia looked at Ginny. "Why don't you watch a bit of TV in your room, Ginny? I'll come get you when dinner's ready."

As Ginny bounded back to her bedroom, Mia turned the stove burner to low and sat across from Lacey in a chair next to the couch.

"So, you're moving to Wilmington?" Mia asked.

"I already did," Lacey said with a full grin that Mia hadn't seen in too long. "I'm staying with Cole until they can start construction in spring. The house is going to be amazing, Mia. The whole east side is going to be glass, for natural light and the view. I'm going to put in a studio so I can start painting again."

That did sound lovely. "I'm happy to hear that." And she was. Painting used to make Lacey happy, plus she was good at it. Talking about her future house had her face lit up brighter than the North Star.

"Guess what else? I worked up the courage to talk to that gardener, Jake. We've been seeing each other for a couple weeks. Can you believe it? He asked me for a real date yesterday, instead of just hanging around the house."

Mia wasn't sure how to take this, so she just smiled as she thought of how to respond. "I hope you said yes."

"After I stopped drooling." Lacey laughed. "I haven't been on a date in a long time. What do I talk about?"

"You'll figure it out. Do your parents know?"

Lacey caught on immediately. After all, if Kathryn Covington went to all this trouble to keep the maid's daughter away from her son, what would she do to keep the gardener away from her daughter?

"They don't know about it. Actually, the day they showed up at Cole's . . ." Lacey trailed off and shook her head. "Never mind. But I haven't seen them since. Father resigned. Did you know that?"

Oh yes, she'd heard. It was the topic of conversation on every news channel. Hard not to hear. "Just be careful, Lacey."

"I won't let them hurt me anymore. Or those I love." Lacey leaned over and briefly took Mia's hand. "You were a better friend to me than the whole of Charlotte society. I won't forget that. And I won't forget how you helped Cole. No matter what you decide."

What did she mean by *decide*? Before she could ask, Lacey let go of her hand and pulled out a large packaging envelope from her portfolio.

"Cole's memoir is going to be published."

Every hair on her body stood up. "What?"

Lacey nodded. "He's opening his own literary agency, too. He texted me earlier. He says you should watch the news tonight. He asked me to give you this." Lacey held out the package.

Surprised by its weight, Mia took it, still trying to comprehend what Lacey had just said. "What is it?"

"The manuscript. Cole wants you to read it. He hasn't signed the contract yet and the book won't be out until late next year."

"Okay," she said on a shaky breath.

Why would Cole want her to have this? And why now? In honesty, she could just wait for the book to be released. Admittedly, Mia wanted to read it. Badly. But to send Lacey here to give it to her in person felt important somehow. Urgent. Final.

"I have to get going," Lacey said, rising. "Can I call you sometime? Maybe we can get together for lunch?"

"Yes, of course," Mia said through a haze.

Lacey turned to her from the door. "I don't want to lose contact again. Come by or call any time."

Mia nodded.

"And get on that soon," she said, tapping the package in Mia's hand.

Mia set the package on the counter and went about finishing dinner. She and Ginny ate together quietly, without the usual chatter Mia initiated. Her gaze kept drifting to the package.

Cole's memoir. Being published.

As Ginny got ready for bed, Mia did the dishes, still staring at the package. Then she remembered what Lacey had said about watching the news tonight. Turning off the faucet, she hustled into the living room to click on the TV.

The local evening news was over and wouldn't be back on until eleven. CNN didn't have anything noteworthy. Not something Cole would tell her to watch for anyway. Wondering what all this was about, she switched to Fox because their nightly news came on an hour earlier than other stations.

While waiting, she finished the dishes, tidied up, put on PJs, and checked on a sleeping Ginny before sitting down on the couch.

Mia watched the broadcast as they reported a man arrested in a child porn ring and then the weather. After commercial she saw a picture of Cole and leaned forward.

"Just a week after John Covington announced his resignation," the anchor said, "the senator's son, Colton Covington, is making his own news."

Mia watched Cole speak to the press about Dean's project and what they intended to do with the property. It was a brief conference, obviously recorded earlier in the day. Cole's smile was easy and genuine, making Mia's heart flutter. He looked good. Really good. Not at all upset or nervous.

Lacey and Cole were following through on Dean's idea. The knowledge made her heart happy. It was such a good way to pay homage to their brother.

The report then showed old news footage of Dean's car from the accident that had killed him, part of the funeral in Charlotte, and a picture of Dean from his college graduation.

But Cole hadn't given her the message to watch for this information about their project. No. Mia had the feeling Cole wanted her to see he wasn't isolating himself anymore. So she could see that he had recovered.

She turned off the television and stared at the package still sitting on the counter. Apparently there was something else Cole wanted her to know.

This time away from him was more difficult than anything she'd ever been through. Like she was slowly dying inside. She kept herself busy with work and Ginny, but at night she still cried herself to sleep wondering how Cole was, what he was doing, and if he missed her with this same hollowing, gutting ache.

She got to her feet and picked up the package, knowing that reading this was going to shred her already broken heart to pieces.

chapter
nineteen

In her bedroom, Mia read through almost half the manuscript before dawn broke and her alarm blared. Today was her day off, but she still had to get Ginny ready and drive her to school. Mia hadn't gotten one wink of sleep.

She showered, brushed her teeth, and started a pot of coffee before waking Ginny. Mia prepared a bowl of cereal with bananas and OJ on the side for Ginny as her sister emerged from her bedroom dressed for the day.

Dressed Ginny-style anyway. Ginny had put on a tank top, skirt, and pants. Mia would help her fix the ensemble after she ate.

Mia sipped her coffee, thinking about Cole's book. She smiled at his title and the note he had handwritten under it. *Aka—Project Mia.*

At least he'd changed the title.

There wasn't anything so far that she didn't already know, except for the fact that the book was mostly about his experiences with her. It was interesting reading about their joint memories from his perspective. Reading in detail about his mother's ultimatum the night Dean died had her anger surging. She'd just gotten past Dean's funeral and Cole's decision to enlist in the army a few years later when Mia had to stop reading.

Fatigued, she helped Ginny fix her outfit and drove her to school on autopilot, functioning on her brief blast of caffeine from that morning before returning home. She knew she needed to crawl into bed and catch a few hours' sleep, but the manuscript was calling to her.

Cole was calling to her. It was crazy. Like her world depended on reading his words. She must have been more tired than she thought. She should give up on this, on the thought of them as a couple. Getting through each day was hard enough.

But Cole needed her to read it. Needed her to know something. And to be honest, now that she'd discovered the main focus of the book was herself, she was curious as to how he planned to end their story. Maybe Shakespearean style, since they were definitely a tragedy.

She reheated another cup of coffee and sat on her bed to read.

Her chest ached as she read about what had happened to him in Iraq and the men he'd lost. About how Cole's will to live was gone as he'd laid in the sand waiting for rescue. So many other men hadn't made it out alive and the one man who wanted to die didn't.

Mia lifted her damp eyes from the page, wondering what would've happened if Cole had not made it home. Lacey would have been devastated. Mia never would've learned the truth. At first, she'd gone to Wilmington for Ginny, to help Cole, and to get closure. Instead, she left with bittersweet memories and the pain of having to let him go again.

Shaking her head, she wiped her cheeks and continued on. She read about when she first arrived and his recovery. So strange, reading about their past, then jumping to recent events. Again, she was intrigued by his version of things. The way he wrote about her was poetic. Like some fictional heroine in an epic love story. Mia didn't belong on the pedestal he'd erected for her.

She set the pages down and headed out to fetch Ginny from school. Today was Friday, which meant pizza night. Ginny's favorite. Mia was just happy she didn't have to cook. Although she felt guilty for the thought, all she really wanted to do was curl up in bed and finish the book. She didn't have much left to read, maybe a chapter at most.

Once home, Mia ordered a pizza and sat on the couch to watch a movie with Ginny, another one of their little routines that Ginny loved and Mia usually did, too. But she couldn't focus. Mia stared at the wall separating the living room from her bedroom as if she could see Cole's pages through the drywall and studs.

Finally, after pizza and another movie Mia couldn't recall, she poked her head in Ginny's room. "Night, pretty girl."

"Night," Ginny mimicked, her hair spread over the pillow. Then she bolted up to sit. "How come you don't have a boyfriend? Like in *High School Musical*?"

Oh boy. Is that what they'd watched? Now Mia wasn't sorry she'd missed it. "Well . . ."

God! There was no answer to this. *Because I love a man I can't have. Because no one else will make me feel like he does.*

"I'd rather spend my time with you." There. Truth.

Satisfied, Ginny laid back down. Mia made a cup of tea

and sat on her bed, grabbing the remaining pages of the manuscript to read.

Cole described, in intimate and embarrassing detail, the many times they'd made love. Her skin heated at his words, at the romantic way he portrayed their love-making. Then his parents showed up. Mia hadn't stuck around to hear what happened that day, but she had been wondering these past weeks.

She continued to read through the pages, then let out a startled gasp. She lifted her head, stared blankly around her bedroom.

The Covingtons were no longer a danger to her. To Ginny. Cole had made sure of that. He'd used the one thing against her that Kathryn Covington feared most. Her image.

Oh God. Mia didn't even dare to hope, because if it was true, if the threat held, Cole would've come back for her. And there was more to read, so Mia knew that wasn't the end. Something else must've happened for him not to try to get her back.

She read on as he explained vaguely to the reader why he didn't do just what Mia was thinking. He didn't come after her because, according to his conversation with Lacey, he felt he made enough decisions for Mia. She—herself—had to decide.

I didn't see Mia Galdon walk out of my life the second time and part of me is glad for that. I can only imagine what she's doing now, how her days and nights are spent. But I'm not so noble as to say I hope she's happy. Well, I do hope for that, yes. I also hope she feels as wretched and alone and miserable without me as I do without her. I can dream she'll

come back then. If that makes me a selfish jerk, then
so be it. I've been called worse.

Alas, I only know two things in life for certain. I
know I love her and I know when her memory of our
time together fades, I'll still feel exactly the same as
I do today. Time is irrelevant, as I once said to her.
And I'm happy wasting every second of it on her.

Mia trembled, eyes welling up and heart pumping so
loud it was like a drum in her head. She could have him.
They could be together.

And the choice was hers.

She'd managed to get a few restless hours of sleep, fighting
the simultaneous urge to run straight into Cole's arms and
hide under her blankets. But as Mia leaned against her kitchen
counter, biting her thumbnail and waiting for the coffee to
brew, she felt like the walking dead. Or leaning dead.

She'd spent the better part of the night hoping. And as
she'd learned throughout her life, hope was dangerous. It
could swallow her whole, chew her up, and then spit her
out and leave her as nothing but a weeping mess on the
pavement. Hope would let her down, laugh at her in irony.

She wanted Cole. Oh, how she wanted him.

Mia didn't know how to be the other half of a whole.
Didn't know anything about relationships. In a way, she'd
used Kathryn Covington as a crutch. She never formed an
emotional attachment to other men she'd dated because Cole
had always loomed in the back of her mind. She couldn't have
Cole because of his mother. It was all too easy to continue
down that same path. There was comfort in her misery.

It was all she knew. Misery.

Now, she had the chance for true happiness. Such a foreign concept. It seemed unreal. A trick. After all, happiness didn't happen to people like her. People like her were meant to only see brief flashes of happiness. A tease.

More than once, she'd told herself she didn't belong in Cole's world. But Cole had created a new world, a new path. A new life. One without his parents. Without the privilege and social standards he'd always attempted to push away and ignore, but was forced into.

She wasn't cut out to play a doting wife and host dinner parties with crystal and fine china. Mia needed to work. Needed to maintain her independence. Would Cole accept that?

Mia wasn't the only factor in this decision, either. There was Ginny to consider. Ginny was only a moderate-functioning Down syndrome teen. To take her sister out of St. Ambrose and move to Wilmington would mean losing her position at the elite school. If this didn't work out between Mia and Cole or if Kathryn Covington rose from the proverbial ashes, Ginny would lose everything. Her sister, her school, her security in knowing someone loved her.

Mia knew what it felt like to have her world stripped bare. She could take care of herself. Ginny couldn't.

She sucked in a breath and let it out slowly, considering for the first time what Cole's decision to publish the memoir meant. Something else dawned on her. Cole never, *never* would have contacted her, asked her to choose him, if he thought Mia or Ginny could be hurt in the process. He'd saved her, protected her and her sister ten years before. He did it again a month ago.

She pressed her fingertips to her lips, remembering Cole's kiss. His kind words. The gentle way he held her. The passionate way he made love to her.

Cole risked his own happiness, more times over, and now he was asking her to give it back. He deserved it, too. Deserved the happiness he never seemed to attain.

Cole loved her. And she loved him. Could it be as simple as that? After all they'd endured?

Ginny's bedroom door squeaked open. Mia straightened and poured herself a cup of coffee. Ginny had dressed herself again, this time in a sweatshirt and jeans. Mia smiled, thankful she didn't have to correct her sister.

"How about pancakes for breakfast?"

Ginny grinned. "But it's not Sunday!"

Sunday pancakes were a tradition for them. "I know, but I thought we could have them today instead, since . . ." Mia trailed off, realizing what she was about to say.

Since we may be in Wilmington tomorrow.

Apparently her subconscious knew what to do, relaying that info to her mouth. Mia knew it in her heart as well—she was just so damn afraid to take that chance.

Mia looked at Ginny, at the one person who she needed to protect, who depended on her, and wondered how her sister would react to getting uprooted yet again. Mia had told Ginny so many times to dream, to go after whatever she wanted. What kind of example was Mia setting for her if she didn't do the same?

She set her coffee on the table and sat down across from Ginny, taking her hand. "Hey, pretty girl. You remember last night when you asked me why I don't have a boyfriend?" Ginny nodded. "Well, there is a . . . man I like. Love, actually. He's an old friend from when I was little. Cole, Lacey's brother. Do you remember him?"

Ginny nodded emphatically. "He's silly."

Cole had been a clown back then. Ready to joke or quip. He'd had a serious side, too, but he hid it so well from others that Mia was probably the only one who had witnessed it.

"How would it make you feel if Cole and I started dating or lived together?"

"Like a sleepover?"

Mia smiled. "Something like that, yes. But it would be a sleepover at Cole's house. We would go live with him."

"Me, too?"

Always. God, always. "Yes. You and I are sisters and I will always love you. You'll always have me, no matter what."

Ginny didn't look scared or worried, but her words penetrated. "But you love *him* now."

Mia tried to find the words to explain. "I've loved Cole since I was your age, Ginny. And I loved you at the same time, since the second you were born. People can love more than one person at a time." How sad that they both had only had each other until now. No one else in their life to love. "The way I love Cole is like a boyfriend. The way I love you is like family. Do you understand?"

"Yeah." By the look on her face, she seemed to.

Mia swallowed hard. "It doesn't mean I love you any less."

"Okay."

"Ginny, if we go live with Cole, it would mean changing schools. Are you okay with that?"

"What about my friends?"

Mia nodded, understanding how important and fragile those ties were. "We can still visit them, just not every day. You're so smart and so funny that you'll make new friends."

Ginny was smiling, but it hadn't reached her eyes yet. Mia wondered what else was going on in her head. "Talk to me, pretty girl. Ask me anything you want to know."

"What about Mama?"

Oh boy. "Honey, Mama—"

"I know. She's dead. With the angels. But no one will visit her rock."

Mama's cemetery headstone. Her grave.

"You know, Mama used to live in Wilmington. We all did. That's where you know Lacey and Cole from. Remember the ocean and the big house?" Mia knew she did because she told Lacey so when she visited yesterday. "We can still go visit Mama's grave, honey, just not as often." Then Mia remembered the perennial garden she'd built for Cole to remember Dean. "There's a garden at Cole's house that's like the cemetery."

"Okay." Pause. "What if he doesn't like me?"

"Cole?" There was no way to explain to Ginny just how big a sacrifice he'd made for them. "He'll love you as much as I do."

"Okay." Then, like a sunburst, the smile reached her eyes.

"We're in this together, Ginny. You and me. We won't go unless you want to."

Please, she silently begged.

The realization hit her, smack in her solar plexus, of how badly she did want this. All the doubts, insecurities, and questions flew out of her head and into oblivion.

Mia watched her sister, still grinning, still happy. Mia knew this was the right call. Knew she'd done something right raising this beautiful kid. Mia would've given anything to have a sliver of that happiness or security at Ginny's age.

"Yeah!" Ginny said excitedly, her voice booming off the paper-thin walls of the apartment.

Mia had to bite her tongue to keep the tears at bay. She hugged Ginny and stood up. "Okay, pretty girl. We'll go. Pancakes first."

chapter
twenty

They'd packed a bag with enough clothes to get both Mia and Ginny through the weekend. If this turned out as planned, Mia could pack up the stuff at the apartment later.

If. It still seemed surreal.

Mia's stomach rolled in nervousness and anticipation more times than freeway exits they'd passed in the three-hour drive. They'd visited Mama's grave and taken a bathroom break twice, delaying the trip.

Mia was both grateful and frustrated by the setbacks.

As they hit the off-ramp in Wilmington Beach and decelerated, Mia nearly tossed up the pancakes and coffee she'd consumed earlier. Thousands of ice shards grew beneath her skin. Her pulse thumped at her temples and neck. Cold sweat laced her palms, making it difficult to steer.

Two minutes and they'd be at Cole's. The palm-lined, two-lane private road to his house seemed to stretch on forever.

Oh God. Oh God. Oh God. Please let this not be some cosmic joke.

The iron security gate was locked. Mia typed in the pass code and the gate swung open. She pulled up to the house slowly, parking in the circular drive, and cut the engine. The edges of her vision grayed.

"It's a castle!" Ginny shouted.

Mia flinched and pressed a palm to her chest to quiet her heart. Her heart didn't listen. She looked up at the house. It had felt like a castle to her, too. Except there was no knight in shining armor. A knight, sure. But her knight's armor was dented and scratched. Not so shiny. Battle worn. She could live with that. She was no damsel in distress or fair maiden herself.

"Come on, pretty girl," she said on a shaky breath.

They got out of the car and Mia noticed Jake's truck parked by the garage next to Lacey's car. She didn't see Jake in the yard. She didn't see Rose or Bea's car either. Then she remembered it was Saturday and they'd be off duty for the weekend.

She wished Rose was here to help her through this.

Wind whipped her hair back, plastering her sweater to her body. The air held the humidity they were used to in the Carolinas, but it was fading and the wind had bite. The salty smell of the ocean caressed her, calmed her, as did the sound of the waves.

Home.

Mia strummed up the courage to move and took Ginny's hand in hers. They climbed the porch steps and rang the bell. Mia had obsessed about what she'd say to Cole during the whole drive. But now that she was here, her mind went blank.

The door opened. Jake stood there. The gardener looked as confused as Mia. "Mia?"

Jake?

Lacey's head poked around his shoulder and before Mia knew what happened, Jake was shoved aside and Lacey was over the threshold and wrapped around Mia so tightly that the oxygen whooshed from her lungs.

Mia dropped Ginny's hand and grabbed the porch rail before they toppled down the steps. "Hi, Lacey," she managed.

"Oh! Oh, Mia. You came!" Lacey stepped back and smoothed Mia's sweater back into place. "What does this mean? Are you staying?"

"She's happy to see you," Ginny said.

Lacey whirled and addressed Ginny. "I'm even more happy to see *you*." Lacey hugged Ginny, too, but Ginny didn't seem to mind.

Jake cleared his throat and raised his brows. He shoved his hands in his jean pockets, stretching his faded gray T-shirt across his sculpted chest.

"Where are my manners?" Lacey said. "Come in, you two. We just finished lunch. Are you hungry?"

They stepped inside, and as Ginny looked around in awe, Mia looked around not so subtly for Cole.

"I'm hungry," Ginny announced, or rather, answered Lacey's question.

"I couldn't eat if my life depended on it," Mia said.

Jake laughed, drawing her attention to him. Mia looked at Lacey in question. Lacey smiled knowingly, reminding Mia so much of Dean it hurt. Lacey stepped next to Jake and Jake's arm slid around her waist, drawing Lacey closer to his side.

"This is a nice development," Mia said.

Lacey grinned at Jake, a full head taller than her. "I think so."

"Lunch?" Jake said, obviously amused by Lacey's distraction. "You were going to get them lunch. It's good to see you again, Mia."

Before Mia could respond, Lacey took Ginny's hand and led her toward the sitting room. No Cole in that room either. Lacey placed a sandwich and some fruit from a tray on the coffee table on a plate for Ginny and sat next to her on the couch. Jake sat on her other side. Mia couldn't move from the doorway.

"You'll find Cole out on the beach, Mia," Jake said in a leisurely drawl that would have any woman with a pulse swooning on her feet.

"Oh yes, of course," Lacey chimed in. "Forgive me. Go on out. We'll stay with Ginny."

Mia glanced at her sister. "Ginny, is that okay if you stay with Lacey for a few minutes? That cute guy there is Lacey's friend, Jake."

Jake actually blushed. Oh yeah, Lacey was doomed.

"Okay," Ginny said, oblivious to everything else in the room but the food in her lap.

"You're safe here," Mia said, one of the things she always told Ginny in a new place. The weight of what she'd just said had her head rearing back.

She was safe here. They were safe here.

Wasting no time, Mia pivoted and walked down the hall, through the kitchen, and to the door. She looked out the glass pane. Cole sat on the dunes with his back to her, watching the water. He had his legs drawn up, his toned arms draped over his knees, as the wind tossed his hair.

She turned the doorknob and stepped out, closing the door quietly behind her. She took two steps down before stopping on the last porch stair. She tried to muster some semblance of courage, but all she could do was stare at the man she loved. Had always loved.

"Cole."

His back tensed. Slowly, as if trying to move through

water, his head turned. His hand came down on the sand to brace himself as he shifted the upper half of his body around to face her.

"Mia?"

He had that same look on his face now that he'd had months ago, when he first saw her in his bedroom. Shocked, hopeful, and like he'd stumbled into a dream. Except now he wasn't the disheveled, broken man who wanted to end it all. Now he looked strong, *was* strong. A man who'd survived hell because he wanted life.

He rose to his feet. "You're here."

The way his voiced sounded made it seem like he'd doubted she would come. She should've packed Ginny up yesterday and driven through the night. Should never have doubted him or his motives for a second.

So, so much time wasted.

"Yes, I'm here."

But then she didn't know what to say and he didn't move. *I love you* just didn't seem to encompass how strongly she felt for him.

"I read your manuscript. You write a hell of a story, Cole, but your ending sucks—"

"I'll change the ending."

He flew across the sand and crushed his mouth over hers. Hard. Fraught. He cupped her cheeks, then changed his mind and slid his arms around her back, hauling her against his solid chest and lifting her feet from the step.

"I'll change the ending," he repeated against her mouth. Kissed her again. "I'll write a damn epilogue." Kiss. "A simple revision . . ."

"I get it," she said, smiling.

She tilted her head, deepening the kiss, fisting her hands in his hair. Her heart spilled over for him. His mouth was so hungry over hers, like if he broke the connection she'd dissolve. She didn't know how she'd lived this long without his kiss. He could make her melt with just his mouth, turn her bones to ash and her will to shards.

"Sweet Jesus," he muttered, his breaths soughing in and out and mingling with hers. "I can't believe . . . you're never leaving . . . I swear to God, if you ever . . ." He growled like a feral, frustrated animal. "I used to be a lot smoother with words. Honest, I was."

She threw her head back and laughed. Loud, long, and freeing. Any trace of uncertainty that remained deeply coiled in her belly unraveled and evaporated. So, this is what happiness feels like, she thought.

"Stop laughing at me and marry me."

She looked into his dark brown eyes, unable to conceal her grin for his benefit. Completely incapable of hiding her amusement. Poor, poor Cole looked so serious. "I love you."

"I love you, too. Now answer the question." Yep. Serious. His voice sounded like pea gravel.

Her eyebrows shot up. "Was there a question in there? It sounded more like an order to me."

From behind her, the kitchen door opened. He turned them sideways until she dangled over the sand. Three heads tentatively popped out of the doorway. Lacey and Ginny stepped onto the porch while Jake leaned against the frame and crossed his arms.

"You brought Ginny," Cole said.

"Yes."

He set her back on her feet, her body sliding down his, but he kept his arms tightly around her. Mia turned her back to the others and looked at Cole, speaking so only he could hear.

"Where I go, she goes. Ginny stays with me. So if you want me, you have to want her, too. Love her, too."

His expression grew fierce. "Have I ever given you cause to question that? She is your family. She'll be my family. I already love her. Love any piece of something that is part of you."

Yeah, he was still smooth with the words. Her pulse tripped. He meant them and she could see the truth in his eyes.

"But there's my family also," Cole said, and she recoiled in familiar fear. "Lacey, of course, but Father, too. He left my mother and . . . he's trying to mend things with us. I have to let him, Mia."

Her muscles relaxed. Her heart swelled. "Then you let him and meet him halfway. I'll be right here with you."

They stared at each other for several beats. His eyes shimmered, but no tears fell. "Please, Mia. Marry me?"

"See, now *that's* a question." She kissed him through a smile. "And that was a yes."

Cole looked over her shoulder. "How's that sound, Ginny? You want a brother?"

Mia bit her lip hard, utterly moved to tears that he'd ask for Ginny's opinion. He didn't need to do or say anything else to prove she was right where she belonged. That they could be a family.

"Yeah!" Ginny shouted.

Mia laughed.

"Ginny approves," he said to her, but he was still looking at Ginny. "I always wanted a sister," he joked.

"You're silly," Ginny said. "You have a sister."

"My mistake. I always wanted *two* sisters. We sure have enough bathrooms anyway."

At this, Jake laughed and Lacey rolled her eyes. Lacey looked at Mia, held her gaze for several seconds. *Thank you*, she mouthed and turned to head inside.

"Where are you going?" Jake asked her.

Lacey looked at Cole, then Mia, and finally Jake. "To paint the happy ending."

Jake straightened. "I don't know where she gets this romantic streak, do you?" Such sarcasm. "Come on, Ginny. Let's leave the love birds alone for a minute."

As the door closed behind them and Mia looked at Cole, the only thing she could think was how wrong Jake was.

They weren't alone. Not anymore.

Turn the page for a preview of the
next book in the Covington Cove series

all of me

Coming soon from Berkley Sensation!

Alec stepped out onto the back deck and braced his forearms on the railing. He breathed in salty air as some of the stress left his body. A soft, humid breeze blew in off the ocean, cooling his skin. He closed his eyes to listen to the surf and the gulls squawking as they skimmed the water, searching for fish.

It had been a long, long time since he'd felt this relaxed. Now all he needed to do was channel that semblance of peace and get a story down.

When he opened his eyes, the newcomer from next door was standing in the surf on the other side of Cole's property. Dark had descended at a leisurely pace, just like everything else on the southern coast, but there was enough moonlight to make out her hair. She stood motionless, facing the ocean with her arms crossed in front of her, so still she could've been made of marble.

Curious, he descended the deck stairs to the beach and

hiked in her direction. If she heard him coming, she gave no indication. Not wanting to startle her, he cleared his throat while he was close enough for her to hear over the waves.

She turned abruptly—she must've forgotten her feet were buried in the sand because she threw out her arms to steady herself. "I'm sorry, I was just . . ." She pointed to the vast expanse of ocean as she righted herself.

Not that he could make out much of her features, but from what he could gather, Alec never would've noticed her in a crowd had they met anywhere else. Plain wasn't the best term to describe her, but it was adequate. Something about her voice knocked him back a step, though. It barely rose above the tide and had a song-like lilt.

She must've taken his silence for something dire, because she wouldn't look him in the eye as she offered her profile. "I didn't mean to disturb you. I'll just head back—"

"You're not. Disturbing me, I mean." He took a half step forward to see her better, but he wound up disappointed because it was too dark. "Besides, the ocean belongs to no one. You're free to walk here regardless of who finds you disturbing."

She didn't seem to locate the humor in his remark, as he'd intended. She rubbed her arms, despite the late evening heat, and turned toward the house as if undecided as to what to do next.

"I'm Alec, by the way. Jake's brother."

"Oh. Yes, of course. Mia said you were coming."

God, that voice. Like a mermaid call from underwater. Fascinating.

Her frame was slender to the point of breakable. The hems of her jeans were rolled to her calves, bearing a flash of pale skin. No polish on the toes. Pity. He had a thing for that. A plain white tee covered most of her torso and was too baggy to determine if she had any curves. His gaze traveled up. Her neck was long, regal almost, adorned with a thin chain that disappeared behind her shirt. Best he could tell, she had a triangular-shaped face and pointed chin. Her eye color remained a mystery.

"And you're Faith, correct? The therapist."

"Er, yes. I'm a special needs teacher, but I have a degree in occupational therapy, too."

He nodded, hoping she'd keep talking. He was getting all kinds of ideas flitting through his mind about a character for his book just by her voice alone. Each time she stopped talking, the ideas drifted away. Which was interesting, because didn't all women talk? A lot. Not her. Maybe she was nervous, given his celebrity. How he hated that.

Just as he was about to encourage more, she pointed to the house. "I should get back inside. It's getting late."

It was barely nine.

She walked away, and Alec watched until she disappeared behind the dunes. Not even a good-bye, or see you later, or nice to meet you. He shook his head and walked back the way he'd come.

Faith closed the back door to the Covington guesthouse and leaned against it. Exhaustion and nerves warred through her body and she fought to rein them in. She wasn't used to all this attention, and today she'd received a lot. Well, since arriving in Wilmington, anyway.

She thought she'd be uncomfortable meeting Cole Covington for the first time, but he was an unusual mix of genuine and nice. Faith allowed herself to relax in his company after a few minutes. Not so with Alec. Perhaps because he'd snuck up on her in the dark. She'd picked the time to go out on the beach when no one else was there and take in her first real glimpse of the ocean. Even the air was different. Lighter, and scented with an odd mix of fresh fish and brine. The water lapping at her feet was cool and hypnotizing. She'd been so wrapped up in a mix of emotions, she hadn't realized she wasn't alone.

What he must think of her. Then again, he probably wasn't thinking of her at all. Why would he?

His fame didn't faze her, and wasn't what brought on a sudden flare of nerves. Authors, even ones as big as Alec Winston, were just people like the rest of them. Flesh and blood and souls in want of something. No, it was the way he stared at her, like he was picking apart her brain. A puzzle to fit together. In all her years, no one had ever wanted to know what made her tick, and in two minutes he gave her the impression he desired nothing more.

Maybe it was a writer thing.

She focused on why she was here, bringing Ginny to mind and smiling. Ginny had been happy to see her. She couldn't remember the last time that happened, either.

Shaking the thoughts away, she shoved off the door and made her way to the living room to get her luggage. Her internal clock was relaying bedtime. She hadn't even really had the chance to settle in, but there would be time for that. Time was something she had in plenty.

Taking her cell phone out of her pocket, she checked the screen. No messages. Same as the last hundred times she looked. A pang of disappointment hit her right in the stomach. She didn't know why she expected her parents to call. And it was after nine. Too late for her to try them. They'd be in bed by now.

She fished her pajamas and toothbrush out of her suitcase

and came across the photo of her and Hope that she'd hastily shoved there before getting on the road. She sat back on her heels and stared at the two of them, her chest growing tight.

Eight years and it still seemed like yesterday that they'd buried her sister. Faith hadn't felt whole since. In fact, the hole in her chest seemed to grow with each passing year. One day it would consume her until nothing remained but a black void.

"We finally made it to the beach," she whispered, tears blurring her eyes.

She hadn't cried in years, and now twice in one day she'd had to bite them back. She sighed and rose to her feet, setting the picture on the small fireplace mantel next to a conch shell. Hope would've loved it here.

Faith turned, doing a quick survey of her new place. The seafoam green walls and white wicker furniture relayed the simple fashion of every beach house, at least the ones in movies. For her, it seemed the perfect escape. She had no expectations, but was satisfied with the amount of room it offered. Yet it wasn't her home any more than her parents' house had been. She got the strange sensation she didn't belong anywhere.

In a few months, she'd go apartment hunting. Once she knew the job was secure and Wilmington was where she'd stay, anyway. No sense in rushing things. She'd built up a lot in savings from not paying rent. Even though the Covingtons compensated her well, she couldn't afford a beachfront location, but perhaps something within walking distance so she could stare at the ocean. There was something almost . . . healing about it.

Mind out of the pity party, she slipped into her pajamas and brushed her teeth. Before turning in, she walked to the bedroom window and looked outside. She wondered if she'd ever get used to the sight. Her imagination didn't do the ocean justice. A full moon illuminated the black ripples, the vastness of water stretching on forever.

Alec wasn't standing in the sand any longer, but she could all but feel him still in front of her. There was a quiet, humming presence about him that his novels' back cover photos didn't portray. His thick, longish black hair curled just above his ears, and though she couldn't see them on the beach earlier, she knew his eyes were bluish gray. The square jaw and a shadow of a beard barely growing in gave him a hint of danger. His wide shoulders and taut muscles were a thing of beauty, if not a little intimidating. He was taller than she expected, too—at five foot five, she'd had to crane her neck to look at him. And handsome, especially when he smiled at his self-deprecating humor.

Turning from the window, she climbed into bed and stared at the ceiling. Her first trip to the beach, something she'd always dreamed about but never accomplished before now, and Alec Winston left an imprint tied within her memory.

Faith hadn't yet decided if that was a bad thing.

Discover Romance

berkleyjoveauthors.com

See what's coming up next from your
favorite romance authors and explore all
the latest Berkley, Jove, and Sensation
selections.

See what's new

~

Find author appearances

~

Win fantastic prizes

~

Get reading recommendations

~

Chat with authors and other fans

~

Read interviews with authors you love

berkleyjoveauthors.com

LOVE
ROMANCE
NOVELS?

For news on all your favorite romance authors,
sneak peeks into the newest releases, book
giveaways, and much more—

"Like" Love Always on Facebook!
 LoveAlwaysBooks